PRAISE FOR

"As terrifying as it is empath
ful horror."
Alison Rumfitt, author
Brainwyrms

"This whip-smart, blackly humorous story of grief and friendship dives deep into the sucking vortex of social isolation. With an achingly relatable protagonist and one of the best monster-villains I've read in years, *Benothinged* lingers in the mind like an unwanted houseguest."
Eris Young, author of *Ace Voices* and *They/Them/Their*

"Alvar Theo writes in such a casual, charming way; whether it be dealing with living in a capitalistic hellscape, transphobia, or immortal demonic entities. They perfectly encapsulate the dark humour in being at the end of your rope, and how sometimes the only thing keeping you going is spite."
Lor Gislason, editor of *Bound In Flesh: An Anthology of Trans Body Horror*

"In *Benothinged*, Alvar Theo asks what if the real monster of queer horror is isolation, mental illness, grief, poverty, and all of the other things that people face in modern day Britain, and if so, how might we defeat that monster? The result is a book that is haunting, bittersweet, and yet also full of tiny joys, as the trans protagonists learn to work together to build a world free of this monster."
Fiendfully Reading

"If you've ever felt swallowed by the shadows, *Benothinged* will strike a chord. Alvar Theo masterfully captures the essence of struggle against an unseen force—The Nothing—that haunts the protagonist, Mask. It's not just a story about fighting ghosts; it's a raw, gripping narrative about battling the very real demons of grief, isolation, and mental illness."
The Horror Tree

HAUNT PUBLISHING

Published by Haunt Publishing
hauntpublishing.com
@HauntPublishing

ISBN (paperback): 978-1-915691-09-5
ISBN (ebook): 978-1-915691-10-1

Cover design by PhaseMoth: phasemoth.com

Typeset by Laura Jones-Rivera: lauraflojo.com

Printed and bound in Great Britain by Clays Ltd, Elcograf S.p.A.

MIX
Paper | Supporting responsible forestry
FSC www.fsc.org FSC® C018072

Published with support by the National Lottery through Creative Scotland

CREATIVE SCOTLAND
ALBA | CHRUTHACHAIL

LOTTERY FUNDED

BENOTHINGED

ALVAR THEO

HAUNT
PUBLISHING

For Christine Matthews & Sammy Lala

Content note

This book contains representations of and references to: anxiety, body horror, depression, domestic abuse, drug addiction, gore, grief, homophobia, misgendering, parental abuse, pet bereavement, suicide, and transphobia.

1

DORIS

There was something I needed to feel bad about. Something from the previous night manifesting as a sense of dread weighing my torso down into the mattress. That was a familiar enough sensation of late, but this one felt especially bad. Then again, it always felt that way. Usually it turned out to be something pathetic that wouldn't have bothered a more stable person.

At some point during the night, I must have pulled the blankets over my head. That was how I woke up: lying flat on my back under a shroud with my arms around my middle. Like I was practising my own burial. It was light enough through the thin blankets that I guessed my curtains were open. The window, too, judging by how loud the chirping morning birds were. Leaving your bedroom window open all night when you live in a bungalow is beyond stupid; an open invitation for any wandering murderer or creature of the night. Apparently, I wasn't tempting enough for any of them.

As often happens if I'm alone with my thoughts for longer than a minute, I got annoyed with myself. I cast the blankets away from my face with a flourish, then screwed my eyes shut at the first awful stab of daylight. Not before I'd spotted it, though.

It all came back to me then.

A long, sleepless night sorting through decades of photos and sobbing my stupid little eyes out. Inevitably, the crying caused a headache so I went to the kitchen for painkillers. There were none. Then I remembered why that was and threw the medicine box across the room. There was much more crying and swearing and kicking things. At some point, I got it into my head to climb on my bed and scrawl the message that was still on my ceiling.

I opened my stinging eyes. Above me hung a single scribbled word: NOTHING. I had apparently deemed the word important enough to balance on my tiptoes, stretching out my arm to write, holding the very end of a Sharpie. My whole body had ached from fingers to toes. It was a wonder I hadn't done my mercurial back in.

"For fuck's sake, Mask." My voice came out croaky and gross, as it often does first thing. At least there was no one around to hear it (and I already hated the sound of my own voice).

Nothing. What had I been going for with that word? I am nothing? I have nothing to live for? Both of those things were true, but it was still shitty of me to say it. Maybe it was 'nothing to get out of bed for'. That was inarguable.

Sam used to be the thing that got me out of bed. Back when he had still been spry enough, he would jump onto the covers and lick my nose until I conceded and got up. He kept that up for far too long, hobbling over to the side of the bed then springing up like Willy Wonka casting aside his cane to somersault. One day, his back legs did not quite make it. The result was like rewinding Willy Wonka on a scratchy VHS. It took a few more painful attempts for Sam to learn his lesson. Finally, he switched to resting his chin on the edge of the mattress and staring up at me. His eyes would gradually get wider and wider until I relented and got up to let him out for his morning piss.

These days, it's my own bladder that gets me up. The first time, anyway. Then it's back under the covers until I get sick of staring at the yellowed polystyrene of my grotty bedroom ceiling. Maybe that was why I'd left myself the message: to give me something more interesting to look at. 'Good morning' would have been nicer. 'Get out of bed, you lazy piece of shit' would have been too long; my back definitely would not have survived.

I turned my head to see the clock. It was just after nine, far too early for me under normal circumstances. Plus, the ceiling graffiti had happened less than five hours earlier which meant I'd slept a maximum of four. I would have been entirely justified in going back to sleep. But if I got up, it meant there was a possibility of my doing something today. I was certainly overdue.

Before I could make up my mind, the postman passed by my window whistling 'Que Sera, Sera', like he didn't know that decent people were still in bed at this hour. Every note was an ice pick into my sleepy brain. Then, of course, the letterbox clanged. I took it as a sign to get up.

I threw my legs over the side of my bed and went to stand. One foot hit the floor, but the other stopped short, my bare sole landing on something stiff, synthetic and out of place. I started back, sending the object rolling across the floor and into my field of vision. The part of my brain that was pure instinct screamed that it was a severed head. Because it was, more or less. Now I'd seen it again, I remembered digging my nan's old wig head out from under my bed. For some reason – despite how objectively creepy it was – I found it soothing to talk to sometimes. It came to a stop with its blank eyes staring at me. Not wanting to touch it, I wished it a good morning and finally got out of bed.

Padding into the hall, still in the T-shirt and boxers I'd slept in, I found three letters. They were all clearly junk. Furthermore, they were all addressed to Ms Deborah Whitehurst. Not worth getting up for, but then what would have been? An invite to a job interview, I suppose, but they generally emailed those. From what I remembered, anyway. I dropped the junk mail back onto the mat and went off in search of breakfast.

Maybe I could use the extra few hours of morning I now had to apply for some jobs. At the very least I could look into doing something to make myself more employable, like a course or some volunteering. Was there any kind that involved zero contact with people?

In the kitchen, muscle memory had me grabbing the big, thick granny cardigan from the hook without looking. Perhaps a soup kitchen or something. That was bound to look impressive, and I doubted homeless people were much for chatting. I had no idea if there were any such places within walking distance, but it would only take five minutes to Google some. I opened the back door. I was picturing the long, productive day ahead of me as I stepped aside to let Sam past.

There was a second – less than that, really – where I knew something was wrong, but I could not remember what. Then I realised I was holding a door open for a dog who had been dead for several days. My gut sank.

Slowly – a picture of purest calm – I pushed the back door shut. Then I opened it a few inches and slammed it a dozen times in quick succession. My eyes welled with tears.

Of all the stupid things to do! Just when I'd been potentially regaining my equilibrium. That was my productive day out the window. Now I was never going to get my life together.

I stumbled back a few steps and crumpled to the floor. Bare legs on cold, filthy tile. I pulled my knees to my chest and rocked gently. If Sam had been there, he would have waddled up to see what was going on. I could almost see him sitting upright and smiling, excited for whatever interesting thing I was about to do. Maybe he would give me his paw, or a sweet, disgusting kiss on the nose. Eventually, he would crack onto the fact that I was just sitting on the floor feeling sorry for myself. Then he would plonk himself down with a grunt and wait it out, his body heat warming up my freezing, raw-chicken legs.

I really was all alone. The last being on this earth who cared whether I lived or died was gone. I wiped at my face.

There was movement in the corner of my eye. My heart stopped when I looked to the back door: a vague human shape loomed behind the frosted glass. A hand reached up and tapped lightly at the frame.

"Deborah, are you okay?" It was an old lady's voice, one I did not recognise.

Fuck. I must have attracted the attention of one of the neighbours I usually avoided, some Doris or Vera or Ethel. Serve me right for having a tantrum.

I attempted to scramble to my feet. At about halfway up, my back went: a sharp pain like a snap near the base of my spine. Crying out, I tumbled forward to rest my hands on my thighs, bent at an almost ninety-degree angle. I'd gone and aggravated the old work injury. Every now and then, it liked to pop up (or out) to remind me that my body was just a mass of sticks and sewage sewn into some worn-out leather. It also reminded me that being in gainful employment really did not agree with me.

The tapping became more insistent; she must have heard me. I needed to open up and speak to her before she went and called an ambulance, thinking I was a fallen comrade. The two-foot journey to the door was excruciating, each shuffle jolting my back.

I unlocked the door, still in my awkward forward bend, and had to scoot back to open it properly. Then I grabbed the side of the door and gradually pulled myself up hand over hand until I reached a standing position. This brought me face to face with the single most Doris-looking woman I had ever seen. In her late eighties or early nineties at a guess. An impressive set of Deirdre Barlow glasses bigger than her face. Wearing a cardigan which… actually looked a lot like the one I had on.

Her thin lips pursed. "Deborah?"

I leaned heavily against the door. "She doesn't live here anymore."

"Who are you?"

"I'm her…" I wanted to say grandchild but worried it would sound like an odd way to put it. I definitely did not have the patience to play the 'awkwardly fumbling for gender-neutral language' game with a random, intruding stranger. "She was my nan."

Two bedraggled eyebrows appeared over the top of the specs. "She's passed away? I thought I hadn't seen her for a while. All on your own, are you?"

With that, The Doris charged past me and was suddenly in my home. The first guest I'd had – wanted or unwanted – in all the years I'd lived there. She did a quick twirl in my kitchen, but made no comment about the state of it. Her eyes briefly landed on the mess of half-empty blister packs scattered across the sides, but then she became distracted by something she spotted in the living room.

"Oh, this is nice," Doris called over her shoulder as she disappeared through the door. I made to follow her, but a flare of pain in my back kept me fixed in place. Lord save me from nosy old women.

Luckily enough, one of the other hooks by the back door held my nan's old walking stick. I tentatively unhooked it and went after Doris.

I found her looking around my grubby little hovel as though it were the most fascinating sight she had ever seen. She peered through the door into the hallway. "It's laid out just like my place next door. Interesting, isn't it?"

It was not even slightly interesting. But at least I knew who she was now: my next door neighbour. I couldn't remember ever having seen or spoken to her. But then I wasn't a 'socialising with neighbours' kind of person. Nan was but she'd been considerate enough not to drag me into it.

"Yeah, that is interesting." I tried to shuffle into position to herd her out of the room.

Doris spun on the spot, putting her well inside the zone of my personal space. She peered up at me, owl eyes enormous under the magnifying lenses of her glasses.

"If you don't mind me saying so, love, you do look tired."

The only comeback I could summon was wide-eyed surprise. I blinked a few too many times for good measure. All right, she had bested me. At that point it looked as though I would have to physically fight her to get her out. Things being as they were, I would not have fancied my chances. Especially as I had reached my limit as far as being upright was concerned. I slinked away from her and winced down onto the sofa.

There was another sofa opposite me, but Doris ignored it. Instead, she continued to flit about the living room, poking her beak into anything and everything that took her fancy. A hoary hummingbird with paper-thin skin. I could do nothing but sit and watch until she tired herself out.

I wrapped the cardigan more firmly around myself. It was a tatty old thing; the acrylic itchy wherever it touched bare skin. But it was warm. What's more, it still smelled, however faintly, of cigarettes and musky Avon perfume. So many hours had been spent snuggled in this cardigan, Sam's head a warm and welcome weight in my lap. I fiddled with the sleeve, my fingers closing on a strand of thick white hair. I rolled it between my fingertips, wondering when I would stop finding traces of him in my home.

When I looked up, Doris was looking down at me. Literally. But probably figuratively as well, given I was wrapped in a granny cardigan covered in dog hair, my splayed legs revealing boxers that had seen better days. Dress for the company you want, not the company you have.

Doris cleared her throat. "You live alone."

It was not a question so much as a statement of very obvious fact. As such, I did not bother to answer.

"Not courting? No paramour?"

My mouth scrunched up tight to keep the laughter in. I had to reevaluate my estimate of her age. Clearly she was not ninety, but an impossibly ancient being. She must have gained immortality by draining the life from young people via tedious questions.

Doris evidently read some kind of answer in my expression, because she pressed on.

"And you're not working?"

I shook my head. There was no obvious judgement in her tone, but I still felt myself getting a little defensive. I briefly considered launching into a monologue about how actually I volunteered to feed the homeless actually and, though it may be rewarding, it actually took up too much of my time for me to have a job as well. Actually. What held me back was the knowledge that I would not be able to bullshit my way through any follow-up questions. Anyway, it wasn't like I needed to impress Doris.

It occurred to me that I should probably stop thinking of her as Doris.

"I'm Mask," I said by way of asking her what her own name was.

Doris had returned to snooping, but that stopped her in her tracks. Her head turned ninety degrees to face me. Then the rest of her body followed. She loomed over me, a coiled cobra watching for the perfect time to strike.

"That's unusual."

Clearly, she wanted me to elaborate. I did not. The awkward silence built up to the ceiling, but Doris did not elect to puncture it by offering her real name. I gave up. If she wanted everything about me down to my very soul but didn't want me to know so much as her name, so be it.

Doris seemed done with her questions for the time being. She hummed around the room, tilting her head at things in a similar manner to Sam when he heard a strange noise. The mantelpiece held her attention for a fairly long time as it was cluttered with Nan's old trinkets. Doris took to picking each one up in turn and making little noises of wonder. Here and there she muttered to herself in a singsong voice. It seemed as though she had forgot that I was even there.

Something clicked into place then: Doris must have some form of dementia. This was not a nosy neighbour jumping at the chance to snoop around someone's home, hunting for something to gossip about. Rather, this was a person struggling to hold on to the steadily unravelling thread of themselves. She lacked the cognitive function to see that she was being rude and obnoxious, whereas I was merely an arsehole.

Planting the walking stick on the ground for balance, I forced myself up with the intention of offering Doris a cup of tea. She would have to take it black without sugar (and quite possibly without tea), but offering was the polite thing to do. I had violated the social contract enough as it was.

I cleared my throat. "Listen, Do–"

Doris spun around again. I could not quite get a read on the expression on her face. It was a smile, but it also very much was not. Her eyes ran the entire length of my body.

"Silly me. You're not well, are you? I've taken up enough of your time."

With that, she was out of the room faster than I could follow with my pained, ramshackle gait.

I found her at the back door. Her face was turned down and the light was gone from her eyes. For a moment, I thought she was confused and there was going to be an extremely unpleasant scene. She perked up when she saw me, though. Like I'd put a pound in a mechanical man at the fairground. Maybe she would grant me a wish to swap my body with someone a good deal sturdier.

She lifted her arms and I thought she was going in for a hug. Instead, she cradled my face with both hands. Her skin was not cold as I had expected, but nor was it warm; she was exactly room temperature. Had it not been for the pressure, I could have closed my eyes and not known I was being touched. Perhaps that was a thing that happened to you when you got this old; Nan had not lived to be anywhere near Doris' advanced age. I expected Doris to smush my cheeks like a TV grandma but, to my horror, her hands began to travel all over my face. She hummed softly to herself as her wrinkled palms rubbed my skin. I only just had time to close my eyes before her soft thumbs smoothed over the lids. Her fingertips slid up to my hairline and then the hands withdrew.

I opened my eyes to Doris' enormous grin.

"I do like that face."

I managed a noncommittal hum, leaning harder on my stick.

"I'll be next door when you need me," she chirped. I was fairly certain I wouldn't.

As Doris finally left, I watched her trundle down the small path that ran alongside our row of houses. She disappeared into the one next door.

I watched for a moment before going back inside. Resting my forehead against the door, I recalled my little tantrum that had summoned Doris. At least the bizarre encounter had distracted me from my grief. Still, it had been unnerving. Silly as it was, I got the urge to draw the top bolt which I never usually do. I even got as far as reaching up for it before receiving a painful reminder that I had a more pressing issue to deal with than an elderly neighbour.

Obviously, I had no painkillers in the house. If memory served, though, there had been a couple of packets of naproxen in the medicine box: my nan's prescription for her rheumatoid arthritis. I would have got rid of them last month when I had my panic-induced tidy-up, but I didn't remember they were there until after I'd calmed down. I wasn't even sure they were there; it had been inconvenient enough to not be worth the effort of checking (plus, I wasn't really in the habit of throwing away things with her name on them; those latest nuisance letters were going to join an enormous pile in the boxroom). There was even an outside chance of the medicine still being in date. I would pop one or two of those and settle down in bed to stare up at Nothing. The day was clearly a write-off.

The medicine box was usually kept on a high shelf in one of the cupboards, but, fortunately, I'd had the foresight to chuck its contents all over my kitchen in a huff. It took some time to find all the medicines: some were in the sink, a few on the hob, some had probably disappeared into gaps between cupboards and would likely never be seen again. Most of the ones I found were useless. Mainly antacids and diarrhoea medicine. There was even an empty box of sertraline, which I had given up on very quickly back in the day when I realised that it was not an antidepressant so much as an industrial-grade laxative. When I finally found the naproxen, I had to squint to read the faded numbers. Very nearly two whole years out of date. Sensibly, I limited myself to one.

There was a sound then, like something brushing hard against a wall. I looked to the backsplash above the cooker; behind that was Doris' house. It would be her living room, if it was set up exactly the same as my place. Or her kitchen, if they mirrored each other. From the position of her back door, I guessed it was the latter.

Was Doris standing in her kitchen right then, facing my direction? Her frail, pained body hunched over as she pictured me, trying to remember everything she had seen on her excursion into my home. Could she even remember coming here? Would the awkward encounter be lost and her brain reset to when a sweet, friendly woman named Deborah had been her neighbour?

I hoped she had someone: a pet, kids, grandkids, a better neighbour on the other side. I hated the thought that this vulnerable old woman was as alone as I was.

2

PETER LORRE

I got dressed up in my nicest, smartest shirt, stuck some clean-ish shorts on just in case, then looked in the mirror and realised how gross my hair was. In the few days I'd spent shuffling around the bungalow with a fucked-up back, showers had been entirely out of the question. I had braved the bathtub exactly once: being submerged in hot water had been heavenly, but hoisting myself in and out via the bars and poles had sucked enough to make it not worth the effort. If only I'd had one of those walk-in bathtubs. Still, at least I was actually using the accessibility aids in my house for once.

I leaned on the bed to check the time on the laptop: exactly seven minutes until the start of my Teams meeting. No time to do anything about my hair. Oh well, at least my camera quality was dogshit.

Plus, it was just 'a quick, informal chat' with some woman from an agency. Just to get to know a little bit more about me. The email request had no mention of it being for a specific job or anything. Still, if there was a chance of it leading to a specific job, I had to put up with it.

My desk was covered in clothes and various crap, so the chat had to take place on my bed. I propped myself up on a load of pillows, set the laptop on my knees and waited.

The nice agency lady, Stephanie, was good enough to start the meeting ten minutes later. A smiling, pleasant-enough face on her. Her hair was in some kind of colourful wrap that I didn't know the name of, and her ears were weighed down by pretty dangly earrings. She apologised for being late and then called me the wrong name.

Now, Mask is very much not my legal name. There are two ways to change your name by deed poll: you can apply for an 'enrolled' deed poll, or make an 'unenrolled' one yourself. The enrolled one is the more official one, where you go through the courts and hand over some cash. For some reason – call it good, old-fashioned, ridiculous British bureaucracy – you also have to put an announcement of your name change in the *London Gazette* and purchase a copy. It must hark back to a time when Sir Charles would have his morning paper brought to him to peruse over breakfast and would read out interesting titbits from the society pages for his good lady wife. A hangover from the dubiously titled 'good old days'. Perhaps the whole thing is just a scam to sell copies of the *London Gazette*. Print is dying, after all. So making yourself an unenrolled deed poll would be the way to go. Except that both versions require signatures of two – TWO – witnesses who cannot be relatives or romantic partners, and they must have known you for at least ten years. Since my relatives are all dead and romantic partners dead on arrival, that left me with no one. As per. Thus, I never got round to changing it legally.

Stephanie, bless her, did not even call me by the right wrong name. Instead, she mixed it up with a similar, slightly more common name. It wasn't worth correcting her; she'd likely figure it out on her own. Or she wouldn't. It hardly mattered.

There was a minute or so of banal pleasantries. Then Stephanie cleared her throat and asked her first proper question,

"So what kind of work are you looking for?"

Oh good, a nice easy one. "Admin," I answered confidently.

She remained silent long enough for me to realise that my

answer had been insufficient. I panicked, struggling for something else to say. Luckily, she asked another question.

"What kind of jobs have you had in the past?"

"Admin." I was significantly less confident with this answer, but it was the best I could do.

Stephanie just blinked, the picture of patience. "Okay, so, when did your last job end?"

That one, at least, had an objectively correct answer. "Six months ago."

"Okay. And what have we been doing for six months?"

'We' had been languishing in misery, thank you very much. I knew that was a wrong answer (see, I was learning) so I told her a palatable version of the truth: I had struggled to find something I could fit around both my elderly dog and my social anxiety (I only told her the first part of this), and that entirely-remote jobs had largely fizzled out. Then, in the last month or so, Sam's health had taken a turn for the worse, so I had to devote all my time to him.

"But now I'm looking to get back into the workforce."

Stephanie nodded as though that all sounded reasonable enough to her. "Are you only considering remote work, then?"

"Well, that would be my preference, but I know that – ah!"

A person had appeared at my bedroom window, hands and face mushed against the glass. As I watched, the hands moved up and out, tracing the edges of the pane. The pattern repeated over and over. I realised then who it was. I'd been wondering when I would see Doris again.

I apologised to poor Stephanie and went over to the window.

When I pulled the disgusting lace to the side, Doris took a step back, grinning up at me. She brought her hands to her chest, tapping her fingers together like an innocuous Mr Burns.

I shuffled over and opened the window – carefully, so it wouldn't smash into her frail body.

"Hi there. Everything okay?"

Doris looked from me to the window she had been using as

a zen garden, down at her little rake hands and then back to me. She leaned forward conspiratorially.

"You need to clean your windows."

Then she turned and plodded off back to her own house as I stood gaping after her.

She was right, obviously, but it did not seem neighbourly to point it out.

I apologised again as I picked the laptop up. "It's my neighbour, she has dementia. I do my best to keep an eye on her."

Stephanie's head tilted, her face softening into sympathy. "Oh, I understand. My poor mother..."

My body froze at the mention of mothers. There was a ringing in my ears that caused me to miss whatever Stephanie was saying about hers. I nodded my head slowly. Hopefully it looked normal to her.

There was another ten minutes or so of chat. If it accomplished anything, it was not obvious. I supposed I would just have to wait to see if I heard from her again.

At least speaking to her gave me the motivation to scroll a few job sites until it got too depressing. It was all of seven minutes later that I shut my laptop off.

The nets were still slightly askew. There was no way I was getting up to fix them. Just as there was no way I'd be cleaning my windows, no matter what Doris said. I wondered briefly if I should check on her, but she seemed well enough during her brief visit.

Thinking of it, there was a possibility that she had dropped by because she was worried about me, if she remembered me being injured and the fact that she had not seen me leave the house since.

Three whole days (possibly, I've never had the best grasp of time passing) of clattering around my house at various degrees until I'd finally been able to stand at a 180 that morning. Three days of going nowhere and doing nothing. Par for the course for me, but the fact I'd had no choice this time felt terribly unfair. I had been, I was sure, on the cusp of getting out, getting active and getting my life fixed.

There are some fun things about not leaving the house for long periods. You can shave off your eyebrows and see what that looks like. You can grow out all your (non-eyebrow) facial hair for an interesting change. You can stay in your favourite pyjamas until they basically disintegrate. Once you really start to embrace freedom (read: have a breakdown), you can conduct some interesting experiments in cutting your own hair with fabric scissors. Not seeing anyone means no one is there to watch you trying to figure out how mullets work. It's all fun and frolics until you have to leave the house. 'Have' being the operative word. The food's all gone, even the last-resort shit, and you've left it too late for an online grocery order.

Plus, maybe going outside would do you some good. Direct contact with sunlight would not cause you to burst into flames, no matter how badly you wanted to be a vampire when you were fourteen (because of Anne Rice; you're too old for *Twilight*). Sure, there was always a chance that you would look at someone the wrong way or misjudge some etiquette that everyone but you just seemed to automatically understand. Then everyone present would freeze in place, point at you and start screeching like Donald Sutherland. A mild chance, but it was still very much there. What was certain, though, was that you needed to get off your arse and stop watching old sci-fi movies all day, relying on tinned soup (purchased by a woman who had long since died) for sustenance.

The timing was right, anyway. You'd had a bath only the night before due to that being the only thing that would stop Satan's minions from pummelling your back with tiny sledgehammers. Because, despite being just north of thirty, you have a physique which would make your new, ancient best friend from next door wince in sympathy. Luckily enough, your bathroom – indeed, your whole house – was designed for someone elderly and/or disabled, and you've finally been putting the various bars and poles to good use. So you're no longer selfishly living in accommodation meant to benefit someone far worse off than you. Anyone watching the house and seeing a hunched-up short-arse with messy, greying hair hobbling around on a walking stick would be very surprised to discover that the seventy-year-old previous occupant was no longer living there – and that the house now belonged to her only grandchild who spent all their time berating themselves via internal monologues in the second person.

Anyway, I got out of bed and went to Asda.

Unwashed (and, thankfully, not recently mulletted) hair shoved into a beanie; teeth brushed as that is the one hygiene norm I always manage no matter how bad I am; clean clothes consisting of jeans that were now a bit too tight and a ridiculously oversized T-shirt to cover that fact. I shoved a facemask into my pocket. It had fangs on it. Because I'm edgy. And, emotionally, still fourteen.

I am neither proud nor ashamed of the fact that I peeped round the door to make sure that Doris was not there before I left. I did not need multiple unsettling encounters in one day.

I made it all the way to Asda without having to deal with anyone.

I never bother with a basket or trolley; I carry a huge Bag for Life around with me and just put everything in there. It saves time and effort and reduces contact with surfaces that others have touched. It's so convenient that it just makes sense. In case it is somehow not obvious: not everything I put in the bag ends up going through the self-checkout.

Towards the end of my trip, I was looking at some magazines I had no intention of buying. There was a free protein bar on the front of some overpriced health and fitness rag that I was considering half-inching. Suddenly, I heard a shuffle of feet. Then there was a horrid tingling sensation all along my spine telling me that someone was right behind me and far too close. I suppressed a shudder and turned.

It was an elderly man, somewhere in the region of Doris' age. Slightly shorter than me (which was a nice treat), bent with age and leaning on a stick. He wore a disposable face mask which looked like it had spent a week in the carpark outside before he just happened to stumble across it and decide to give it a new home on his face. It rose and fell with his breath in an unsettling way. It was probably doing him fuck all good. At least he was keeping a nice, safe, two-centimetre distance away from me.

He nodded at my bag, now full to the brim. "I hope you're going to pay for all that."

His voice was so weird that I didn't immediately process what he had said. It was nasally, but also like there was a lot of fluid in his throat.

"I said, I hope you're going to pay for that."

I looked down at the bag, then back up at him. I should have told him to mind his own business, but I was just so thrown by the encounter.

He scowled, as far as I could tell from the visible section of his face. "The security guard's already watching you."

I looked up and down the aisle. "Where?"

"Up at the front on his little monitor thing; I've seen him."

"You've seen him watching me?"

"Obviously not you, specifically. He's watching, though. Stealing's far more trouble than it's worth."

I had thought he'd been having a go at me, but that last part sounded like a genuine warning. Then again, he sounded like Peter Lorre partially submerged in a bubble bath, so his tone wasn't exactly easy to judge. I decided to take it as friendly advice.

"Right. Thanks."

I took a couple of steps to the left, manoeuvring my big old shoplifting bag around him. At no point did he shift to make it any easier for me. I felt his eyes on me the rest of the way around the shop.

My bag was overspilling by the time I got to the checkout; I had to shove a couple of things under each arm. My own stupid fault for underestimating how much I would be getting. Annoyingly, I intended to pay for it all as well. Peter Lorre had sufficiently put the shits up me.

As usual, I passed a rack of Bags for Life just before the tills. Then I backtracked. Among all the cartoon anthropomorphic fruit and generic flowers was a print of a Border Collie puppy sitting on a doorstep. Head tilted, one ear sticking up as the other flopped down. I stared at it long enough to suddenly become self-conscious when I realised what I was doing. I just about managed to pick it up with my last two remaining free fingers.

I did not pay for it. I couldn't. It felt like something that was owed to me. Without bothering to check that no one was watching, I pressed 'I have my own bag' and set it down in the bagging area.

On autopilot, I put everything else through the till and split it all evenly between the two bags. It all worked out so perfectly that it seemed like fate. My head was blissfully free from thought until the moment I made unfortunate eye contact with the security guard on the way out.

There he was, behind his little monitor thingy as foretold by the unlikely prophet. He must have seen something on my face because his eyes narrowed in a cartoon parody of suspicion. He got up and stood in my most likely path to the exit.

I could not very well turn and walk in another direction. Far too obvious. I could make a big show of forgetting something and going back for it, but that would just prolong the anxiety and I was not sure my fragile psyche could take it. There was nothing for it but to keep on walking towards him, act surprised when he stopped me and attempt to bullshit my way out of it. There was every chance he would overlook the bag in favour of its legally purchased contents anyway.

He shuffled on his feet as I approached him. Readying himself for some sort of altercation. I doubt I gave him the impression of a fighter, but perhaps he expected me to make a run for it. He stepped in front of me. I raised an eyebrow ready for my 'shoplifting? Moi?!' act. Then he cleared his throat and opened his mouth to speak.

There was an inhuman cry. For one very confused moment, I thought it came from the security guard – my Donald Sutherland-based paranoid fantasy finally come to life. But then it became obvious that the sound had come from behind me.

I turned to see poor Peter Lorre a few feet away. Stick abandoned at his feet, he was leaning over with his hands on his knees, wheezing so badly that my own throat ached in sympathy.

The security guard looked between the two of us. I saw him do the mental calculation and opt to help the possibly dying old man.

I heroically left him to it and fled the scene.

On the way home, it dawned on me what was weird about the old man's mask: when he breathed in, far too much of the material was sucked back. His mouth must have been huge, and a very peculiar shape. Perhaps it was some kind of facial injury, something that would also affect his voice. Fuck, I hoped he was all right. As hand-wavey as my morals sometimes were, the idea of benefiting from an old man collapsing and dying did not sit right with me. Then the ridiculous thought occurred that he could have distracted the guard on purpose. He had warned me about him, after all. It made zero sense, of course; it had to be just a coincidence. The world and everyone in it did not revolve around me.

I barely thought about the bag that nearly got me arrested. I could have been sitting in a police station at that very moment, crying to anyone who would listen about my dead dog. Did they let people off with crimes for being so pathetic that it brings down the whole vibe in the cells?

It was a relief to reach the small row of bungalows. It always was.

There were four to a line, not separated by any kind of fencing. We did not have individual gardens, rather a sort of shared green space. It probably would have been quite cosy if I actually got on with any of my neighbours. On my particular stretch was a woman I'd never spoken to but who always seemed to glare at me whenever I saw her. I had no idea who, if anyone, lived next door to her. Then there was Doris' house, and mine on the end.

From the corner of my eye, I saw curtains twitching in the second house. Not empty, then. I risked a look over and stopped dead in my tracks. The old man dropped the curtain and backed away from the window faster than I would have thought him capable.

But then, he must have been fast to beat me home. Even if he hadn't had time to remove his useless mask.

3

SIGMUND FREUD

Curtains twitched in my hand – my wrinkled, liver-spotted hand.

Beyond the nice, clean nets was the footpath in front of our row of bungalows. It took me a second to recognise it because I was viewing it from an entirely new angle. Like I was in one of the neighbouring houses rather than my own.

There was nothing of any obvious interest outside until a woman walked into view with her dog. Had I been myself, or had any degree of control, I would have gasped at the sight of them.

It was Nan – hale and hearty – walking my young, beautiful Sam. It was *so* clear. Much clearer than a normal memory. Precious details I had long forgotten were now right in front of my eyes. A gift from the subconscious that usually hated me.

Dream Me's hands tightened on the curtains.

"That thing better not shit in me petunias," I said in an old-man voice. The statement was weird enough to pull me out of the dream.

I opened my eyes to a peculiar kind of darkness. Not normal blackness, but like the shading in a pencil drawing, except it appeared to be moving, along with the walls and ceiling. A shifting, twisting animation of my bedroom. It was as though I had awoken in a nightmare cartoon, the kind that traumatised kids for life.

I tried to turn my head, but it would not move. In a panic, I tried and failed to move any other part of my body. My frantic, non-thrashing left me breathless. I gave up with a pathetic whine. At least I could still do that.

I lay there watching black patterns swirling around my ceiling as I calmed my breathing. This was another dream, obviously. Or sleep paralysis. Either way, there was nothing I could do but let it play out.

And so, it began to play.

Doris emerged from the wall to my left. Dragging one leg behind her, moving in a jerking motion. She came to stand at the side of my bed and peered down at me, pouting in sarcastic sympathy.

I tried to say her name (not that it was even her name). All that came out was an awful choking sound. I tried and failed to twist the noises I was making into recognisable words. The whole time, Doris half-heartedly suppressed her smile; the corners of her mouth still sneaking up here and there.

There was movement in my periphery. My eyes shot over to the right. A maskless Peter (not that it was even his name) glowered at me. Almost the entire bottom half of his face was missing, as though it had rotted away. From the nose up it was business as usual, but beneath that was jagged flesh, exposed gums and a set of somehow perfectly intact false teeth. The tiny flaps of skin around the hole where his mouth should have been fluttered with every breath.

I gagged.

Just in case – just in fucking case – I tried to move again. All I could manage was to twitch my fingers. It caught the attention of my elderly visitors. They looked down at my hands. Then, ever so slowly, they both turned to look in the same direction: towards the end of my bed. The mattress dipped down by my feet.

My heart raced so hard it was painful. Surely that would wake me up.

"Mask? Oh, Massy, Massy, Maa-aask?"

The voice was croaky. Inhumanely so. As though the speaker's throat were full of shrapnel. They pressed their hands down just above my knees. There was precious little weight behind it.

"This is no way to live, is it? All alone. You haven't even got that stupid dog anymore."

The hands slipped off my legs. The mattress shifted as the person – if it was a person – crawled up the bed towards my face.

"You don't have to live like this. I can take it all away."

I still couldn't move my head; I could only look to Doris and Peter for a reaction. They stared blankly at the thing crawling up my body, their slowly turning heads tracking its movements. I scrunched my eyes shut. A single tear ran from each one. Dry flesh rubbed over my face; a hand cupped my cheek. A tear hit it, pooling against the little wall it made. Not a single fucking thing could have convinced me to open my eyes.

"Well, look at you tucked up safe and warm in Grandma's bed."

It lay down on top of me. Still so light, I could easily throw it off if only I could move. I had to assume the things that ran over my lips then were fingers, but the shapes were all wrong, the sizes inconsistent.

"Oh, Mask, what a big mouth you've got."

It gripped my ears, yanking my head from side to side until I cried out.

"And what delicate ears."

It let go. Both its hands slid down to cover my face. I wept beneath them.

"And what fragile little eyeballs." It pressed down hard on my eyelids.

I opened my mouth and screamed. I shook my head until its hands shifted. My eyes opened as a reflex.

I saw its face.

My body moved before my eyes were even open, hurling itself out of bed. Up, up, up. Foot caught in one of the blankets, crashing to the floor. Pain shooting through my arm. I struggled to my feet and slammed my hands against the wall until one landed on the light switch. I pressed my back flat against the wall and stood there trying – and largely failing – to breathe normally.

I was awake. Properly awake. There was no one in my room but me. Nothing in my room but the usual mess.

What a fucking horrible dream. What was wrong with my subconscious that it cooked that shit up? And was the nice but weird snapshot of Nan and Sam just to lull me into a false sense of security? Christ, what a shitty, spiteful brain I had.

Well, that was my sleep fucked for the rest of the night.

Images flashed up in my mind: Doris' impassive face, Peter's ruined one. And finally, the creature: a cracked, black skull only partially wrapped in loose, grey skin; two empty, elongated eye sockets. Its whole face was longer than it should have been, as though it were part way through melting. There was no doubt that I would be seeing it every time I closed my eyes for weeks.

There was a long mirror about a foot away from me. I rolled along the wall until I could peer into it. My face was blotchy, my eyes red. My ears were red too. I stared at myself for a minute before becoming paranoid that something awful was going to pop up behind me. I got back into bed, gathering my tangled mess of blankets.

Sometime in my teens, I stayed up and watched *The Exorcist* after Nan had gone to bed. Except, I did not watch *The Exorcist*. I watched right up to the spider-walk down the stairs scene and shat myself so thoroughly that I turned it off and ran up to my room. Nan told me the next morning that she'd woken up from the noise and I lied about tripping on the stairs. I don't think she bought it.

For about a year after that, I was plagued by a recurring nightmare. Once every few weeks or so I would 'wake up' paralysed on the bed. It was always dark, but my eyes had adjusted enough that I could see everything. Not that there was anything to see, I was just painfully aware of the fact that the devil was coming to possess me. After a minute or two of struggling, I would start to feel something moving through my body in a wave. It started down at my feet and I always managed to scare myself awake before the sensation reached my head.

I had no idea why I was suddenly being visited by the pumped-up, adult version of my adolescent nightmare. Nothing had scared me recently. There was my near miss with the security guard, but I doubted that was who the creature represented.

I sat there, focused on my breathing and attempted to apply some logic to the situation.

Thinking about it rationally, it wasn't all that strange that I'd had such a fucked-up dream. I had been having weird dreams for a while (and I knew why), they just hadn't been anywhere near this intense or terrifying. The content of the dream wasn't even that hard to decipher: Peter's face must have been what I was imagining under the mask; Doris had appeared out of nowhere twice now. I had no idea what the thing crawling into bed with me was, or why it had decided to fuck up my face fairy tale-style. Then again, Doris basically shoved her fingers in all my face holes the first time we met so perhaps it came from that. Maybe all these encounters with people nearing the end of their life had me freaking out about my own mortality. That was what that decrepit nightmare creature had represented.

Satisfied that I had rationalised away all the horrors of my subconscious with my big, adult brain, I settled down in bed and did not sleep another wink.

*

The next day, I decided to check in on Doris. I felt guilty about being subconsciously afraid of her. She was a harmless old woman who had lost some of her mental faculties and I was having nightmares where she gleefully witnessed me being taken by a monster. In all honesty, it would have made far more sense for her to be scared of me.

I peered through her front window before trying her door. I couldn't see anything; the curtains were dark and thick and still drawn despite it being midday. I knocked three times, counting to fifty in between each one. When all three knocks went unanswered, I took a few steps back until I hit the public footpath that ran along the front of our houses. That gave me a view of Peter's house as well. Both looked empty: unkempt grass around their doorsteps; dead flowers in a hanging basket between them; curtains pulled haphazardly in both windows. It was odd to see them bookended by the two houses where people still obviously lived. Not that mine was in a much better state than either of theirs. I wanted to knock at Peter's door too, but it would be just my luck if he answered. What would I say to him, exactly? Thanks for the possibly-on-purpose-but-probably-accidental rescue? If he hadn't meant to be a distraction, it must have looked to him that I saw him struggling and skipped off home. He might even be offended that I had not recognised him as my neighbour. Him looking out his front window to find me staring at his house would most likely not go down well. I left it about another minute before I went back inside.

Standing in my hall, I was considering trying for Doris at the back door when there was a knock behind me.

I hadn't seen the postie or anyone else approaching. I could not see a lot through the narrow glass panels – just that it was a shortish figure with a mop of grey-white hair. I opened the door to find Doris beaming brightly.

"Did you knock for me just now?"

"I did, yeah."

"You have to give me longer than that to get to the door; I don't move so quickly these days."

I had been out there for several minutes, definitely longer than I would have thought she needed. She certainly barged past me and into my living room quickly enough. I felt a familiar stab of outrage and had to remind myself that I'd been the one to call for Doris.

I followed her and asked if she wanted a cup of tea. I had purchased tea. And sugar. And oat milk. The host with the most. Maybe I should have splashed out on some Ferrero Rocher, really spoiled her.

"No milk or sugar for me, please," Doris said, rendering two-thirds of my purchases obsolete.

I sulked into the kitchen and put the kettle on. She scuttled loudly enough behind me that I knew she was there.

"What did you want me for?"

That's right: I'd been the originator of this social interaction, not the elderly woman who had made the long, and possibly painful, journey to her front door only to find out that I'd given up and buggered off. Who had then been forced to chase after me.

"I just wanted to check in. How are you, Doris?"

If the odd little smile she gave then was any indicator, she was touched by my question. I tried not to think of the very different smile from my nightmare.

"I'm well enough, sweet. You don't have to worry about old Doris. It's you I worry about, all alone at your age. A nice young thing like you should be out enjoying yourself: girlfriends, boyfriends, whatever."

It became imperative then that I completely turn my back on Doris for several minutes in order to make her tea. Alas, due to her spartan tastes, there was little I could do to draw the process out. Tea bag in water and done – it was unsatisfying, somehow. An incomplete ritual. I turned back and handed her the steaming cup.

"Careful, it's hot."

She took it with both hands and held it close to her chest. "I like it like that. Warms my bones." She brought it up close to her face, but did not take a sip. I lost her for a moment as she stared into the mug.

Rather than stand there listening to the clock in the living room tick, I decided to ask her one of the many questions I'd put on my mental list.

"Do you know the man who lives next door to you?"

Doris shrugged, tea sloshing right up to the brim but failing to overtake it. "Can't say I do. Why do you ask?"

"I ran into him the other day; just thought he was a bit odd."

"It's just old age, comes to us all. It'll even get you in the end." She looked thoughtful for a moment. "Unless it doesn't, I suppose."

I tried to think of a way to ask about Peter's face that did not sound horribly ableist. But then, maybe Doris didn't know herself if she hadn't had much to do with him. I moved on.

"How about her on the end?"

"Rude bitch."

I snorted. "Doris!"

Doris looked thoroughly pleased with herself. "Well, she is. I don't much like that son of hers either – when he deigns to pop round. Deborah was the only neighbour I really liked. Lovely woman, she was."

A lump threatened to form in my throat. I leaned back against the fridge, aiming for casual but probably looking like I'd collapsed on a fainting couch. Spiritually, I had. "Yeah."

"You must miss her something awful. And your mother, of course."

I had no idea what Doris knew about my mother or what had happened to her. I knew I didn't want to talk about it, though.

"Do you have any family, Doris?"

She took a break from almost dipping her nose into her tea, looking away wistfully. "There was a sister. Audrey, her name was. Lost her marbles, poor thing. Awful way to go."

My heart clenched in my chest. Poor Audrey. Poor Doris. "And now?"

"Now? Oh, they're all gone now; it's just me these days. I suppose we're in the same boat, really."

Fuck, that was grim. I should have made myself a cup of tea; I could have done with having something to shove my face into.

Doris got a tiny lightbulb above her head. "We could do this regularly." She gestured with her cup, nearly scalding us both. "Tea and a nice little chat every now and then."

"I'd like that." It was out of my mouth before I even knew whether or not it was a lie. A moment's thought told me that it – somehow – was not.

Doris smiled. She placed her cup in the sink.

"How about I let you get on with your day? I'm sure you've plenty to do."

I couldn't tell if this was sarcasm or not, so I just nodded.

"I'll drop in on you sometime." She left by the back door and skipped past the kitchen window.

I had no idea why I was suddenly in the market for elderly friends.

Oh, fuck that. I knew exactly why: I was lonely. Plus, it was always better than having elderly enemies.

As I went to wash up Doris' mug, I marvelled at how together she had been. Her dementia – if that was even what it was – must be something that came and went.

The mug in the sink was still full to the brim; Doris couldn't have had so much as a sip. She must have forgotten. Or maybe I'd ruined it by leaving the bag in. I was severely out of practice at hosting.

That, apparently, was all set to change.

4

IRENE

Irene had fucked up.

She had originally planned to go to the library on Friday, but when the time came, she was far too tired. She definitely could not have gone without her chair, which meant getting a taxi there and probably back as well. There was no way she had the energy for rooting around the house for taxi fare. Assuming that a taxi would even take her with the chair – she had been abandoned on the roadside before. If she left it until the next day, she reasoned that she might feel up to the twenty-minute walk so long as she went first thing. Plus, if she stayed the whole five hours until the library closed, the librarian, Mae, might give her a lift home as she sometimes did. That same librarian also tended to pack a much larger lunch than she needed. And had pastel-dyed hair, bright golden-brown eyes and adorable dimples. With just over a week to sort the mess she had found herself in, Irene reasoned that one more day would not make any difference.

Thus, she spent the whole of Friday trying to find a comfortable position in bed so she could sit and draft a letter to the council. Apart from the bathroom, for obvious reasons, she was keeping to one room in order to conserve heat and electricity. The kettle was plugged in on the floor for tea to stave off hunger pains; the last of the foodbank stuff had run out on Wednesday. She could always ask Mae to drop her off near there on Saturday under some pretence. There was a decent chance Mae would see through it; she had a map of all the local foodbanks on her desk that she photocopied for anyone who asked. Without a doubt, Mae would take Irene straight there if asked and then insist on waiting to drive her home as well, but that all seemed too much of an imposition to Irene.

They had been to the foodbank once, but the pretence had been Mae's. On one of the Saturday lifts home, she had asked if Irene minded that they stop at the post office on the way. Irene had of course said that was fine, and then Mae parked outside the post office that just happened to be next door to the foodbank.

"I'm going to be a while in the post office; do you want to get out and stretch your legs?" Mae was a picture of innocence. It was impossible not to smile back at her. If anyone else had pulled a stunt like that, Irene would have found it patronising. But Mae was always so earnest in everything she did.

Once they were back in the car – Irene with a few days' worth of food, Mae with a cheap packet of envelopes – they said no more about it. Then Irene had gone and spoiled it when they pulled up at her place by thanking Mae with just a touch too much emotion in her voice. Mae had placed a hand on Irene's wrist (oh so close to her hand) but then she said what she always said when Irene thanked her.

"Don't worry about it. I'm a librarian, it's what I do."

She never could figure out if Mae liked her back or was just doing what she had convinced herself was a librarian's duty.

Irene's new plan to go to the library a day late ended up going to shit the night before. Her stomach started playing up, her joints felt as though they had doubled in size, she was exhausted but could not have fallen asleep if she'd clubbed herself with a hammer. The sun was rising by the time she finally slipped from consciousness into a series of bizarre dreams.

Death came for her: a dark, vaguely human shape. A rotten skeleton partially covered in wispy, crackling skin. Irene had the sense that, if she touched it, its body would crumble into dust. Not that she would have touched it in a million years. It sat on the end of her bed humming to itself as it watched her. That was all it did, every time. It moved around the room in each dream, but it was always humming and always staring straight at her.

By the time Irene woke up, it was just after two in the afternoon. The library closed at three on Saturdays. The public computers automatically shut off fifteen minutes earlier than that to get people to leave. Even if she skipped the bathroom and just threw some clothes on over her pyjamas, she would be lucky to get there in twenty minutes. Even if there was a free computer, she couldn't do everything she needed to in so short a time. She was fucked. The library wouldn't be open again until Tuesday morning. Nearly three whole days without the internet. Or, at least, sufficient internet to do the mountain of things she needed to do to dig herself out of this hole.

Irene lay back down and tried to focus on her breathing. Her empty stomach whined.

She thought back to the days she had wasted calling the Universal Credit helpline. Holding through insufferable music, hoping the call would be picked up by someone young enough and new enough that they still thought they could help people. That they still *wanted* to help people. She went through the story several times: she had missed that interview because they had told her the wrong time. She had even arrived early for the time she thought it was, using money she didn't have to spare on a taxi. They all just kept telling her the same thing: she needed to appeal and would receive no money until she did.

That had taken up so much of her energy that she'd let everything else slide. When she finally sat down to open all her post, she found a dozen pieces of junk mail and an eviction notice. The bastards were coming on Monday the seventeenth.

Today was Saturday the eighth. When she finally got to the library on Tuesday the eleventh, she would need to send an email to the council informing them that she was about to be made homeless and ask for assistance. What were the chances of them getting something sorted for her in six days?

Her stomach whined again. It went on for so long that she thought it was going to implode, finally giving up and eating itself. When it eventually stopped, there was another noise she did not immediately recognise. A chill went through her when she realised that it was someone humming.

Another dream, it had to be. She must have passed out again.

Irene turned her head to see Death sitting in her wheelchair, rolling slightly back and forth as it hummed to itself. It smiled down at her, tilting its head so quickly Irene thought it might fall off.

"Look at you, poor little thing! So tired. You don't want to be dealing with all this, do you?" It gestured at the pile of papers on her floor. Then it leaned forward to read the nearest one. "Dear homelessness team, my name is..." It sat up and – for want of a better word – pouted. "Well, that can't be your name."

It was her deadname. Across all the letters: the sanction notification, the eviction notice, her own appeal for help. She had said it over and over on the phone, trying fruitlessly to win back her Universal Credit. She had been called it throughout the assessment that deemed her fit for work despite her lack of ability to stand up for more than ten minutes on a consistent basis. Again and again she had to pretend to be someone else for people who barely saw her as human, let alone a woman. Death was right: she was fucking tired.

"What is your name, sweetheart?"

"Irene." It came out in a whisper. It was all she could manage.

Death stood and slowly came towards her. "Oh, Irene, don't you want all of this to be over?"

It suddenly became clear: this was not a dream; Irene was dying. She had long suspected that she wouldn't reach forty.

Whether it was malnutrition or organ failure or one of the other millions of things that could kill such a fragile human being, Death had come for her. She felt no fear. Only relief. No more pain or hunger; no more infuriating bureaucracy designed with cruelty in mind; no more struggling to stay alive in a world that only hated her.

There would also be no more Mae, of course, but that was a fool's dream anyway.

Death crouched down, bringing their faces level.

"Say the word, sweet Irene, and I will take you away from here."

Irene smiled. A single tear slid from her eye. This was the happiest she had been in years. Finally, she would be at peace.

"Do it," she said. "Take me away."

It did.

5

VINCENT

Insomnia.

I don't believe in any kind of afterlife, mostly because I don't want to. That said, if I were to imagine Hell, it would be like insomnia. Lying there alternating between staring at the ceiling and forcing your dry eyes shut. Time somehow coming to a standstill despite the fact that every tick of your bedroom clock is like jabbing a Stanley knife into your brain. Just one excruciating, endless night alone with your thoughts.

That's not a million miles away from how I used to picture death as a kid. Conscious and immobile for all eternity. Horrifically aware of the passage of time. Unable to do anything about it. I was an intense child. My mom used to say I depressed the hell out of her.

I have never been fantastic at sleeping. Probably dates back to childhood when I would lie there in the dark thinking, 'This is what death is like'. Then came adulthood and my body flat out deciding that it hated me. Now, of course, there are the sleep pattern disruptions that come from both taking and ceasing to take medication, and that was all before I started dreaming about decaying neighbours and a grey nightmare creature that probably represented death.

They had all appeared in my dreams again. I barely remembered, though. It was all short, blurry snippets. The one upside of a distinct lack of the old Rapid Eye Movement. If it weren't for the vague sense of dread that I woke up with (more than usual, I mean), I probably wouldn't even have noticed.

I try not to buy medicine to help me sleep, especially when I suspect it would be a bad idea for me to have any kind of drugs in the house. They never work for long and the sleep it does give you is an unnatural one that doesn't even leave you refreshed afterwards. But sometimes it's worth it just to not spend another night awake mentally screaming at yourself.

That was how I found myself in town again, a tote bag containing night-time cold medicine on my shoulder.

I could hear a busker somewhere – way too early in the day – starting a song I knew I was going to recognise once they got to the words.

Town was not too busy given it was fairly early, but there were still too many people around for my liking. I get frustrated having to weave my way around and through people, having to watch where everyone else is going because they evidently do not bother.

An old woman I had been trying to pass came to a sudden stop in front of me, causing me to almost crash into her. When I stepped around her, my foot slid in something mushy. I turned, dreading what I would see. Luckily, it was the remains of a pasty or something. I checked the bottom of my shoe – nothing that wouldn't just come off as I walked. When I looked up again, I noticed a man dawdling a few feet behind me. I turned and walked away as though I had not seen him.

It had only been a moment's glance, but I noticed something off about him. From the unwashed, overgrown ginger hair and the clothes – dirty joggers with holes on the bottom, several layers on top including a faded flannel and a jacket that was far too big for him – I thought he might have been homeless. Obviously that was not the problem, it was the way he was standing in such an awkward place. He had also clearly been looking at me until he saw me spot him. Hopefully, he'd just seen me step in something and was being nosy. A minute or so later, I looked over my shoulder as casually as I could. He was coming my way and seemed to be watching me again. I went into the nearest shop.

It was a shoe shop. Small and cramped with the unpleasant aroma of cheap leather and glue. I wandered around idly, one circuit of the floor. When I got back to the door, I almost walked into him as he entered.

He backed up to let me pass. Once I was out, I stopped by the door and knelt down to tie my laces. I watched his feet shuffle, knowing I had backed him into a corner. He either had to go through with the pretence and enter the shop or stand there and wait for me to finish so he could start following me again. After a moment of indecision, he went inside.

I sprang up and rushed around the corner, heading for a small health food shop a few doors down. I went as far inside as I could while still being able to see the windows. Less than a minute later, the guy walked past. He was clearly looking around for me.

I leaned against a fridge and tried to calm down. Would he double back when he couldn't find me? Whatever nefarious deed he intended to commit upon my person surely depended on the element of surprise. Now he'd lost that, he'd have to give up and go home. Or pick on someone else. Rather them than me.

The busker must have been close – I could hear him clearly now. The song was that starry night one by the 'American Pie' guy. I decided to use him as a timer: once he got to the end, I'd risk sticking my head out the door to see if the coast was clear.

By now I was getting odd looks from the woman behind the till. I picked up a protein bar – the nearest thing – and pretended to read the back of it. What I was actually doing was listening to 'Vincent', mouthing along with the words beneath my mask. Such a lovely song. I hoped I'd be able to listen to it again without having flashbacks to hiding from a man who undoubtedly meant to do me harm.

The music stopped suddenly. The singer had been mid-sentence; I finished the line unaccompanied. I waited a moment for it to start up again. When it didn't, I was struck with the bizarre certainty that something awful had happened to the busker.

It didn't take long to spot him when I left the shop. I would have seen him on the way in if I hadn't been freaking out. Just across the way and a few shops down. His guitar was on his back and he was frantically trying to gather up the change he'd collected in the case at his feet. For a second, I thought perhaps a PCSO had told him to move on. Then I saw who was stock still and staring at him as he panicked.

As predicted, my stalker had decided to pick on someone else.

I could have turned and walked in the opposite direction. Beat myself up for being a shitty human being from the safety of my own house. But, it seemed, I was walking towards them.

Stalker guy had moved in on the busker, getting right into his personal space. Town wasn't busy, but it was hardly empty. No one looked in their direction. In fact, everyone was Not Looking at them so much it was like their eyes were being repelled by magnets. Two homeless guys fighting – a lanky white one apparently bullying a shorter, Black man – was something that people Did Not Look at. Some of them were probably secretly pleased that the busker had been interrupted.

As I barrelled towards them without a plan, I tried telling myself that this shit was all confidence and bluster. Two things from which I usually suffered a severe lack, but hey-ho.

The busker was upright now, clutching his cache of coins to his chest. Stalker guy was an inch from his face, saying something I couldn't hear.

"Hi!"

It came out of my mouth so loud that the two of them jumped. A couple of people who'd been steadfastly ignoring the scene until then finally turned to look.

The busker's eyebrows raised; his eyes filled with hope. I fumbled around for a follow up.

"Do you know *The Flight of Dragons*?"

Stalker guy took a few steps back. The busker righted himself. "Do I know what, sorry?"

Judging myself sufficient distance from the two of them, I pulled my mask down from one ear so he could hear me more clearly.

"*The Flight of Dragons*. It was a movie I was really into as a kid and it had this title song and it was by the guy who sang that one that you were just doing. It was really good. The song and the movie. It's about this guy who…"

I stealthily watched the two of them as I launched into the synopsis of a forgotten classic of fantasy animation from 1982. The busker looked from me to the stalker and back. I could see that stalker guy was also looking at me, but I kept my eyes forward, willing him to disappear.

"I don't know it, sorry."

I fished my phone from my coat pocket. "I'll find it for you."

Stalker guy tossed his head back with a snort. Then, finally, he gave up and walked away. I had to bite down on the urge to swear loudly in relief. I kept up my act of pretending to look for a song.

"Is he gone?" I asked, without looking up.

"Yeah, he's gone."

I put my phone away and got my first decent look at the busker: maybe a couple years younger than me with a patchy beard. No hair showed from under his cap, so it must have been very closely cropped. He was a little taller than me and pretty skinny. Ripped jeans and a grungy jumper, neither of which appeared to be sartorial affectations.

"Do you know him?"

He nodded, watching the crowd, probably for stalker's return. "Ginger? Yeah. Hadn't seen him in a while. Hoped I was free of him."

"He was following me before he came over to you."

That made him look at me. His eyes were wide. Then they softened into something sorrowful.

"I'm sorry."

That threw me. If it hadn't been for the look on his face, I would have thought he meant he misheard me. I had no idea how to respond.

"Right, well, I'd best be getting on. Take care of yourself."

I gave him a quick smile before fixing my mask. As I turned to walk away, he stepped forward.

"Don't! I…"

I waited.

"I like your nails? Very Fraulein Sally Bowles."

I looked down at my hands. A spout of insomnia-induced boredom had driven me to paint my nails in the dark green shade my nan had always favoured. As wary as I am that it increases my chances of being read as a woman, I do like having painted nails. Plus, it is getting more common for people of any gender to do it; the busker's nails – I could see where he was still clutching coins to his chest with one hand – were black.

"Thanks. I like yours, too."

He held up his other hand to better demonstrate them. "You know, a drunk girl gave me this? She offered me some change, realised she didn't have any and then started crying. I was trying to calm her down and she was just frantically searching through her bag for something she could possibly give me." He chuckled fondly as he remembered the tale.

There was a raggedy woven bracelet around his wrist in very particular shades of blue, white and pink. I almost asked if the same girl had given him that as well but, if it did mean what I thought it meant, drawing attention to it was likely to make him uncomfortable.

"Why don't I walk you home? Or wherever else you're going. Just in case Ginger isn't really gone."

I took a quick look around the square; there were no obvious hiding spots. The busker had appeared to keep his eye on Ginger the whole time as he walked away. I didn't think it was likely that he'd make a sudden reappearance, but I had no idea what I would do if he did. Then again, I could be jumping out of the frying pan and into the fire if I just went off with another stranger. I knew on an objective level that his likely being trans didn't necessarily make him a safe person to be around, nor did his knowing *Cabaret;* it still put me slightly more at ease, though. Plus, he'd indulged me bollocking on about a childhood fave and that was the sort of thing that endeared someone to me for life.

"That's probably a good idea."

He visibly relaxed, his shoulders dropping from around his ears. He had a killer smile on him.

"Great. Just let me sort my stuff out. I'm V, by the way."

He turned and began to gather the rest of his things.

"V? What's that stand for?"

He settled his guitar case onto his shoulder and we started walking.

"It varies, to be honest. I'm feeling Vincent at the minute, but I don't really want to commit to anything."

"Sounds like my approach to gender."

We shared a quick little smile then. I took it as confirmation from him. It was in contention for one of the most awkward, clunkiest things I had ever said, but it got the point across. Actually, I was glad to get that information in as smoothly as I did; the second I'd realised he might be trans I had wanted to point to his bracelet and shout, "That! Me too that! Friends now!"

I had intended to only walk with him for a while and make sure we separated before we neared my home, but then we got to talking. He asked the usual sort of stuff like my name and then why the hell was that my name. There was, of course, a story behind said name, but I changed the subject in case it set me off. I asked him about busking. That went on for a while. Then out of nowhere he asked me if I wanted to hear a story.

"What kind of story?"

We were just a couple of streets away from my place. I would have felt guilty about having him walk that far, but he seemed to be enjoying my company. That was a fun little first for me.

"It's a bit of a spooky story."

"Sure." I figured it was safe, seeing as I would be having a chemically induced sleep that night.

"There's this terrifying monster called The Nothing."

"That's what I'm afraid of."

He looked up, confused.

"Nothing."

His laugh sounded forced.

"What does it do? Eat you?"

"It's probably more accurate to say that it consumes you. It picks isolated people like the elderly or the homeless. Once it takes you, it has you, body and soul. It feeds on you."

"What's it look like?"

"The people it takes. It can wear their faces. That's how it gets close to people in the first place. It needs to know that you're all alone, that no one wants you. Then it pounces."

"How do you fight it?"

He shrugged. "I guess you just have to find somebody to want you."

"Well, that's me shit out of luck."

He flashed me a weak smile. He was giving off a weirdly intense vibe, staring at the floor and brooding.

"But then again, I'm not elderly or homeless so I should be all right."

"I hope so," V said, far too seriously for the conversation I thought we were having.

We came to the start of the bungalow row, and I had enough sense to stop there rather than let the nice stranger see exactly where I lived.

"This is me."

V stopped and looked around. I got the impression that he was surprised, like he'd spaced out and not realised how far we had walked.

"Do you want some bus fare to get back to town?"

He shook his head. "No, I'm staying out of town for the rest of the day. I don't want to chance running into Ginger again." He smiled down at me. "Take care of yourself, Mx Mask."

"You too, Mr V."

I waited for him to walk away first. It had been nice to talk to someone. Obviously, I had spent some time with Doris, but it wasn't quite the same thing as talking to someone roughly my own age who I actually had some things in common with. Plus, I hadn't been constantly watching out for signs that he wasn't okay and needed my help.

I went inside and tried not to let my imagination run away with me. He was homeless. I most likely wouldn't be able to find him again even if I went looking. There was zero reason to assume he wanted to make friends with some random person anyway. I just needed to write it off as a pleasant encounter with a person I was never going to see again and let it go. I was too old for making a new friend; I'd missed the boat on that one.

When I entered my bedroom that evening, I found the wig head wearing make-up. Lipstick was smeared over her mouth and her eyes were blacked out with mascara. I had no memory of doing that, but I'd certainly done crazier shit when I couldn't sleep. Plus, I could recall finding Nan's make-up when I was looking for nail varnish.

Instead of dwelling on my nocturnal nonsense, I took a huge shot of the night-night drugs and passed out somewhere around nine. No staring into space, no driving myself crazy. Just sweet, blissful nothing.

6

PROFESSIONAL ZACHERY

My head shook so violently that my eyeballs hurt. Caught between sleep and wakefulness – and given all the weird shit that had happened lately – I assumed I was under attack.

I shot up in bed, throwing my arms out in front of my face. The pain in my head stopped, but the noise continued: a dull, muffled buzzing. It clicked then. I fished around under my pillow and pulled out my phone. The call was from an unknown number and could thus fuck off. I did not answer phone calls at the best of times, let alone when they woke me up like that. It stopped ringing, but flashed up with a notification telling me to charge my phone and calling me a useless prick for leaving it on and under my pillow all night.

I tossed it onto the bed where it bounced across the mattress, and sat there rubbing my eye. When I looked down at the end of my bed, I had the strangest sensation. Vaguely akin to déjà vu. Something bad that gave me a sinking feeling in the pit of my stomach. And then I remembered the dream.

Ginger sat at the end of my bed. Legs crossed, elbows on his knees, head resting in his hands and staring at me the whole night. He did not move, no matter how much I cried or desperately attempted to yank the blankets over my head. Just sat and watched. It had felt like hours, but dreams don't always obey the regular rules of time and space and what have you.

The fucked-up dreams were getting really old. They had been vaguely amusing right up to the one where my elderly neighbours summoned a Fuck Demon. Just regular weird, absurdly whimsical stuff that I could tell people about, if I knew anyone, and they'd be like, 'Huh, weird.' Now it was all this terrifying nightmare wank. My subconscious needed to have a word with itself.

The phone buzzed again. This time, the little symbol for voicemail appeared in the corner. I took that to mean the call had actually been important. I grumbled onto the floor to plug it in and called my voicemail.

It was Stephanie? From the agency? We had a little chat last week? Remember? Well, anyway, she forwarded my CV to a few people and one company got back to her this morning. They wanted to interview me, but it would have to be today. She left a number for me to call her back. I did so: a temporary admin position paying decent money. I said I could be there for two.

And just like that, I had my first job interview in over three years.

Trying to remember the last one inevitably skipped to that final meeting where they'd told me that they would not be renewing my contract. Despite several warning signs, my naïve arse had not been expecting it. It was obvious they hadn't liked how much time I'd had off when Nan died. Or how miserable and, consequently, inefficient I'd been once I came back. That had been fairly early on, though, and I thought I'd turned a corner. So much so that I had started to assume my contract would be renewed. I even asked about it a few months beforehand. For someone with a paranoid streak, I sure took all the vague assurances I was given at face value. It was all the more shocking when they finally gave me the boot. Then there was some time spent wallowing and refusing to look for a job that was just going to waste several years of my life and then crush me beneath its heel. By the time I was over that particular tantrum, Sam was clearly on the way out and I needed to take care of him.

Now, how to explain that all to an interviewer while still making myself sound employable? I could start by reassuring them that there was no one else left to die on me.

I left via the back door. As if by magic, The Doris appeared. We managed to scare the absolute shit out of each other.

"Fuck. Sorry, Doris." I leaned against the door, trying to get my breath back.

Doris, for her part, seemed completely recovered. "It's fine, luvvie. Where are you off to?"

"A job interview." I straightened up and dusted myself off. "Wish me luck!"

She looked less than enthused. "You never mentioned."

"Yeah, they only called this morning."

Doris frowned. "That's very short notice. Are you sure you're ready?"

I shrugged. "Ready as I'll ever be." As I walked away from Doris Downer, I called over my shoulder that I'd pop round to see her when I got back.

Hopefully, I'd have some good news for her.

*

I allowed far too much time to get there, arriving at the building nearly thirty minutes before my interview. I killed a bit of that double- and triple-checking that I had the right place, switching between the sign on the building to the map on my phone to the note I'd made myself. I checked my appearance with my phone – it was fine as far as my face went. When I switched to a different angle, a man appeared behind me on the screen. I started, then stepped out of his way.

"Sor…"

Our eyes met and I almost screamed.

It was Ginger. There was no doubting it. He was even wearing the same clothes. We stared at each other in silence. Then he walked past me and onto the steps leading up to the building. For a moment, it looked as though he was going to go in, but he just turned and sat down on the bottom step. He placed his elbows on his knees and his head in his hands and stared up at me, face impassive.

I blinked a few times. My heartbeat thundered in my ears. I took a few steps back, then turned and started walking.

Had he followed me there? That didn't make sense. He must have just happened to spot me and decided to take revenge for foiling whatever it was I foiled the day before. Phenomenally shit luck on my part; I wasn't even close to the place where we'd last ran into each other. My phone was still in selfie mode, so I used it to check if he was following me again. Luckily, he had not moved. He just sat on the steps, watching me go.

There was a shop about five minutes from the office building, so I headed there. Hiding in a shop from the same creepy fucker for the second day in a row. I still had no idea what he even wanted from me. If he were just a mugger, he could have had my phone out of my hand and been off in a matter of seconds. Maybe intimidating people was all he was into. That would explain the bad feeling between him and V. It probably gave Ginger a cheap thrill to have people scared of him without having to do anything that could get him arrested.

The fuck was wrong with people?

I did enough aimless wandering in the shop to attract the attention of the person behind the till. Their eyes remained fixed on me for the rest of my visit. I know I have no right to be offended – given certain proclivities – but I was. After maybe twenty minutes of vamping, I grudgingly bought a bottle of Coke for appearances.

I sipped it as I made my way back to the building. Hopefully – logically, even – Ginger would have got bored of sitting there waiting for someone he couldn't even be sure would return. If he was still there, I was just going to have to stride right past him.

As I rounded the corner and saw him standing in front of the building, I felt a cold stab of panic. Then I realised he was talking to someone on the steps. A moment later, a security guard stepped into view. He must have confronted him about loitering there. Ginger appeared to be arguing. The security guard jabbed a thumb over his shoulder at the building. I assumed he was threatening to go back inside and call the police. Ginger shook his head and walked away – in the opposite direction to me, thankfully.

It was over. And I wasn't quite late for my interview yet. I ran to make it over to the building before the security guard went back inside. Right before I made it, my foot caught on a paving slab. I hit the ground hard, pain shooting through my leg. My Coke rolled away into the road where it fizzed out furiously onto the tarmac.

The security guard dragged me up by my arm. I wished he'd let me go on lying facedown on the floor for the rest of the day. Or maybe the rest of my life.

"All right?"

He didn't look all that concerned, more annoyed that someone had given him a dose of second-hand embarrassment and inconvenienced him.

"I'm here for an interview," came my pathetic voice.

He looked me over, but didn't say anything. I must have been filthy. My knees felt grazed and possibly even bleeding. Coke had soaked through my nice, smart shirt. He silently led the way into the building.

I signed in as a visitor in something of a daze. I wrote 'Mask' and then had to write over it. The receptionist clearly clocked it. At least she looked vaguely sympathetic to my plight.

The lift was out of order, so I had to further annoy the guard by having him escort me up three flights of stairs.

I arrived at the interview five minutes late, dishevelled, out of breath and on the verge of tears.

Somehow, it did not go well.

On the walk home, I swung wildly between keeping an eye out for Ginger and hoping he would sneak up behind me and snap my neck.

When I reached my back door, I looked over to Doris' house for any sign of movement. Selfishly, I hoped she didn't remember I'd said I would come round. What a horrid gremlin I was.

I must have yanked my keys out of my pocket too violently because they sprang from my hand and landed in the grass beside the doorstep. Kneeling to look for them had me hissing in pain. I took a seat on the doorstep instead, rolling up my trousers as far as they would go. Both knees were a mess, like something I would have done on the playground twenty-five years ago. I was just a child playing at Big Boy Things like getting a job and being a functioning human being. I slammed my head against the door hard enough to hurt.

My nan used to sit out here to smoke. She said the effort it took to go outside every time helped her cut down. Not long after I moved in, I found a few old fag butts wedged down the side of the doorstep. I made a little pile of them, then sat there trying not to cry until the woman who lived in the end house walked past glaring at me.

What kind of pathetic creature is reduced almost to tears by sitting on a doorstep? Perhaps the same kind that blows their first job interview in years by being a stupid, clumsy coward.

I closed my eyes and tried to imagine what realistic changes I could make to my life in order to be happy. When that came up empty, I went to unrealistic changes: lottery wins; celebrity without any of the negative side-effects; twenty more years with my nan; any years with my mother; Sam just fucking devolving into a puppy in my arms instead of dying; some form of romantic partner even, seeing as that's what apparently made other people happy.

None of it moved me. If I'd been offered a Faustian bargain for the lot of it right there and then, I would have left the devil on my doorstep and gone inside to bed.

Doris' slippers scraped on the concrete. I hadn't even heard her door open, so absorbed was I in my own misery. I wanted to keep my eyes shut and refuse to respond to her. She'd forget it eventually.

I reminded myself that being sad was no excuse for being a cunt.

"Hi, Doris."

She had settled on her own doorstep facing me. It was close enough that I didn't have to shout.

"Did it not go well, sweetheart?"

I looked down at my knees. There was witch hazel in the house somewhere. They would sting horrifically as I cleaned them. I was looking forward to it.

"No."

Doris smiled. I think it was supposed to be reassuring. "At least you got an interview. That's good."

"It's not good. It's worse." I should have left it there, but it all came spilling out as though someone had slit me open. "Because then you get your hopes up thinking maybe this'll be the thing to finally fix your sad little life. Then it doesn't and you feel fucking worse for having tried. I should just accept that there's nothing I can do to get myself out of this hole I've dug, and let myself rot in it."

Feeling calmer now, I looked over to see what effect my outburst had had on Doris.

Nothing. She was sitting there with the same small half-smile on her face. Not a care in the world.

I laughed. Doris did too, possibly not even knowing why. There was an amiable enough minute or two of silence before Doris spoke up again.

"Have you thought about going to the doctor? Maybe he can help."

I laughed again, bitterly this time. "Doctors are useless. I keep going through these cycles where I finally admit something's wrong with me, so I psych myself up to go to the doctor. They prescribe me something. I take it, have shitty side-effects for a couple of months, spend another few months trying to figure out if it's working, decide it isn't and come off it. Then it's the withdrawal symptoms. I was actually on fluoxetine until a few weeks ago when I had to throw them all away."

When I realised Sam was going to die, I had to make a difficult choice with regards to my medication. I could keep up with it, hoping it would lessen the grief, or I could throw it all away so there was nothing in the house on which to overdose. In the end, I made the sensible choice. There were several times when I absolutely would have done it. Now, I was in the midst of withdrawal: constant headaches; fatigue; terrible digestion; really fucking weird dreams.

"Oh, Mask." Doris' voice startled me; I had forgotten she was there. "What sort of a life is that?"

Not a good one. Not one worth living.

I turned to Doris to say something. The expression on her face stopped me. She looked pleased. I knew it made no sense, and it was likely just her illness messing with her normal emotional responses. Still, her reaction chilled me to the bone.

I made my excuses, fished my keys out of the grass and went inside. Naturally, I immediately filled with guilt at the thought of leaving her on the doorstep. To make up for it, I kept watch through the window until I saw Doris had got back up and gone back inside. I had to shake off this daft paranoia before I alienated the only person still bothering to give me the time of day.

Doris was a sweet old woman who wanted to befriend me. Ultimately, she had my best interests at heart. Just a cheerful, confused guardian angel watching over me.

7

RAYMOND

The whole point of moving into this stupid bungalow had supposedly been to avoid things like this. There were two bars at the side of the bath and a big bloody pole in the middle of the room. Still, somehow, Ray had managed to fall. Once the pain had mostly subsided, he could do nothing but lie there on the cold tile building himself up to attempt to stand. The better part of an hour had passed before he admitted to himself that it was not happening.

He should have an alarm or something. One of those pully things they have in disabled toilets or even just one of those little noisy things women have in their handbags. Something that could be heard more than his feeble shouts. The woman who lived in the house to the right of his had gone away with her son – he had seen them loading up the car the day before yesterday. The one on the left was too far away; if he had fallen somewhere on the other side of the house, he would have had a chance at rescue. If someone came to the front door, they could possibly hear him. The only person likely to do that was the postman in the morning. Ray had no idea if he could last that long.

It was all Tyler's fault for leaving. He had been perfectly fine in the boxroom, lazing about playing stupid games on his phone. Then one day he'd announced he was going to join his mother in Australia, leaving his poor grandad to fend for himself. Ray knew from when Helen had done it that emigrating took a lot of time and organisation. Yet, Tyler had only bothered to inform him the week before he left. And the way the little brat spoke to him on his last night there! He was lucky his grandad was in no fit shape to give him a good hiding. All this nonsense about the way he talked to people who were 'just trying to help' him. And, 'You should go see Aunty Sharon and Aunty Meena' – he actually called the big, butch thing his other daughter married 'Aunty'. Ray made sure to tell him where to stick that idea.

As though he owed Sharon anything after the way she had conducted herself. She had put her 'wedding' all over Facebook for everyone to see. It had been mortifying. They had kids as well. Adopted, of course. Foster services were so bursting with unwanted brats that they handed them over to literally anyone these days. The poor things never stood a chance. Would have been better off drowned at birth.

Ray winced at the pain in his ribs. There was a decent chance they were broken. The absolute best-case scenario would be horrific bruising. And that was if someone came along and found him.

He tried to remember the last person he had spoken to. It must have been that woman who randomly turned up at the house the other day.

Ray had come back from the shop to find a tall, skinny woman staring at his house. It was the weirdest thing. She turned when she heard him coming and immediately offered to help him get his bags inside. He should have told her to piss off, but he was tired and aching and he really needed the help.

What he had not needed, though, was her life story. Apparently, she used to live there before him and just fancied seeing the place again. Ray had been told that the previous tenant was a lowlife benefit cheat who left behind enormous arrears and an abandoned wheelchair. He said as much, but she dismissed it with a wave of her hand. She followed that up with a load of questions about Ray that he initially refused to answer. But then she had to go and ask about grandchildren, finally giving him the opportunity to go on at length about that ungrateful little waster, Tyler. It all seemed to come pouring out of him then. His own life story. When he finally ran out of things to say, it occurred to him that he had not thought to ask her name.

She had been looking at the front of the TV guide he'd just bought. The cover story was about someone dying or nearly dying or some other nonsense in *Coronation Street*. She looked up when Ray asked the question. There was an odd little pause.

"Gail," she said. "My name is Gail."

Sometime before, Ray had received a postcard obviously intended for a former occupant. He could not remember the name it was addressed to, but was pretty sure it wasn't Gail. It was signed, 'Your librarian'. It mentioned something about not seeing her for a while and hoping she would pop into the library soon. Ray was struck by it because it was so odd to see the library advertising, and in such a personal way. The postcard was actually still on his fridge, picture-side up. It made it look as though someone away on holiday had been thinking of him. It could even have come from Australia.

When she finally left, Gail mentioned she might pop in to see him again at some point. He did not see why she should and even said as much to her, much to her amusement. He would give anything for her to do so now.

Since then, she had popped up several times in his dreams. Not in a pervy way – he was long past that at his age – she just sat there and talked at him. It was always stupid questions: aren't you lonely; isn't it a shame Tyler left you; why did one daughter move to the other side of the world; why had the other one never driven ten minutes to see him. He had never put much stock in dreams; they meant nothing.

Ray shivered at the cold, then winced when the movement sent fresh pain shooting through his whole body. His eyes scrunched tight and he felt tears threatening to come. He would not cry; old age had not robbed him of his manhood. There was a noise above him, and then something blocked out part of the light. He opened his eyes to find Gail standing over him.

He blinked a few times. Surely she had to be a hallucination. "Are you really here?"

She nodded. Slowly, she slid down to sit cross-legged at his side.

"What are you doing? Call me an ambulance!"

"You're an ambulance," came her monotone reply.

That was it, Ray could stand no more. He let out an awful wail so loud that surely someone who could actually help would hear. But, at the end of it, he was still just left with Gail.

She stared blankly at him. "Do you feel better for having got that out?"

He began to sob.

"If you want me to, Raymond, I can make this stop. You will never feel pain again. Doesn't that sound nice?"

That sounded like she was willing to kill him to put him out of his misery. Cold, naked, hurting and – he had to admit – scared, that sounded appealing. He gave a tiny, pathetic nod.

Gail's smile was big and warm and the worst thing that he had ever seen.

"Let me take you. Just say the words. Your suffering will cease."

Ray swallowed a lump. More than anything, he wanted to be able to reach up and wipe the tears from his face.

"Take me."

This time, Gail's smile showed all her teeth.

8

VAL

Deborah was crying. Poor Deborah. No one should have to go through that.

Through what? I was not sure.

I also wasn't sure where we were. Not my house, nor any house the two of us had lived in previously. It looked like an old woman's house: cosy armchairs, little knick-knacks and a dated décor. I was old too, from the feel of things. My arm around the weeping Deborah's back felt frail, as though her wracking sobs could snap it if they became violent enough. Luckily, it appeared that she was calming down.

"It's just so awful! How can I possibly…" The words dissolved as she was hit with a fresh wave of tears.

Her voice. Nan's voice. After three long years. Was that really how she had sounded?

She turned to me, face wrecked with emotion. "My little girl! My Gracie!"

I snapped out of the dream, opening my eyes to that peculiar darkness again.

I knew I was still asleep, still dreaming. Unfortunately, knowing it was happening didn't translate into being able to stop it.

I was on my side being spooned by what I assumed was the nightmare creature. It was next to weightless, but I could feel its bony arm lying across my ribs. Its crumbling lips must have been right up against the back of my neck; all the hair there tingled unpleasantly. When it spoke, the voice reverberated down my spine, making my back jerk painfully.

"What a sad little life, Mask. Can't even remember your loved ones without dragging up all the pain they caused you. Best just not to have loved ones, isn't it? Best just dig yourself a safe, dark hole and allow yourself to rot down there. What a waste."

Working hard to ignore what it was saying, I wondered if what had happened to my back meant I could move this time around. I didn't dare to try while that arm was still around me, though. Said arm then slid up and a skeletal hand came to rest lightly on my throat.

"All we want to do is help you."

Three faces phased through my bedroom wall: Doris, Peter and Ginger. The heads hung there a moment like traitors' on pikes, then the rest of their bodies slipped into view. The three of them stepped towards me, legs working in eerie unison. I subtly tested my own legs, getting them to twitch.

"I could take you away from all this, you know." The hand spider-crawled up to my face. "I could make you feel so loved."

The decrepit sticks it had instead of fingers forced their way past my lips and into my mouth. My tongue tasted salt.

"If you'd only let me in."

At least that was so horrific it finally woke me up. Still on my side, my arms were wrapped around something. The one on the bottom was almost completely dead. I looked down to see the thing I clung to in my restless sleep was Nan's wig head, lipstick no doubt smeared all over my pillow. Perhaps that was what had caused my fucked-up dreams. I rolled one way and let the wig head roll the other. Gradually, the feeling came back to my arm.

I lay there for a while in a pool of what was most likely my own sweat, but I guess could have been an extremely impressive piss. My bladder, however, informed me that was not the case a moment later. That was something, at least. Not having pissed myself was likely to be the highlight of my week. Maybe I did have a sad little life.

Ridiculously, I spent a good five minutes in the bathroom gargling with mouthwash. I kept going long after the spearmint started to burn. It came to an end when my absolute bitch of a brain made me imagine fingertips reaching the back of my throat. I gagged, choked and finally coughed the mouthwash into the sink. Sadly, there was no spearmint-flavoured rinse for my mind.

I had too much to do that day to spend it dwelling on a withdrawal-induced nightmare. I tried to yank a mental curtain around it, but it kept getting caught on the rail. Realistically, it was going to be the backdrop for my whole day. I just had to get on with things. Proactive was the name of the game. I was going to find some info on my homeless stalker to avoid any more incidents like the previous day (I stamped down on the memory of the actual incident, lest I spend the rest of the day wincing). Chiefly, I wanted to know how likely he was to keep harassing me and how much danger I was actually in. There was only one person who was likely to be able to help. I set out on a busker hunt.

It did not surprise me that the spot where I'd met V was empty – he was probably avoiding Ginger too. Hopefully not so much that he was too scared to come into the town centre. If that were the case, I'd have no hope of finding him again.

I wandered around for the better part of an hour before I heard music. 'Valerie' by The Zutons; V must have had a gimmick. I found him right at the other end of town. Doing decent business by the looks of things, as far as busking went. I watched for a while, not wanting to interrupt. I clocked the precise moment he saw me, his eyes going wide. I put it down to shock at recognising someone when he hadn't expected to, but I couldn't help notice he seemed more alarmed than surprised. Perhaps he thought my presence would summon that fucker; he surely wouldn't thank me for leading Ginger back to him.

The song came to an end, so I approached. V looked around for… help? We had parted on good terms, I thought; maybe he just wasn't used to people seeking him out for a nice reason. I tried for a reassuring smile.

"Hi, V, remember me?"

He looked on the verge of running.

"Mask?"

"Yep. Can I buy you lunch?"

He narrowed his eyes and tilted his head. Then he shrugged. "If you're eating, too."

Ten minutes later, we were squeezed into two separate sections of a bench with an anti-homeless bar in the middle.

Lunch consisted of two lots of meal deals from the first shop we came to. Sandwiches, crisps and a drink. V watched as I took my mask off to eat. He made no move towards his own food until I had taken a couple bites of my sandwich. I assumed it was a point of etiquette. Then he tore into his own food with such intensity that it was a shame to have to interrupt.

"You still going with Vincent?"

He shook his head, swallowing the last of his sandwich. "I kinda like Val now. Like that old actor, Val Kilmer."

Either the two of us had different standards as to what counted as an 'old' actor, or V was an actual baby. I'd thought he was around my age, but clearly I needed to reassess. Asking was probably a bad idea, as the answer would most likely depress me.

"So I wanted to ask you about Ginger."

V paused wiping his hands on his jacket. "Because you saw him again?"

I nodded. "Ran into him on my way to a job interview. Fucked the whole thing up the wall. Why would he be following me?"

"Because you're alone. An easy target." V leaned towards me, becoming more animated as he went on. "He sees someone weaker than him, scared and alone, and he just zeroes in on them. He was always like that, even before."

"Before?"

V blinked a few times. He leant back in his seat. "I just meant, when I knew him before."

"Did you ever try going to the police about him?"

V snorted. "Homeless, Black trans man, remember?" He flattened his empty crisp packet between his hands and started to fold it up. "How are your dreams?"

I didn't remember telling him about my dreams last time, but I must have. "Still pretty messed up. I think my sleep paralysis demon wants to fuck me."

He laughed at that, his face lighting up. "What makes you say that?"

"Well, it's always all over me and telling me how it could make me feel loved if only I'd let it in."

I had expected another laugh at that. Instead, it was like I'd thrown a bucket of ice water over V: his smile vanished, his mouth dropping open. He went to say something, but then he closed his mouth and looked down at his hands. There was an awkward, silent beat. Then he placed the folded-up crisp packet onto the bar between us. It was now an origami frog.

"That's so cute!"

He pressed down on the tail end of the frog, making it jump.

I barked out a delighted laugh. He smiled at me, but his eyes were still sad.

"Can I tell you some more about The Nothing?"

It took me a moment to remember what that was. I shrugged. "Okay?"

"The thing about The Nothing is it can't take you unless you let it."

"So it tricks you?"

He shook his head. "It wears you down. It shows you your life in the worst possible light. You're never safe from it, asleep or awake. It gets into your dreams."

That sent a chill through me. I couldn't be sure if that was just part of the story and me mentioning my dream had reminded him, or if he was making it all up as he went along and using what I'd told him to scare me.

"Then, when you're just about ready to curl up and die, it tells you it can make all your suffering end. Promises to take you away from all this. Tells you it can make you feel loved if only you'll let it in."

A direct quote.

"Fuck you, V."

I got up to leave. He grabbed my sleeve.

"I'm not fucking with you. You're in danger."

I shook him off and walked away. He caught up with me, cutting me off. I think I growled at him.

"Please, just watch out for strangers suddenly trying to be your friend."

"Like you?"

He stepped out of my way. "Take care of yourself, Mask."

I didn't look up as I passed him. I resisted the urge to look back. When I put my hands in my pockets a short while later, one of them closed on what felt like rubbish. I pulled out V's origami frog. Quite when he'd slipped it to me – or why – was a mystery. I shoved it back in and stomped the rest of the way home.

I slammed the front door behind me.

V was either trying to wind me up or he had a mental illness that made him genuinely believe all the shit he'd said. Either way, I was not likely to see him again. I hadn't wanted to admit that I was excited at the idea of making a friend, but I was. What a pathetic little creature. It was only twenty-four hours earlier I'd given a speech to Doris about how awful it was to get your hopes up only to have them dashed. Why didn't I ever learn?

I threw myself facedown onto the sofa.

My last actual friend had been a guy from school. Stewart. We lasted past school and well into my twenties. I thought he was my best friend, not least because he was the only one.

We saw each other a few times a year to go out drinking. The last time, I'd been doing some reading and had come to a few conclusions. I wasn't sure whether to mention it or not, but I was excited to talk about it. When you find answers to a lot of the questions you've had about yourself for years, it's natural to want to tell someone. I sat there for hours plucking up the courage. Finally, I was drunk enough to come out and say I thought I was non-binary, asexual and maybe aromantic. He laughed at first, then asked me to explain. I did, including definitions I'd memorised for that specific purpose. When I finished, he sat there thinking for a while. Then he wrinkled his nose like he could smell shit and said,

"So you're nothing?"

I pretended to laugh it off, but it stung. That was when I realised I didn't have a best friend so much as an occasional drinking partner. It wasn't even me who ended the friendship. He stopped being the one to text first. Then he stopped responding to my texts. And then I didn't even have an occasional drinking partner anymore.

Not long after my nan died, I went round to Stewart's house. His mom remembered me, calling me by my old name. She was surprised I didn't know he'd moved out a couple of years earlier. She offered to write down his address in Derby for me if I wanted it. I declined.

Adults did not want friends. They wanted lovers, spouses, kids. Making their own new families even as they got to keep the old ones. New work colleagues could be tolerated, but anyone approaching you with an offer of friendship was a fucking weirdo not to be trusted.

A click interrupted my thoughts. It was followed by the sound of the kettle boiling. I jumped to my feet.

Doris hovered in the kitchen doorway.

"I've just stuck the kettle on; you looked like you needed a cuppa."

She turned and made for the fridge. I could do nothing but follow.

"Doris, how…"

"The back door was unlocked."

The fuck it was. I never leave the house without double-checking it. Then again, I was not exactly on top form lately. How else would Doris have got in – could my nan have given her a spare key for emergencies?

Doris had the mugs and tea bags and milk ready to go. She hummed to herself as she waited for the kettle to boil.

"You should have knocked or something."

"I did." Her face was pure innocence. "I have no patience now that I'm an old lady. If you keep me waiting too long, I'll go ahead and let myself in."

"I don't know how I feel about that." I did know how I felt about that and how I felt about it was uncomfortable.

She shrugged, spilling the milk she was pouring into my mug. She handed me my tea and watched as I took a sip.

"There you are, isn't that better? You should know by now that old Doris just wants to take care of you."

I looked down at my tea. I didn't know how to react to what she'd said, but I hoped it was true. It was nice to think someone cared about me.

9

DORIS DAY

The next week passed in a blur. Truthfully, it might not have even been a week; my relationship with the passage of time became even worse than usual.

Doris was there a lot. Constantly in and out. Asking me about my life, wanting to know what had upset me. And there was so much tea. I had only fallen into the habit of drinking it to be companionable. Plus, I needed to use up the milk and sugar that Doris didn't take. Not that she even drank the tea most of the time. I was forever finding cold cups of it all around the house. She never took any of the biscuits I dug out for her either. I hoped she was eating right when she got home.

I told her bits of what had happened with V. She listened and nodded, leaning against my sink holding tea destined to be tipped away. When I finished, she looked thoughtful.

"So you told him you were having nightmares and he made up a story to scare you?"

"Pretty much."

"He doesn't sound like a very nice young man."

I shrugged. I had reached my limit of wanting to talk about it. I certainly did not want to get into why it had upset me so much.

"And to think, you'd thought you found a friend. You must have been crushed."

God damn, Doris, just reach into my chest and rip out my heart next time.

I tried to think of a subject change, but my brain was operating at minimal efficiency due to misery and lack of sleep. Doris beat me to it anyway, announcing she was off home for lunch. She tipped her own tea down the sink, which was helpful. Then she left me alone in my empty house.

Trying to fill the time between visits from Doris and what little sleep I managed to get was not easy. I watched a couple of shows I had already seen several times before. I got fixated on this American comedy about a group of adult friends (not that one, a better one). The characters didn't even particularly like each other, but there was a found-family element to it that I used to upset myself. Those unpleasant fictional characters all had each other, they were trapped together forever. Why couldn't I trap someone with me?

When I got too upset for that show, I went through the big Cary Grant boxset I bought for my nan a few Christmases ago. I had to turn *Arsenic and Old Lace* off as it reminded me of Peter and therefore my dreams about his missing face. *An Affair to Remember* made me cry. So – ridiculously – did *The Grass is Greener.* Luckily, *To Catch a Thief* wasn't in there. I did wonder why my mom hadn't continued the tradition and named me after a classic Hollywood star; I would have liked being a Cary. Finally, I had to pack in watching those movies when one of the Grant-Hepburn pictures confused the hell out of my gender envy.

The only other option was sleep. By which I mean lying in bed staring at the ceiling. I adamantly refused to leave the house for cold medicine to misuse, so my sleeping pattern was once again fucked. It got to the point where I would have welcomed dreams of that monster finger-fucking my mouth all night so long as I got some actual rest.

The next time I saw Doris was after an hour-long turbulent sleep in the middle of the afternoon. I opened my eyes to find my ceiling graffiti had changed: it now read BENOTHING. I had no memory of doing that and I didn't even know that was a fucking word. I was about to find my phone to look it up when Doris loomed into view, hanging over me. I froze. For a second, I was hit by the absurd thought she had been the one to write on the ceiling.

"Doris?"

"That back door again – you really need to start locking it." Her eyes ran over me, fully dressed with a blanket half pulled over my torso. "This is no time to be sleeping, luvvie."

I huffed in annoyance and clambered out of bed with the intention of very gently throwing her out. When I stood facing her, her hands came up in front of her chest and she looked around the room frowning.

"Unless… it is time to sleep?"

My annoyance melted away instantly. I reached out and placed a hand on one of her bony shoulders. "No, it's not. I was just being lazy. I should probably eat, actually. Do you want anything?"

She perked up, her arms dropping to her sides. "Oh no, not for me. I wouldn't say no to a cup of tea, though."

As Doris led the way to my living room, I tried to remember if she had last been round yesterday or the day before. There was even a chance it had been that morning. I really needed to sort myself out.

I left Doris settled on the sofa as I went to make tea. It occurred to me to try the back door while I was waiting for the kettle to boil: locked. Doris must have done it after she let herself in. I couldn't see where she'd put the key, though. I had to remember to ask her. Hopefully, she remembered herself.

Doris was fidgeting with the cushion behind her when I brought her tea through.

"Comfy?"

"Yes, love. Don't worry."

I took the seat opposite her and tried to think of something for us to talk about. Then I spotted the boxset on the floor by Doris' feet.

"Do you like Cary Grant?" I sat forward and pulled the box over. "We can watch one if you like."

Doris' eyes had gone wide. "No, don't bother."

I pulled the lid off the box, only half listening to her. Not all of the DVDs were in there. I was certain they had been, but the remaining ones had tumbled slightly like interrupted dominos. I straightened them out. Judging by the gaps in Mr Grant's face, three of them were missing. So odd.

In the corner of my eye, something darted past my vision. My head shot round. Nothing. Definitely no movie-stealing spiders. I must have reached the stage of sleep deprivation where you started seeing things. It made sense that I'd misplaced some DVDs and forgot about them. They were bound to turn up somewhere stupid like in my bed or the fridge or something.

Doris made an odd little noise to get my attention. I was probably freaking her out. "Never much saw the appeal of Cary Grant. Debbie was a big fan though, wasn't she?"

It took me a moment to realise she meant my nan. She was always Deborah. Like Deborah Kerr.

"Kerr rhymes with star," I muttered to myself.

I looked up to see that Doris' eyebrows were almost at her hairline.

"Erm... yeah, she was. Big fan." I replaced the lid and shoved the box down by the side of the sofa.

"I remember her showing me that boxset, actually. 'Look at what Piglet got me for Christmas.' Dead happy, she was."

'Piglet' made my breath catch. I hadn't heard that in so long. I had to blink away the beginning of tears.

"So proud of her only grandchild. Although – and I do hope you won't mind me saying this – I know she wished you would visit more."

I had wanted to, I really had. Whenever I happened to be in gainful employment, that was all I ever had time for. I would be exhausted at the end of every day and need the weekends for catching up on errands. Whenever I wasn't working, I was sleeping on the air mattress in Nan's spare room that was basically a cupboard and spending all my time looking for a job. I loved my nan, but I could not put up with constant questions about when I was going to find a job or a partner or why I wasn't out with friends. She loved me, but laughed herself into hysterics when I told her what I was thinking of changing my name to. The only time I ever heard her comment on anything trans-related was to roll her eyes at a trans woman on TV and mutter something about young people these days. I could never tell her who I was. It would have shattered my tightly held image of her as a wonderful, selfless person and fractured our relationship forever.

She raised me while grieving a daughter who had completely cut contact. I could barely be around her as an adult because I hated myself and my life and everything around me. I couldn't even face her when we found out about my mom.

Doris popped her cup down on the table between us. Still full, no steam coming off it.

"I shouldn't have said anything. No point getting yourself all upset about it; it's too late now. Far too late."

I needed to be out of that room. Away from the sweet old lady who seemed intent on eviscerating me. I picked up the cold tea.

"Do you want a fresh one? Or shall I warm this up in the microwave?"

Doris shrugged. "Whichever one is less effort, love."

I shoved it in the microwave. There was no sense in wasting a second cup when she was most likely just going to leave it. Maybe I should stop making them for her. I found the back-door key while I was waiting; it had fallen on the floor by the doormat. I put it back in the lock where it usually was.

The cup came out of the microwave almost too hot to hold. I carried it in with the intention of setting it down on the table and forbidding Doris to touch it. As I did, something caught my eye again. My head turned automatically. Then I tripped over my own feet and tumbled forwards, showering Doris with scalding-hot tea.

"Fuck!" I was up and darting around the room before it even registered that the thing I was looking for was my phone.

Doris stood, dripping tea. Her blouse was soaked through. "It's fine. I'm fine."

If her condition somehow prevented her from feeling pain, then I was fucking grateful for it. I ran into my bedroom to find my mobile.

"I'm gonna call an ambulance, Doris; everything's going to be fine!" I called in full knowledge that I was reassuring myself, rather than her.

I could hear her going on about how she wasn't hurt and not to trouble myself, as I searched through my blankets and found my phone. To my relief, there was still some charge in it. Rushing back into the living room, I messed up the pin and failed to unlock it. I swore at myself, then stopped and took a breath. I looked up at Doris.

She was bone dry.

Her face was clear, her blouse was back to its normal white. The wet patches on the floor and sofa were still there, but otherwise there was no evidence I had spilled anything.

"Doris?"

A friendly smile spread across her face, somehow filling me with dread. "See? I'm fine. You didn't even get me."

My head shook in a mad, diagonal pattern. "No. No! It was all over you; you were seriously hurt."

The smile turned patronising. "I think you might be seeing things, luvvie. Are you getting enough sleep? You do look tired."

I was seeing small, black, wispy things in the corner of my eye, worlds away from what I had just witnessed.

"Doris, I don't know what's going on, but…"

"Oh! Is that the time? Must be getting on." She turned and sped into the kitchen.

I ran to follow, too fast to stop myself slamming into the back door. It was still locked. The key still in the lock where I had put it all of five minutes ago. What the fuck was going on?

"How did she…"

"I never left, luvvie."

I yelped, spinning round.

There she was on the other side of the kitchen. I had run right past her without seeing her. Except that was impossible. I had momentarily glimpsed the spot where she was standing and could say with confidence that it had been empty. I couldn't be seeing things and also not seeing things, could I?

Doris shuffled forward. I stumbled back against the door. Tears welled in my eyes.

"Doris, what's happening?"

"Nothing. You just need to get some sleep, sweetheart. You're a mess. Now, why don't you move so I can go home. You can watch me do it if that'll set your mind at ease."

I kept my eyes on her as I pushed away from the door. We very slowly swapped places: Doris standing at the back door, me over by the fridge. I held my breath as Doris tried the handle.

"Oh, now that is very silly."

She spun round far too quickly, making me jump right out of my skin.

"Give me the key, Mask."

I shook my head. She took a few shambling steps towards me. There was something off about her movements that I couldn't put my finger on.

"I hate to have to take this tone with you, but you need to give me the key and then you need to get a fucking grip on yourself."

I actually gasped at her swearing. Her face was alive with quiet fury. I could no longer look her in the eye, so I glanced down at her feet.

One foot was still facing the other way. It had not turned around when she had.

She must have followed my line of sight. I saw her look down.

"Oh dear, that's rather spoilt things."

Doris leaned to her left, lifting her backwards leg up. It snapped itself back into place.

I heaved, falling against the fridge. The noise drew her attention back to me.

"Oh, Mask," she said with a smile, "if you didn't like that then you are going to hate this."

She widened her stance and dropped down into a deep squat. Her knees made an awful crack, but no pain showed on her face. Once her knees were level with her chest, she began to lean back from her shoulders. Her hands fisted into her skirt, dragging it up with her movements. By the time the hem reached her shins, Doris' knees were bent at a right angle while her torso balanced perpendicular to the floor.

I had never seen a body do such a thing. I could only watch in horrified silence as Doris hung there, suspended.

Apparently, there was worse to come. Doris' head appeared to be sinking down into her neck which in turn sank into her shoulders. She was like an inflatable losing air. The only part that seemed to retain its size was the big grin on her withered face.

Movement down near her skirt caught my eye. Two claw-like hands slipped out from under it and wrapped around her ankles. They were grey and black and gnarled, the digits all different lengths from where parts of them had... broken off? Rotted away? Either way, those hands were unsettlingly familiar.

A groan filled the room. It came from between Doris' legs. Her skirt rose like that trick with a ball under a cloth. I only caught glimpses of what was underneath, but I had the sickening feeling that I knew exactly what it was. I tore my eyes away long enough to see that there was almost nothing left of Doris above the shoulders and those shoulders were hunching down into her chest. Whatever was coming out of her did so at the same rate that the rest of her was disappearing.

It was like watching a glove turn itself inside out. A single tear ran down my cheek; I had not felt it coming. More followed, soaking my face. My wide-open mouth tasted salt.

One of those monstrous hands slid upwards to grip the hem of the skirt. Then it was tossed back with a flourish, revealing the head and upper body of the creature from my nightmares. Its shoulders were bracketed by Doris' knees. It was not looking up at me, apparently too focused on degloving itself from my kindly old neighbour. Thankfully, the skirt covered the part where it was still joined to her body. It fixed its hands back on her ankles, bracing its forearms against her shins. It heaved itself theatrically. I had the impression it was putting on a show for me.

Suddenly – too quick for my eyes to follow – the creature sprang into the air. The skirt fell down around the crumpled remnants of Doris. Then it vanished. All that remained was the nightmare creature, head held high and arms spread at its side. The posture was oddly angelic. It was not looking at me. I got the impression that its eyes would be closed, if they had lids. It just swayed slightly, bathed in the fluorescent kitchen light.

This was the clearest view I'd had of it so far: long, thin body bent at odd angles; here and there I could see through to blackened, cracked bone; what skin it did have was dark and rubbery up to the edges where it resembled burnt paper; in some places there was a layer of red and yellow viscera visible between skin and bone.

Its head jerked down to stare at me with empty eyes.

My body woke up with a jump. I screamed all the oxygen out of my lungs. Then I fell back against the fridge, gasping for breath.

The creature darted forwards, hands slamming on the fridge door either side of my head. I must have had enough breath again because the screams ripped out of me. And then the creature's fingers were in my mouth, stifling me. I gagged around them, but it wouldn't let go. It used its grip on my jaw to drag me down to the floor. It brought its skull face down to mine and I screamed around my awful gag.

"Shh, shush. You can shut up, or my fingers can rot in your mouth. Understand?"

I nodded. It slipped its fingers out, taking hold of my jaw instead.

"Where's Doris?" I gasped. I needed to know if she was safe.

Eyeballs rolled into the creature's empty sockets. Regular human lips grew around its dry ones. Doris' eyes and mouth in that thing's face. When it spoke, it was with her voice.

"I'm right here, Mask." The rest of her face grew back around the eyes and mouth. "Goodness, you look a state. How about we have a nice cup of tea?"

I unleashed a noise somewhere between a scream and a sob.

"Oh dear, do you not like this face?"

The eyes rolled back until they were white. Then they kept rolling until they were someone else's: its face became Peter's, with his awful, ruined mouth, then the snarling face of Ginger. Finally, the features sank back into the nightmare creature.

"What are you?" I pleaded.

"Me? Oh, I am nothing you've ever seen before."

The Nothing. Like V had said. He'd been trying to warn me.

"V..."

The Nothing shook its head. It shook my head too. "V, V, V, that naughty little boy. What did he tell you about me? That I'm a monster who eats people? No," it leaned down into my personal space, "I save people. I take poor little nothings such as you and I give them purpose. A *home*, deep within me. Nobody needed or wanted them, but I do."

Tears were pouring down my face. "You eat them."

It grinned. "What's more needed or wanted than food?"

I choked on a sob.

"Oh, shush, don't start that nonsense. I'm not going to hurt you, Mask. Didn't that little street urchin tell you that I don't take the unwilling?"

I shook my head as much as I could with the monster gripping my face. "I'm not willing."

"You will be." It darted forward and licked my face with its stinking black tongue.

The Nothing got to its feet and stepped back. It affected something like a grin. "I'll be next door when you need me," it chirped.

It ran through my kitchen wall and vanished without a trace.

I sat staring at the floor. My mind was filled with images of Doris' leg snapping back into place, then her face shrinking away. My kindly, old neighbour who could barely take care of herself. There was a banging noise somewhere behind me, but it failed to reach me through the memory of Doris' voice changing into the creature's. Then I heard my doorbell. Who the fuck was calling at a time like this?

I walked through the house in a daze. As silly as I knew it was, I half expected Doris to be at the door, back to normal and demanding tea to not drink. Instead, it was the woman who lived on the end of the row.

"What was all that noise just now?"

The noise had been my terrified screams. Someone who was not a rude bitch would have been full of concern. She was just pissed off.

"Sorry," I muttered, because what the hell else could I say?

She pursed her thin, old lady lips. "Just pack it in or I'll have to call the police."

I nodded. I could have had quite an interesting conversation with the police just then. Maybe being sectioned would keep me safe from The Nothing.

The old lady walked away. I stepped outside.

"Wait!"

She turned back, looking enraged at the interruption.

"Do you know the woman who lives next door to me?"

"What's that got to do with anything?" she said with a scowl. "Yeah, what's-her-face. Hadn't seen her around for a while. Thought she'd died, even."

None of that was useful. I wasn't even sure why I'd asked.

"Can I go now?"

I stared at my feet. She huffed and left, muttering.

When I looked up, Doris was pressed against her front window. She grinned at me with a rotten mouth. Her eyes were black.

I ran back inside and slammed the door. I locked it, threw the bolt and did the chain.

Then I remembered that the monster I needed to hide from could just walk through my wall anytime it pleased.

I had no idea what I was going to do.

10

VIGGO

I wandered from room to room, unable to settle anywhere. My bedroom was a no-go due to all the awful things I had dreamed in there (whether they had been dreams or real or somewhere in between was something I was looking forward to obsessing over). I wanted to keep an eye on the kitchen wall – for all the good it would do me – but I was not sure if I'd ever be able to enter that room again. Eventually, I parked myself on the living room floor where I could see into the kitchen from a safe distance.

My thoughts raced with the revelation that almost everyone who had recently popped into my life had been the same shape-shifting monster intent on eating me: Peter, saving me from the consequences of my actions because he wanted me for himself; Ginger, following me around to prevent me getting a job; finally, Doris, a woman I believed to be my nan's only friend and then mine. Had she even been called Doris? I tried to remember when she had actually told me her name, and realised that she never had. Doris had been my name for her in my head and I didn't even notice when I started saying it aloud. That thing must have thought I was a fucking idiot. It was one hundred percent right.

Every 'Doris' encounter now took on a different hue. From our very first meeting where I initially wrote her prying questions off as nosiness and then dementia, to the last week where she had been over constantly. At some point in the middle, she started referring to herself as the false name I gave her, internally laughing at me every time. She had begun by scoping me out for a potential victim, then readying me to be one. All the comments about how I'd let my nan down and what a sad little life I had – chipping away at my spirit under the guise of being socially awkward due to illness. And I had fallen for it despite my natural paranoia and slight misanthropy. And despite being literally warned about it twice.

What had V said about The Nothing? Had there been anything on how to beat it? I fetched myself a notebook and pen so I could write down everything I remembered.

It consumes you.

It had confirmed that itself.

It picks isolated people whom no one would miss.

I could not have tailored myself to its needs any more if I had fucking tried.

It wears the faces of its previous victims to get close to you.

Between my new best friend, my supermarket helper and my homeless stalker, it had got pretty damn close to me.

It makes your life a misery until you agree to let it take you.

Ha! Poor Doris had missed the boat with that one. Obviously, she could scare me plenty, but just how was she conceivably going to make this shitshow any worse? I could not fathom being lower than this.

There was one other thing V had said that I needed to ponder – that Ginger had always been a prick, even 'before'. In hindsight, that obviously meant before The Nothing took him. V must have known the real Ginger. That had to be important. Even if it wasn't, the fact that he knew all this stuff about The Nothing meant I needed to see him again. Even if he didn't know a way to defeat it, he must at least know how to survive an encounter with it. I hoped so, anyway. I resolved to find him in the morning.

I spent the night on the floor staring into the kitchen. I jumped at every noise, every mild hallucination. By sunrise, I had almost convinced myself that none of it was real and I could go get in bed and sleep soundly until midday. What stopped me was unlocking my phone. It opened on a dictionary site where I had apparently looked up the definition of benothing at some point in the night.

Benothing: to destroy completely, reduce to nothing. Annihilate.

I needed to find V.

*

He wasn't anywhere I had seen him before. I couldn't hear his guitar no matter how many times I walked up and down the town. Eventually, I collapsed onto the bench where we had eaten lunch. My eyes closed involuntarily.

They opened again when someone shook me.

From my point of view, V was outlined by a perfect blue sky, his eyes filled with tenderness: the beautiful boy that I hoped was going to rescue me. Wasn't I just a little Disney princess?

"This bench is specifically designed so that people can't sleep on it." He smiled down at me.

"Well, no one in history has ever been as tired as I am right now."

He slid into the space next to me. "You've seen it, haven't you? Properly, I mean."

I nodded, bleary eyes barely staying open.

"Who did you see it as?" V asked.

"My neighbour. She seemed like a nice old lady. What about you? Was it always Ginger?"

He hesitated before answering. "No, it was an old man before that."

"Was there something wrong with his mouth?"

V's eyes flitted away for a second. He tilted his head. "No? I don't think there was."

So not Peter? Or just Peter pre-whatever the fuck happened to his face?

"That's why you know about it, because it took someone you knew?"

V picked at a hole in his jeans.

"Was he your friend?"

He snorted at that. "I wasn't lying when I said he was a piece of shit. I didn't exactly miss him when he was gone. Couldn't have if I'd wanted to – I was busy being terrified for my life."

"Can it be stopped?"

V looked up at me, his eyes roaming over my desperate face. "No."

My head dropped back. Tears came to my eyes; I was too exhausted to fight them.

"There are ways to avoid it, though. I think names are important to it. That's a big part of why I never settled on one. I move around a lot and the busking means that people notice me, even if they don't want to. And there is zero privacy for the homeless: there's no way it would ever get me alone enough that it could do anything to me."

Looking up at the sky, I saw the tiny figure of a distant plane. I tried to imagine the people on there. Travelling abroad for business or pleasure. A hundred people (I don't know how big planes are) all with minds just like mine, their own intricate, tiny worlds with themselves at the centre. It hurt my brain. The light hurt my eyes and looking up hurt my neck.

I sat up properly, righting myself. "It knows my name and where I live. I can't just up and leave. And I don't know how to make people pay attention to me without humiliating myself – and I couldn't keep that up for long."

We sat in silence for a minute or two. I watched people milling around town. I couldn't see V well enough to know what he was doing.

"Why does people noticing you help?"

I saw him turn to face me from the corner of my eye.

"I have a theory that it can't take you if there's someone who would miss you, even if it's not immediately obvious. I've seen it back off when a familiar person approached."

"When?"

He shrugged, looked away. The pause before he answered was way too long. "Just when Ginger saw someone he knew for a minute."

Something didn't ring true about that, but I didn't push him. Instead, I spun in the seat so sharply that it visibly startled him.

"Would you miss me, V?"

His smile was fond. "When did you last sleep?"

"Just now, remember. On this disgusting capitalist bench."

He barked out a laugh at that. "I would miss you, Mask."

"Do you think that's enough?"

"I honestly have no idea."

He looked so sad for me and probably himself too. We were two people in the same bizarre situation and the only ones who could help each other. I was struck by a genius idea that was definitely not a product of sleep deprivation.

"Move in with me."

V raised an eyebrow. Then he burst out laughing.

"I'm serious. There's an air mattress and something of a spare room. You could have a warm place to sleep and a ridiculous amount of tea."

"What if I killed you in the middle of the night?"

"Then the monster who wants to devour my soul doesn't get me." I leaned forward enough to slip a hand onto his forearm. "Doesn't it just make sense?"

He closed his eyes for a moment. "Mask, we've met about three times. You can't just go around inviting near-strangers to live with you."

"Not normally, no, but I'd say these are pretty fucking exceptional circumstances." I could see that he was turning it over in his mind. "It's the only way to test your theory, isn't it? Either you're right, Nothing backs off and we're safe, or it doesn't back off and we know to try something else."

"It's The Nothing, don't just call it 'Nothing'."

I had to laugh at that. "I take it you came up with the name, then?"

"It's a good name!"

He pouted. It was adorable. I have literally never wanted to take someone home with me more.

V fished something out of his pocket. "Do you want to split my chocolate with me?"

My stomach growled, but I had to decline. "I'm a vegan, dude, didn't I say?"

I tried not to be offended by V's worried expression. He reached into his other pocket and handed me a can of Coke.

"Thanks," I said, opening it. "Why do you keep trying to give me stuff, though?"

I noticed he waited until I had taken a big gulp to answer.

"I have a theory that The Nothing doesn't eat or drink," he said, watching me.

It was so obvious now it had been pointed out. All that disgusting cold tea. The fact that Doris had never taken so much as a biscuit from me. It probably would have occurred to me if I'd been capable of thoughts more complex than, 'Please help me'.

Something dawned on me, then. "Wait a minute, you thought I was The Nothing?"

V shrugged. "I knew it was trying to get the real Mask. Then you showed up here all vulnerable and appealing for my help, then you invited me to live with you: a tempting offer that would also mean I was alone with you. It's exactly the sort of thing it would do. If you're offended then, you know, soz."

I wanted to be offended on principle, but he had a point. I drank the rest of his Coke in a way I hoped conveyed that there were no hard feelings.

V stood up. He turned and looked down at me. "Wanna walk me home?"

I jumped up, ready to feel like an idiot if I had misunderstood.

"You won't regret this V, I promise."

"I already do," he said amiably. We set off.

"Hey, are you still thinking Val?"

"Nah, I like Viggo at the minute. I only picked Val because that actor was in the first Batman movie I saw as a kid."

Batman Forever, 1995. So V wasn't necessarily a baby, he just considered actors who peaked in the 1990s to be 'old'. Perhaps I would be able to get him into my Cary Grant boxset during our cohabitation. We could have movie nights.

As we walked, I let myself get my hopes up. There was a chance that this was it: The Nothing would leave and I would have someone in my life who would give a shit if I suddenly disappeared. It would serve that stupid thing right if it accidentally improved my life.

11

IRE

As a child, Irene had liked the *Mog* books by Judith Kerr. She had campaigned for a cat of her own only to be constantly disappointed. As an adult, she could barely afford to feed herself, let alone a pet. Whenever she pissed away a couple of quid on the lottery, she fantasised about a quaint cottage full of cats.

One day in the library, Irene had to sit and wait for a computer to become available. She happened to spot an unfamiliar *Mog* book on the returns trolley: *Goodbye Mog*. She swiped it and sat down to have a read. If she had known that Mog died in it, she never would have picked it up. She was glad she did, though. The little cat from her childhood passed away on the very first page, only to hang around watching her loved ones cope with her death. Eventually, the family got a new kitten. Mog watched over them all until she was satisfied that they were all right without her, and then she moved on.

It was exactly how Irene had always pictured death: your spirit remaining as your loved ones healed and then disappearing peacefully. The fact that she no longer had any loved ones was neither here nor there. Maybe she would see her family, witness them hearing the news. They would be sorry, wouldn't they? They had to be. She would stand back and watch them realise that they loved her and should have been there for her. The guilt would eat them alive and Irene would move on to rest in peace.

Her death had not turned out like that. If anything, she was enduring a sick perversion of the concept. Her spirit lingered, watching people go on with their lives. But her body was also still there, and it was under the control of something monstrous.

There had been darkness at first. Then she was suddenly standing outside her house. She heard her voice telling the old man that she used to live there. The thing that controlled her body introduced her as Gail.

It was odd to experience panic without the physiological reactions. She felt as though she couldn't breathe, but she wasn't breathing. She thrashed around without moving an inch. She screamed and screamed and screamed and the monster told the old man that it would be coming back to see him again.

When it did, the old man was on the bathroom floor. It promised him everything it had promised her. He was fooled, too. She could not remember it taking her. Agreeing to it, yes, and then being within it, but not the actual act. She witnessed it consuming the old man. She felt it too. Both bodies breaking down in order to be forced together. How could she feel pain when she had no nerves? Perhaps it was merely psychological.

There was darkness again. Her consciousness blurry and confused. Then she was out in a part of town that seemed to be largely populated by homeless people. Presumably, this was where she would have ended up had she lived.

A boy sat on his own, tuning his guitar. As soon as she saw him, she knew the monster had set its sights on him. His loneliness shone from every pore.

It took a seat next to him and introduced itself – Gail again; Irene wondered if it was attached to the name or just couldn't be bothered to think of another one. The boy gave a small, shy smile. He went back to tuning.

Irene tried her best to will him away. She focused all her energy in his direction. Nothing was likely to happen to him with so many people around, but it only had to lure him into an alley or somewhere else isolated.

Her voice asked him for his name. He mumbled something she didn't catch. It asked about his family, no doubt noticed the tiny expression that passed over his face before he steeled himself and remained silent. If Irene could have forced the words out of her stolen mouth, she would have asked him if there was anyone he could go to, even if it seemed impossible. Or, at least, if he had friends on the streets. Someone should have been looking out for him.

"I think you need someone to look out for you."

Had it heard her? Or was it just that obvious?

He shrugged with affected nonchalance. "Doing all right so far."

Surprising Irene, the monster leaned over and brought her hand to his face. It let it rest just shy of touching a graze on his cheek, just enough to get the message across. "Are you?"

He jerked away. Irene thought he would kick off. Instead, he pouted, making himself look ten years younger.

"Can't do nothing about that. Unless you're gonna go shank the prick who did it."

The monster laughed lightly. "Maybe I will; it's been a long day."

The boy's face was tilted away, but Irene saw him smile. He spoke again without looking up. "I'm V."

"V? Is that your whole name?"

He shook his head. "I don't have a name yet. Haven't decided. I'm sure it's gonna start with V, though."

"Maybe I can help you pick one."

"Yeah, we'll workshop it." His head was up now and he was smiling at them.

The monster was smiling back. Irene could feel it stretching out her face.

It looked away from V to fiddle with its sleeve for some reason. Irene watched in suspense. It pulled off her bracelet, the shitty little woven one she had bought from her first Pride a few years before. It was decidedly past its best. She only kept it for stupid sentimental reasons. The thing that had killed Irene held her bracelet up for the boy to take.

V just blinked at it at first, as though he did not understand the concept.

"Present for you. Take it."

He treated the two of them to their first shot of his smile truly unleashed.

Irene watched him slip it onto his wrist, the picture of happiness. She did not know which one of them she wanted to weep for more.

Time was not the same inside the monster. It stretched due to her constant impotent terror, but it also seemed to fly by. Her best guess was that it had been a week or so after their first meeting with V when it happened.

V had spent the morning trying out busking for the first time. It had gone surprisingly well, in that no one had attacked or threatened him. He had made about five quid in change. They were on what he'd called a lunch break, sitting on a wall a little farther out of town. The monster held the chips he had bought for them in her lap, never eating any. It never ate, awkwardly changing the subject when V offered. Occasionally, it picked up a chip or two and brought them up to her mouth only to crush them and stealthily toss them away. V noticed none of this, as far as Irene could tell, he just sat messing around with his guitar. He played something Irene didn't recognise, admitting halfway through that it was his own song. Then he had blushed and launched into something else.

Despite everything, Irene felt pretty peaceful listening to him play. As long as the monster kept quiet and still, she could pretend that it had never happened. This could be her: outside on a warm, sunny day, hanging out with the young man she had taken under her wing. Maybe it was her actual lunch break, and she was due back at work any minute. Maybe she was a secret lottery winner and she was waiting to surprise V with that fact. Maybe the two of them were going to be all right after all.

Irene noticed her before the monster did. Just there in the very corner of her eye. A woman in a sundress staring in their direction. Petite and radiant, a sunhat atop her mass of mermaid-coloured hair: Mae, the librarian. Her librarian. There was no way she hadn't recognised Irene. Suddenly, Mae was striding towards them. If Irene had still been the main occupant of her body, her pulse would have shot up, her heart beating out of her chest. For the briefest of moments, she felt hopeful. But, of course, librarian or not, Mae could do nothing to save her.

The monster turned her head, making Irene dizzy. She could see Mae properly now, meaning that it could too. It jumped to its feet. Again, Irene had a sickening sense of vertigo.

"I have to go."

It didn't even look at V as it said it. It just burst into a run that Irene's body would not have been capable of back when it was hers.

She couldn't look back to see if her librarian was following. She couldn't gather her thoughts in time to wonder why the monster was running. All she could do was watch as it shoved past people until it rounded a corner to an empty side alley.

Then everything was blurry again.

12

GRACE KELLY

It felt weird to have a guest in my house. Obviously, Doris had been a guest at first. But, given the way that she was, I had been able to let loose around her. The Nothing had seen me in stained T-shirts and tatty boxers so often, it was a miracle it still wanted anything to do with my wretched little body.

Things were different with V. It hadn't occurred to me when I'd invited him, or on the walk home, how awkward it was going to be. I excused the mess that the house was in and how tiny it was about three times within the first sixty seconds. Then I remembered I was talking to a homeless man.

It was still embarrassing showing him the place I intended him to sleep: too small to be a bedroom, too big to be a cupboard. It had mainly become a place to shove shit I didn't need but didn't want to throw away. A lot of my nan's stuff, obviously, plus everything from the flat I'd been renting before I moved back in. Sam's bed had been thrown into the corner at some point. His lead was probably buried under a mountain of things, seeing as he'd had no need of it for a long time before his death.

The airbed was easy enough to find, the pump less so. I offered to start inflating it while V took a shower. That would have been a perfectly fine and normal thing to say, had V mentioned wanting a shower. Or even if I had asked him first.

V blinked at me a few times. "Erm, yeah, maybe a shower would be a good idea."

He left for the bathroom. I seriously considered just letting The Nothing have me. At least I redeemed myself by getting the airbed (partially) inflated and making the room tidy(ish) by the time he got out. Plus, I had found some of my most presentable clothes for him to wear.

Things only really picked up when I found a forgotten bottle of Malibu behind some books. My guest and I retired to the living room with the intention of getting a little bit pissed.

An hour or so later, I was sitting listening to his life story and trying to not get annoyed by how good he looked in my clothes.

"Dad was always bitching about having three daughters. Like it was some great injustice that he never had a son. One day, I snapped and told him the good news. Turns out, he was a lot more okay with having daughters than he thought."

"Did he throw you out or did you leave?"

"Somewhere in the middle."

"What about your sisters? You ever see them?"

Something passed across his face. He took another drink before answering. "No. They would, I think, but I don't want to create a situation where my sisters have to choose between my dad and me. If they made the wrong choice, it would crush me."

"I get that." I did. I had never told my nan anything for pretty much the same reason.

I leaned forward to put my empty glass on the table. It slid from my fingers with an inch to go, landing with a clunk. I sat back, fighting drowsiness; getting drunk when I'd gone thirty hours without sleep was probably not a great idea. I needed V to keep talking so I could stay awake.

"Wasn't there anyone you could stay with?"

V sat swirling his drink. "For a while. I sofa surfed for a couple of years. Eventually, I ran out of friends."

"I haven't had a friend in years."

It must have been my maudlin tone that made him turn and affect a grin. "Until now," he said. Then he held his hand out for a fist bump.

I placed my hand over his fist – paper defeats rock. He laughed more than the gag was worth. Perhaps he really was my friend. It occurred to me that I should probably offer him some facts about my own life in the spirit of friendship, but I struggled to think of any that weren't depressing.

"I went through a phase of eating polystyrene as a kid." Sadly, that was the best I could do.

V nodded his head slowly enough that I realised it had been an odd thing to come out with. "Okay? Is that an autistic thing?"

Shit, was it? "You think I'm autistic?"

"Obviously, I don't know you all that well. To be honest, though, I thought that was why you called yourself Mask."

Well, there was a connection I'd never made. Perhaps he had a point. The natural follow-up to his comment would be to explain the origin of the name. He must have read my reluctance in the silence that followed because he went ahead and changed the subject.

"Whereabouts are you from, anyway?"

I boggled a little. "Here? I've lived within a ten-mile radius my entire life."

"Oh. It's just, you don't sound very… what you call it?"

"Black Country? Yam Yam? That's ten-plus years in customer service for you, sir."

He smiled at that. "You do kinda sound like an automated recording."

Was that an autistic thing as well? "Did you say where you were from?"

He smirked. "Yes, you ignorant fuck. I'll cut you some slack because you look seriously sleep deprived. It's Redditch."

"Ah," I said, "you know what they say about blokes from Redditch."

"What."

"Nothing. Who the fuck thinks about Redditch?"

Luckily, he laughed. "Do you know anything about the place?"

I searched my memory banks and came up with, "Redditch Festival? Like the one in Leeds?"

V shut his eyes for a second, taking a deep breath. "Do you mean Reading Festival? The one that's in Reading?"

I shrugged. "Am them different places?"

He bent double laughing, nearly spilling his drink. He had got it down to a chuckle by the time he straightened up. "Was that for my benefit?"

"Of course. If you want me to Yam Yam it up, I am only too happy to oblige."

"You slipped back into automated recording then."

I couldn't think of a response, so I just made a face at him.

V drained his drink and set his empty glass next to mine on the table. He patted his thighs to signal activity, then bounced to his feet. "I'd better finish inflating the bed before it gets too late."

I shuffled forwards to follow him, but he held up a hand.

"You look seconds away from passing out. Have a lie down or something."

I huffed, but immediately did as he said. My eyes were closed before he had even left the room.

When I opened them, the light had changed. A little darker with a slight greyish tinge. Doris crouched on the floor in front of me. Hunched up with her hands flat on the rug like a frog. Hopefully, I wasn't about to see her give birth to herself again.

She tilted her head. "Oh, Piglet, how long do you think this is going to last?"

To my surprise, I was able to open my mouth. No words came out, though, just a groan. Doris patted my head.

"He'll leave, you know, and you'll feel all the worse for having let someone in. You really would be better off with me. The sooner you agree, the sooner you can stop worrying about V or anyone else."

I lay there working my jaw. The dream paralysis felt like a dead limb; I was convinced I could break out of it by forcing myself to make tiny movements.

Doris leaned in. "Want to know what it's like for them inside me?"

I very fucking much did not want to know, but I lacked the ability to communicate that to her.

"They feel so safe and warm. They're all together in here. They had no one before, now we all have each other for ever and ever."

"Bollocks!" I was proud of myself for getting the word out, but it completely zapped my energy.

At least Doris seemed to get a good laugh out of it. Her grin became feral. Her eyes appeared to grow to the size of her ludicrous glasses.

"They're watching, you know. Do you want to know what they think of you?"

An awful thought occurred to me. "Are they… aware?"

"Oh yes. Every moment. They see everything I do with their body; they feel every piece of them I take."

I snorted. "I thought I was supposed to come willingly. You're not really selling this, Doris."

"Oh, I know letting me have you wouldn't be a dream come true for you. I might have been able to sell that to others in the past, but not you. Only the truth will work on you now."

"What truth?"

"Between me and any other future you're likely to have, I am the better option."

I laughed, despite it stinging.

Doris rose suddenly; I had to roll onto my back to keep sight of her. She stood over me with her hands clasped, head still tilted to one side.

"How did Grace Kelly die?"

For a moment, I stopped breathing. It took considerable effort to force out, "A car crash."

Doris chuckled lightly. "Silly thing, I didn't mean Princess Grace of Monaco. I meant Grace Kelly Whitehurst."

I couldn't let myself cry; it would not be productive. I placed my palms on the sofa and pushed until I was in a semi-sitting position. I rested my head against the arm.

"If you think that bringing up my –"

"It was a rhetorical question, sweetness, you don't have to answer. I am very much aware that no one knows how she died." Doris began to pace the room like a sinister orator. "Imagine a body decaying so badly before being found that a post-mortem cannot determine a cause of death to a reasonable degree of certainty. How long must she have been there?" She stopped, affecting a thoughtful expression. "I do hope it was quick. Imagine lying there knowing that no one was coming to save you, that no one would even miss you."

I pushed myself further up with my legs. I could sit mostly upright so long as I leaned back against the cushion.

"I am going to –"

"You hurt your back when we first met, do you remember? What if you hadn't been able to get up? How long would it have been until they found you? Starving to death must be an awful way to go. You didn't even have a dog left to eat you."

My hands twitched. I took a few deep, cleansing breaths.

Doris sidled up to me. She bent at the waist, slapping her hands down onto my thighs.

"You don't want to end up like her, do you? Think of all the indignities she would have been spared if only I'd got to her first. I'm sure it's safe to say she would've been exactly my type."

I leaned forward, pressing my forehead to hers. I let the tears flow. Doris cooed at me as she stroked my hair.

"I know, I know. Let it all out – you'll feel so much better."

I got a mild friction burn where our faces met as I slid my head upwards. Then I opened my mouth and sank my teeth into Doris' nose.

The Nothing screamed. It jerked away from me, but my

teeth held tight, taking a chunk of its nose. The flesh crumbled to ash in my mouth.

The Nothing stumbled backwards across the room. I got to my feet.

"You were right: I feel so much better."

Its hands were over its face. One glaring eye appeared through the gap in its fingers. "You'll rot with or without me, Mask. Why not be food for another living creature? You might as well make yourself useful in death, seeing as you never were in life."

Barely standing, I launched myself at it. We fell to the floor, a mass of flailing limbs and gouging fingers.

My eyes opened on V's horrified face. He had me by the shoulders – had he been shaking me?

"What?"

V looked on the edge of tears. "You were screaming and flailing and you didn't even wake up when you hit the floor."

A quick look around told me that I was indeed on the floor next to the sofa.

"Was it The Nothing?"

I nodded. To my surprise, V pulled me up into a hug. As my arms went around him in return, I tried to remember the last embrace I had been in. If forcibly hugging Sam didn't count, then it must logically have been my nan. But the actual last hug itself was not in my memory bank. I clung to V and sobbed. He held me through it, occasionally rubbing my back and making soothing noises.

We were interrupted by someone hammering on the front door.

V stiffened. My heart rate shot through the roof. We separated, helping each other up.

Obviously, it was not The Nothing. Why would it be banging on the door when it could come through the walls? I couldn't think of anyone else it could be, though. Whoever it was, it was most likely not good.

I couldn't see anything but shadow through the door's frosted panels. I was glad to have V behind me. As soon as I had that thought, he ducked into his room and hid. I would have laughed if I hadn't been shitting myself.

The impatient fucker knocked again. I swung the door open.

It was just the woman from the end of the row. She looked furious. My sigh of relief appeared to enrage her further.

"What the hell was all that noise?"

Fuck, I must have really been loud. Still in somewhat of a daze, the best I could think of was, "Spider."

"A spider?" She rolled her eyes. "This is two days in a row now. Keep it up and I'm getting the police involved."

I nodded, pulling the door slowly to signal to her to leave.

"Who's that lad?"

I looked behind me. The hallway was empty; V was still hiding.

"The one I saw you with earlier. Black chap. Looked like a junkie."

Why was I putting up with this vile old woman?

"None of your fucking business, you nosy cow!" I slammed the door in her face.

V poked his head out from his room. "Neighbour?"

"Yep. Last one standing, unfortunately."

"Any chance we can point the vicious, soul-eating monster in her direction?"

I smiled. "I honestly don't think it would stand a chance."

13

CLAUDE RAINS

I had a dream. A mercifully Nothing-less dream. Just me watching some movies and eating popcorn. The popcorn was off, though. I chewed and chewed, but never swallowed. Still, it was the nicest dream I'd had for a while. Peacefully, I opened my refreshed eyes to find that I was chewing on the wig head's nose.

I gave a little yelp and threw her away from me. Unfortunately, almost all her nose was still in my mouth. I gobbed it into my hand and tossed it across the room. After a minute or so of gagging, I apologised to the wig head and went off in search of something that would cover the taste of polystyrene.

When I entered the kitchen, I discovered V cleaning it. Not even just putting things away, but doing stuff I basically never did like cleaning the cupboard doors. Forgetting about breakfast, I stood watching him for a minute before announcing myself.

"You didn't need to clean up."

Luckily, he did not scream and spray me with cleaning fluid; he just turned and smiled. His nose was oddly red – I wasn't sure whether to mention it to him or not.

"I did. It was an absolute shit-hole."

I laughed. He continued, "Seriously, how can you live like this?"

"You sound like The Nothing."

"Well, it does occasionally make valid points."

He motioned for me to let him pass. I followed him into the living room. He had evidently cleaned up in there as well. He leaned down and picked something up from the table.

"I wasn't sure where these went."

It was a small pile of DVDs – the ones missing from my Cary Grant collection. I took them from him.

"Where were they?"

"Behind the cushion on the sofa."

My mind supplied me with an image of Doris fiddling with the cushion behind her. Had that been before or after they went missing? I flicked through the titles: *Bringing Up Baby; Holiday; Sylvia Scarlett* and *The Philadelphia Story*. Just what the hell did that mean? Maybe it was that I had left them there in my depression fugue. I had certainly done weirder things than that in the past.

I shrugged. "I'll stick them back, don't worry about it." Now I had a closer look at the reddish mark on his nose, I wondered if it could be an allergic reaction. I nodded towards it. "Is that from the cleaning stuff? Has it irritated your skin or sinuses or something?"

His hand went to the tip of his nose, touching it lightly. "Oh, no, I just woke up like this. I feel fine. Maybe something bit me in my sleep." He grinned suddenly. "Between the two of us, I don't think I'm the one that's allergic to cleaning."

"Unnecessary."

"Accurate, though."

I rolled my eyes and went to put the DVDs away like an adult who was capable of keeping their own house in order.

A blissful few days passed with no sign of The Nothing. It was not even turning up in my dreams. I knew it was foolish, but my hopes started to creep upwards.

To be honest, even if the two of us were just putting off the inevitable, I was still glad for the time I spent with V. Not counting

Doris for obvious fucking reasons, it had been years since I'd had a friend. And I had never had a friend I could entirely be myself around. There was no way in a million years that V would have ever wrinkled his nose at me and called me nothing.

A lot of my childhood (and then the subsequent two decades) had been spent wishing I could have friendships like the ones I saw on TV. Orphans who became like siblings; noble heroes who sacrificed their lives for each other; my own little Scooby gang. I even envied all the friendships that were presented as unhealthy – from mean-girl frenemies to co-dependant adolescents who egged each other on to commit shocking crimes. At least they had someone. While I did not figure out either my gender or sexuality until well into my twenties, I always knew there was something up. At the very least, I knew the relationships I longed for were platonic. Or filial. In my more sentimental fantasies, my mother turned up on our doorstep with some new half-siblings who were somehow my age despite that making no logistical sense. Maybe they were step-siblings, and we would initially be hostile towards each other before bonding over some childhood adventure.

No one is lonelier than an abandoned child who is aware of their own otherness.

Speaking of my childhood, cleaning out the boxroom had led to me finding both an old television/VCR combi and a box of videos. Thus, I was able to force V to watch *The Flight of Dragons* with me.

We sat on the floor in front of the sofa, the better to see the set where I'd perched it on the table. I excitedly jabbed my finger at the screen when the theme tune started.

"That's it! The song I told you about. Think you'd be able to play it?"

V shrugged. "Probably. I am a musical genius."

We mostly watched the film in silence, me in a nostalgic haze and V probably bored out of his mind. As the credits rolled and the theme tune started up again, I asked him what he thought.

"I get why child-you liked it. Dragons and shit."

I pouted. "You didn't like it?"

"It was fine, I'm just not massively into fantasy stuff. Plus, how he ended up defeating the bad guy was stupid."

"He defeated him with logic."

"He talked him to death! An omnipotent monster wizard!"

"It worked! It made sense within the narrative."

V huffed. "You have a really questionable taste in '80s movies, you know? Apart from *Labyrinth*, I suppose."

"Everyone loves *Labyrinth*. It's barely even a cult movie anymore." I remembered that I knew a potentially interesting fact about *Labyrinth*. "Hey, you know the whole 'remind me of a babe' bit?"

"Yeah?"

"That comes from a Cary Grant film called *The Bachelor and the Bobby-Soxer*. He says 'a man' rather than 'the babe', though. Is that interesting?"

V chuckled. "I suppose. I know a *Labyrinth* fact you might like."

I made a show of readying myself to have my mind blown.

"Apparently it was originally meant to end with Sarah just beating the fuck out of Jareth until he shrank down all tiny."

I liked that. More stories should climax with the protagonist decking the all-powerful antagonist.

"So… would that have been a better or worse ending than *The Flight of Dragons*?"

V rolled his eyes with a sigh. "I'm not getting into that again. What are we watching next?"

"*Rock-A-Doodle*."

"What's that one about?"

"What if Elvis were a chicken?"

The back of V's head hit the sofa and he let out an almighty groan.

*

My bubble was burst about a week after V moved in.

I was on my way back from the shop with enough groceries to feed two – TWO – people for up to a week.

I saw movement in the window of the end house but pressed on, ignoring it. I swore under my breath when I heard a door open behind me. Perhaps she just happened to be on her way out somewhere.

"I want a word with you!"

No such luck.

I turned, but didn't stop walking until I was certain it was me she wanted. "What's up?"

"Tell your boyfriend to back off!"

That was just about the last thing I expected her to come out with. "V?"

She smirked. "That's his name, is it? He wouldn't tell me. I know what name to give the police now if he turns up at my house again."

It was not exactly a lot for them to go on, but she seemed pretty pleased with it.

"He came round your house?"

She huffed. "As if you don't know. Round here telling me to keep my nose out your business. He's the one who needs to watch his back, not me."

With that, she stomped back into her house and slammed the door.

I entered my own house in something of a daze.

V was sitting on the floor in his bedroom. The room looked as though a hurricane had torn through it. Had I not been so shaken, I would have given him shit about actually being the messy one.

"Did you go see the woman on the end?"

He looked up, raised an eyebrow. "The nosy old bitch?"

"Yeah."

He shook his head.

"She says you did. Says you told her to mind her own business."

"A: she should and B: she's talking shit. Just bored and trying to start trouble."

"I suppose."

I looked at the floor. I was certain that V's room had been immaculate the last time I looked, despite the pile of my old things in the corner.

"Were you looking for something?"

He stared blankly at me. I gestured to the mess. He looked even more confused.

"You didn't do this?" he asked me.

"I wouldn't trash your room, dude."

"I thought maybe you'd been looking for that letter and then forgot to put everything back."

"What letter?"

"The one on my bed."

There was indeed a letter lying on top of the airbed. It was addressed to Deborah Whitehurst at the house she had lived in before this one. That made it ten years old at least. I dropped my shopping on the floor to pick it up.

It was handwritten on lavender stationary that was vaguely familiar to me. So vague I could not be sure if I were imagining it or not. My eyes skimmed it, zooming in on the last line: *With Love, Your Grace.*

Either Nan had secretly been a bishop, or she had been in communication with my mother much later than I thought she was.

From the floor, V looked up at me for a reaction.

"I, erm…"

I ran from his room to mine, slamming the door behind me. About a minute later, I heard V dragging the shopping bags into the kitchen. The poor guy really deserved a better housemate than me.

I settled onto the bed and studied the envelope in my hands. A faded postmark told me it had been sent on the ninth of October. The first three digits of the year were 201, but the last one was illegible. That narrowed it down to the decade, at least. I turned it over and over in my hands, unable to start reading it. Then I felt brave enough to skim it. It was so short, nothing really jumped out at me apart from the fact she had signed it 'Grace'.

My mom had not liked being called Grace Kelly. As pretty as it was, it was still a name with a gimmick. She went with just Grace throughout school, before deciding in adulthood that it was just Kelly. I'm not sure why she changed it, maybe to reinvent herself. There was certainly an element of twenty-something adolescent rebellion in there. A rejection of her own mother who always insisted on calling her some variation of Grace. That she signed it as such seemed like an act of contrition, like she wanted to make peace. The only way to find out if that were true was to read it.

Dear Mom,
I'm sorry it's been so long. I'm doing okay at the minute. There's a man on the scene that I'm pretty serious about. If we do end up making things official, I want the two of you there.

Where the fuck had that serious man been when she died? More importantly, where had he been before she died?

There was a section in the middle where she went on about me, asking how I was doing. She referred to me first of all by my legal name, then the childhood nickname she had given me. The former was same old same old, but the latter was a shock to my system. I had forgot she even called me that. I had not let anyone use the name since she left. Piglet – my Nan's mercifully unisex favoured term – had long since replaced it.

I know you're probably not thrilled with me making contact with the child I gave up, but please pass the letter on. I don't care if you read it before you do, just make sure that you do.
With Love,
Your Grace.

I read through the last few lines a second and third time just to make sure I had understood. A second letter. One obviously meant for me. I tore the envelope to pieces just in case, but I already knew that it was not in there. Where the fuck was it? Why the fuck had Nan hidden it from me? Who the fuck did she think she was? I had been an adult in 2010, for fuck's sake. A stupid tear rolled down my cheek. My mom had tried to contact me; what if she'd wanted to meet me, build a relationship again? There was a decent chance I would have turned her down, but that should have been my choice to make.

Fighting back more tears, it finally occurred to me to question where the letter had come from if V had not been the one to dig it out. Someone must have got into the house without us noticing and found this out specifically to mess me up. There was only one being who would – or even could – conceivably do such a thing.

A noise came from the living room. It sounded like something brushing against the wall. Thinking about it a moment, I had heard the same sound after meeting Doris for the first time. The brushing became a loud, harsh scratching. Glass smashed.

I got off my arse and ran into the living room. V had already beaten me there.

A couple of my nan's pictures had been knocked off the wall. Along the wall itself were deep gouge marks, like the claws of an enormous beast.

I turned to V. "Did you see it happen?"

He shook his head. "I was in the kitchen."

We stood staring in silence at the wrecked room.

I cleared my throat to speak. "I think –"

POP!

I leapt about a foot in the air at the sound coming from the front of the house. V stumbled back. The pop was followed by an angry hiss. We ran into V's room to find his airbed shredded.

I took a deep breath in an attempt to control my terror. "It's still here, isn't it? And it wants us to know."

V didn't answer me. He just stared down at the ruins of his bed.

He slept in my room that night. Mercifully, he did not comment on BENOTHING. I saw him clock it and vowed to get rid of it at the earliest opportunity. The two of us settled down into bed together; we were both too scared for it to be awkward. We probably would have held each other all night if one of us had been brave enough to initiate it. I awoke alone the next morning.

The curtains were open, presumably V had done that. He also must have put the wig head on the windowsill, facing outwards. That was strange, but hardly worth getting out of bed for. So I lay there staring up at the ceiling, running through my options with the graffiti. I would try covering it up with paint or something first. If that didn't work, I would have to remove the tiles completely.

As I continued to stare up, an odd scratching sound came from the ceiling, as though someone were running their nails up and down the length of it.

Then the ceiling tiles exploded. Polystyrene rained down upon me like a blizzard. I screwed my eyes shut to protect them. When I opened them, I could see that my bare ceiling had been carved into over and over again.

Benothing and Benothing and Benothing.

There came a sound from the window. I bolted upright to see that the wig head had moved ever so slightly. It was still for a moment, then it spun around to face me. I yelped at the movement. Then I screamed when my brain processed what I had seen.

The wig head's nose that I chewed off had been replaced with a human one. There were human eyeballs in her sockets as well. Thick lines of blood dripped down her inanimate face.

I scrambled out of bed and into the hall, calling for V as I went.

Someone banged on the front door, causing me to yelp. My fucking nosy bitch of a neighbour, at a guess.

I opened the door ready to scream at her. Instead, I found my postman white as a sheet except for his red-rimmed eyes.

"Are you okay? What's happened?" Had he seen my gory window display?

He opened his mouth, but no sound came out. Slowly, he sank to the floor. He sat there, staring into the distance.

I turned to shout into the house, "V, get out here!"

Barefoot, I stepped out and crouched in front of him. "Do you need an ambulance?"

He shook his head, still staring over my shoulder. I followed his line of sight to the house on the end of the row. The front door was wide open.

I shouted for V again. When he did not make an appearance, I was forced to leave the poor postie on his own. He made a strangled noise as I walked off in the direction of the house. Quite why I was doing so was beyond me.

The smell hit me first. Like sewage perhaps, but with a fishy undercurrent. The blood that covered the hallway was too dark for me to actually recognise it as such but, logically, what else could it be?

"Hello?"

I didn't expect an answer, but I didn't know what else to do. I stepped onto the doorstep, but that was as far as I was willing to go.

"Hello?" I heard my voice breaking.

The scene was such a mess that it took me a moment to pick out her corpse. My nosy bitch of a neighbour, covering most of her own hallway. Her head was facing away from me, but it didn't take a genius to guess where the wig head's new features had come from.

Of course, as soon as I'd had the thought, her lifeless head spun to face me, providing me with gory confirmation.

14

RAY

Ray was rotting. That probably was not the right word for what was happening to him, but he had no idea how else to describe it. Every moment, he could feel himself getting smaller and weaker within his former body. It was not a million miles away from how he had felt about getting older. The main difference now was that his body had been hijacked by the woman who had tricked her way into his home. That was what you got for being polite.

There had been a similar feeling of impotence when Ray found out that his daughters had got together behind his back and decided to move him into his own bungalow. He still remembered their pitch: a whole house to himself, rather than just a room at Helen's and it was all designed in a way that he would have an easier time getting around. With Helen in the middle of organising Australia, he hadn't had much choice in the matter. By that time, Sharon had known better than to suggest he move in with her. It was a shame that he had left no body for them to find, let them see what their neglect had wrought. His ghost would have derived a grim sense of satisfaction from their guilt. It certainly would have been better than what he was actually left with.

Ray stood in front of the mirror in his bedroom. Or, rather, Gail stood in front of the mirror. She grinned at him, giving his face a sinister edge he was sure it usually lacked. She must have known he could see her; she seemed to delight in that fact. He didn't notice that she was moving at first, she had his arm creeping up so slowly. It was only when she took hold of the jumper he was wearing that he realised what she was going to do. Still going slowly as though to build anticipation, she lifted the baggy material until Ray's torso was exposed.

Whole sections of his skin were black and porous. There were actual holes in his flesh. If he could have vomited at the sight, he would have. He wanted to scream, force his eyes shut, run and never look back. The grin on his face just got bigger.

Suddenly, the jumper dropped back down over his fragile body. Gail tilted his head as though she could hear something. Ray strained until he thought he caught the sound of sobbing coming from outside.

Gail ran into the living room and pressed his face up to the back window. Two of his neighbours were out there: the old bag and the younger one with that rabid dog. They were hugging each other, the younger one weeping on the shoulder of the older one. A lot of silly noise. Ray wished he could bang on the window to get them to shut up. Gail, apparently, found it interesting enough to creep over to the back door and peep out.

Those bloody women showed no signs of letting up. There was a lad in a baggy black hoodie walking up the path behind them, leading the neighbour's Border Collie. Must have been the grandson, unless she had money to waste on a dogwalker. When he reached them, he just stood there awkwardly. The dog bounced around happily between the three of them. And Border Collies were supposed to be smart.

The women finally pulled apart, to the visible relief of the young lad. The older one patted the crying one on the arm.

"You know where I am if you need me, love." She turned and went back to her own house.

The other one gave her grandson a quick hug before going inside. The lad happened to look in Ray's direction as he followed his nan. His face was red and blotchy like he had been crying as well. Actually, thinking about it, the lad might well have been a girl. You could barely tell these days. Whatever went on in young people's heads was a mystery to Ray.

Once they were gone, Gail stepped out onto the back doorstep.

"You know what that's about, don't you?"

Gail turned, bringing Ray face to face with the neighbour from the other side. He had not heard her come out. She was beaming so much that perhaps she had floated out, giddy on the potential for gossip.

"They've found her daughter, the one who dumped the kid on her. Apparently, she'd been dead for years, but no one had found her. It's been all over the news this week."

For a moment, Ray was back on the bathroom floor awaiting a rescue that would never arrive. He watched his corpse decaying there in fast-forward until someone thought to break in to see what had happened to him. A sorry end indeed. He could not say if he was better or worse off now. Maybe he was still there hallucinating this entire thing.

"Do you know their names?"

It was a shock to hear his own voice. Gail had not spoken to him since she had taken him.

The nosy neighbour shrugged. "I think the one with the dog is called Debbie. Not sure about the one with the glasses. Does it matter?"

Apparently, it did, but Ray had no idea why. It did not seem likely that Gail was just making conversation. But then, Gail often did things that were a complete mystery to him. A while back, she had been searching his house and just happened to pick up the postcard on the fridge. She didn't seem too interested in the front, but reading the back made her give a theatrical little gasp and clutch it to her chest. It stayed on her chest as she twirled around the kitchen, humming. The postcard now had pride of place on the mantelpiece.

Gail turned her back on the nosy neighbour and went inside

without saying another word. Ray wished he could have seen her face at that.

Once inside, Gail turned the telly on – the first time Ray had seen her do so. The channels were flicked through until they eventually found some news. There was no mention of what Ray had just heard until the main show ended and the local one began. Sure enough, the headline was about a woman's badly decomposed body that had been found in some grotty bedsit.

Ray had been the one to find his wife's body when it happened. Actually, according to the autopsy, it was a good few hours after it had happened. It was perfectly normal for Josephine to spend all morning in the garden while her husband watched television in the living room. It was also normal for him to doze off for a few hours in front of the telly. There had been a black-and-white film on when he woke up, some daft farce. Venturing out into the garden had been an odd return to the world of colour. In his recently awoken haze, he thought Josie was also napping when he saw her on the floor in front of her beloved petunias. Then the fog cleared and he realised how daft that was. There was no movement when he called to her. Her body was already cold when he reached her. A heart attack, they said.

That was when things with his daughters had begun to go south. Even though Helen moved him into her place, their relationship had become frosty. The girls had always favoured their mother, and Ray was sure he wasn't imagining the air of resentment from both of them. He never quite figured out whether they thought he could have saved her or if they were just angry at him for being the one who survived.

As the sickening details of Debbie's poor daughter were relayed on screen, Ray could feel Gail's grin spreading across his face. It surprised him when she spoke again, apparently to herself.

"Oh, Grace Kelly Whitehurst, you would have been delicious."

15

JAMES STEWART

Going down to the police station to give a statement about finding your neighbour's corpse is exactly as fun as it sounds. What's even more fun is knowing that the creature who did that also wants to kill you, but in a much slower and more intimate way. For fairly obvious reasons, I did not include that in my statement. The wig head had disappeared by the time I returned home, so I didn't mention it. Nor did I tell them how many times my neighbour had threatened to call the police on me. I'm sure it would have pleased her to know that I did end up having to talk to them because of her.

I tried to be sad about the dead woman. I really felt as though I should have cried for her. But I went through every interaction I could remember and just could not feel it. It was not as though I would have wished her fate on her; there is not a single living person I would want to die like that. I just could not drum up a single bit of grief. Then I remembered that she had a son. He probably even knew by now. He would be dealing with the reality of his mother dying in unpleasant and mysterious circumstances. He would never get to know the truth about her death. Obviously, that got to me. At least no one on the bus wanted to sit next to the crying weirdo.

When I got home, V asked me if I was okay, but I could tell

that he was just doing so to be polite. He stood there fidgeting until he finally gave in and asked what he actually wanted to ask.

"You didn't tell the police about me, did you?"

I shook my head.

"And they're not going to need to speak to you again?"

I shrugged.

He must have figured out that I needed looking after then. He led me to the living room and sat me down on the sofa, before disappearing into the kitchen.

My thoughts were filled with blood and flesh; I was never going to get over that smell. It was fortunate that I had stopped eating meat as a teenager otherwise I would have had to clean out my freezer. Next time I passed a butcher, I was likely to puke.

Dealing with the police had been no picnic either. Having to answer to my legal name, second-guessing every question they asked and how they looked at me. Knowing that I was lying, but not being able to tell the truth even if I wanted to. There was about a minute where I zoned out and missed half the conversation because I had been staring at the officer's nose, picturing it being torn from his face. I couldn't even be relieved to be home because I knew something awful was waiting here for me.

A cup clinked down on the table.

"Wasn't sure how you liked your tea, but sugar is apparently good for shock so hopefully you like half a kilo."

He took a seat next to me.

"I know you're freaking out, but there's a silver lining here: The Nothing isn't likely to show itself for a while with the police sniffing around."

I nodded towards my fucked-up wall. "It doesn't need to show itself."

He did not have an answer for that.

I picked up my tea just for something to do. A single sip told me that half a kilo had only been a mild exaggeration. Perhaps it would help. Something had to.

"Has it killed anyone before? Like, actually murdered them?"

V shrugged. "I didn't think it did that. People are food to it; I wouldn't have thought it would waste them."

"How do you know so much about it? You've never really explained."

"I told you: I met it before."

"And what? What exactly happened?"

V looked away. I waited for some kind of answer. Our stalemate was interrupted by the doorbell. V jumped up to get it only to immediately return.

"It looks like police again."

I swore under my breath as I got up. V disappeared off somewhere behind me.

The officer was not one of the ones I had seen earlier.

"I already gave a statement."

He raised an eyebrow at my rudeness, but didn't comment on it.

"I just wanted to know if you knew the neighbours. We could do with talking to them, but no one seems to be in."

I had to put some thought into answering that. Doris and Peter were most likely not legally dead, seeing how their bodies had been consumed. Were still being consumed, really.

"My nan was friends with the woman next door, but I think she died not long after Nan did. I've never even seen the man next to her. I'm pretty sure both houses have been empty for a long time."

He frowned, eyes darting over to Doris' place. "You wouldn't happen to have a key for next door, would you?"

"Sorry."

"Don't worry about it; we'll find out if it's rented and talk to the landlord. Does the same person own your place?"

"I own this place. Inheritance."

He gave me a once-over. "Yeah, you don't look like the usual residents. Have a nice day."

I had the door shut before he had fully turned away. Hopefully, that would be the last time I would have to deal with the police. At least for today.

Something occurred to me on the way back to the living room. I turned to V.

"Say you're elderly."

"You're elderly," he deadpanned.

"You're old and alone and good friends with the woman next door – you'd give her a key in case of emergencies, wouldn't you?"

He shrugged. "Spose."

It made a great deal of sense for the real Doris to have given Nan a key. It also made sense that I wouldn't notice a spare key lying around in all my years living here. I even knew where it was likely to be: in one of the kitchen drawers that were filled with random shit. I left V gawping to go and look.

Twenty minutes later, I had found a dozen or so things I hadn't been looking for but was pleasantly surprised to find. I had a small pile going on the side. Next to that was a smaller pile of keys. Some of them were tiny and I couldn't begin to guess what they were for. One of them was for a Volvo I couldn't remember my nan ever owning, and one of them looked exactly like my backdoor key, but cleaner and newer. It was attached to a keyring with a faded black-and-white photo of who I thought was maybe Katharine Hepburn. Surely this had to be an emergency key for Doris' house.

After watching my frantic search for a few minutes, V had retired to his bedroom. I found him checking over the carcass of the airbed, the room around him now spotless (I probably should have offered to help him clean up, but it was too late now). I brandished the key at him.

"I have a really stupid idea that would most likely achieve nothing – are you in?"

*

It killed me to agree to wait until after dark to get into Doris' house. I would have gone the second I thought of it if V hadn't been there to stop me. Given his repeated insistence that it was both dangerous and ridiculous, I was surprised he agreed to come with me. Maybe he was worried about me.

Doris' house had the musty smell of stale air. It was as though no doors or windows had been opened in a long time. I was relieved that was the worst of it; a repeat of my visit to the house on the end of the row would not have been welcomed.

The kitchen light flickered a few times before finally coming on.

V frowned. "We probably shouldn't have the lights on if we're breaking in."

"We're not breaking in. Plus, all my neighbours are too dead to call the police."

I pulled open a random drawer just to feel as though I was doing something. It was the cutlery drawer – I couldn't even pretend that was useful information.

"What are we doing here, Mask?"

"Looking for clues." I said it with about as much conviction as I felt.

The truth was that I had no idea what I hoped to find in Doris' house, but the police had put the idea into my head and it was difficult to get out. It was not likely that The Nothing had hidden the secret to destroying it in its lair, along with helpful instructions, but nothing ventured, nothing gained.

Being in a house from the same model as your own is an unsettling experience. Everything is exactly the same, but somehow different enough to be uncanny. The fact that it mirrored my home, so everything was backwards, only made it worse.

The living room was tidy enough, but just about every available surface was covered in a layer of dust. I gravitated towards the mantel where there were several framed photos. There were a couple of black-and-white ones of two little girls that I took to be Doris and her sister, Audrey (assuming that The Nothing had told the truth about that). Then some with a more sepia tone showing the girls growing up until there were full-colour ones of two grown women, one of whom was clearly Doris. The most recent one by far appeared to have been taken at Christmas. Initially taking it to be another one of the sisters, I did a double-take before picking it up for a closer look. It showed Doris and Nan sitting on the sofa wearing paper hats. Sam lay at their feet, only partially in shot. In Nan's lap was the as-yet-unopened present I had just given to her: the Cary Grant boxset.

I had taken that photo.

Christmas Day roughly five years ago. I dropped by after lunch. Nan's friend was just about to leave when I arrived. They got me to take a picture of them first. Then Nan and I exchanged presents and Sam insisted on a walk and I never once thought about Nan's friend for the rest of the visit.

I had met Doris. The actual, real Doris. She really had been friends with my nan. Then they had both died and Doris had been utterly forgotten. In my defence, I had only seen her for a minute or so that day. The second she was gone, I started badgering my nan to open her present so I could see her reaction. She loved it, of course. Then she got one DVD out at random and said something about the actress in it. Something I could not quite remember.

There was a creak behind me. I turned to find myself alone in the room. I hadn't noticed V leaving. When I moved, I felt the key in the little front pocket of my jeans. Doris' spare key which was attached to a Katharine Hepburn keyring. Oh, of course.

"V!"

I ran for the hall. V appeared in the doorway, and we almost smashed into each other.

I held up the photo. "Katharine Hepburn!"

V squinted at the picture. "No, it isn't."

"No, I met the real Doris, just for a second. Then after she was gone, Nan told me her name was Katharine Hepburn. I can't believe I forgot that."

"Is that one?"

I stared blankly at him.

"Is that a clue? Like you were looking for?"

I shrugged. "Maybe. She..." Something occurred to me. "She hid all the DVDs in my collection that had Katharine Hepburn in them. The Nothing didn't want me to know her name. That has to be important."

V looked thoughtful. "Gail did give me a fake name."

"Who?"

His head shot up, eyes wide. "Erm... Gail. That's how The Nothing first appeared to me."

"You said it was an old man."

He shrugged. "Does it matter? It's a shapeshifter, you know that. If we're finished here, we should really get out of its lair." He pushed past me, heading for the door.

"V, is there something you're not telling me?"

He turned back. "There's lots of things I'm not telling you; we barely know each other." He grinned to show it was a joke. Then he left the house without looking back.

V opted not to sleep in my room that night. Instead, he made himself a nest out of the airbed remnants and some blankets and cushions. He seemed content enough.

I lay in bed turning everything over in my head. Names were important to The Nothing. But why? Could I do something with my knowledge of Doris' real name now I had it? I couldn't imagine what that could be. And then there was the issue of Gail, and V not telling me the whole truth. I resolved to get it from him the next day no matter what.

16

I

In another universe, no doubt, Irene had asked the cute librarian out within minutes of meeting her.

The first time they met, the library had been busy. It was summer and the schools were out. Irene had thought that would mean no kids would be in there doing their homework. It turned out to be bustling with children doing something called the Summer Reading Challenge. She was pretty sure that hadn't been a thing when she was a child.

Irene had noticed her hair first – a fading blue with a lot of black roots showing. The next thing she noticed was how busy she was. She thought about leaving until she saw what she had come in for – a form to apply for a library card. She took one, neatened the pile and found a table to sit at and fill it in. She waited for all the children to leave before taking it to the desk.

The problem came when the librarian asked for some ID. Irene's heart all but stopped. She mumbled something about not having any with her. The librarian told her she could bring some in next time and collect the card then. Not sensing that anything was amiss, she then launched into a list of the various forms they would accept. There was nothing else for it. Irene checked there was no one else within earshot, then leaned over the counter.

"Look, I… I haven't got any ID with my name on."

The librarian scrunched her nose in adorable confusion. "Nothing at all? Can't you get something?"

"Not with this name on it."

Irene saw the exact moment she twigged. Then the two of them held a brief contest for the most awkward smile.

The librarian turned to her screen and clicked the mouse. "Right, I'm just ticking this little box which says I've seen some identification." She reached under her desk and pulled out a small black card. She wrote Irene's name on the back with a Sharpie.

"It means peace, doesn't it?"

Irene had been staring off into the distance, trying to make sense of what was happening. "Sorry?"

The librarian looked as though she regretted speaking. "Irene means peace."

"Er, yeah, from the Greek goddess of peace."

"It suits you."

It was such an obvious, clumsy attempt to broadcast that she was Okay With That Sort Of Thing, but Irene didn't mind. It even made her just a little bit bold.

"What's your name?"

"Mae."

Irene wondered if that was short for a longer Asian name, but it felt rude to ask. Instead she said, "That's cute."

Mae smiled, sliding Irene's card over to her.

At that point, Alternate Universe Irene asked the cute librarian out. Maybe they had gone out a handful of times. Maybe Mae had eventually moved into the bungalow with her. That version of Irene was safe at home helping her girlfriend dye her hair, maybe being persuaded to try something a little more colourful herself. Alternate Universe Irene had no idea monsters existed. Not literal ones, anyway.

Regular Universe Irene had a theory that the monster did not always have a corporeal form. She suspected that was what happened when things went blurry – it stopped existing in the physical plane. It must have done that for a long time after the run-in with the librarian. Irene was aware of nothing but a constant feeling akin to motion sickness the entire time.

Eventually, Irene found herself wandering through town, presumably looking for V. Irene hoped he had moved on, maybe even got himself off the streets. When she finally caught sight of him, it was bittersweet. She was happy to see him again, but she was not the only one seeing him.

His face lit up when he saw them. He rushed over and pulled the monster into a big hug.

"I was so worried about you! I've been having all these anxiety dreams about you and some, like, demon thing."

The monster patted him on the back to end the hug.

"I just needed to get away for a few days. How've you been?"

V shrugged. "The usual shit." He was still smiling, though. "Hey, that woman came by looking for you."

"What woman?"

"The one you saw that day? Early thirties, Asian, multicoloured hair? She was asking people if they'd seen you."

The tension was palpable. Irene had no idea how the boy could not see it.

"Did you speak to her?"

"No, I've been avoiding her. I figured you ran away from her for a good reason." He beamed up at her, so obviously hoping for her approval.

Irene felt her facial muscles pull up into a smile. "You wanna go for a walk?"

They ended up down by the canal. A nice enough place if you were a creature who did not need to fear being mugged.

V chatted on about how his nascent busking career was going. He apparently did pretty well in the warmer weather. Someone had even offered to buy him an ice cream on his break the other day, but V didn't fuck with dairy. Oh, and another day a little girl tried to teach him this song about a baby shark. Her parents looked embarrassed, but it was really sweet.

The monster was silent the entire time. Irene knew what was coming; her heart broke more with every word V spoke.

Just as they were passing under a bridge, the monster reached out and stopped V. They turned and faced each other in the shadows.

"Are you happy, V?"

He frowned in confusion, then shrugged. "Yeah, things are going okay: the weather's better; I'm making the odd bit of cash; it's been a while since I've seen..." He trailed off, a haunted look coming over him.

If Irene ever got her body back, she was going to find the person who hurt V and tear him to shreds.

"Is that happy? Or is that making the best of things?"

He shrugged again. "All I can do, innit?"

"It's not all you can do. What if I said I could take you somewhere you would never be cold or hungry or tormented again?"

It lied. That was the worst thing. It didn't trap you with clever wordplay or grant your wish with an ironic twist. You could not examine its speech for a loophole to save yourself. It just lied to you. Then it tormented you for the rest of time.

V was listening to neither the monster's lies nor Irene's internal monologue. Instead, he was staring over their shoulder.

"It's her."

The monster turned to look.

Mae was rushing along the canal path towards them. She could have had a superhero cape billowing behind her and it would not have seemed out of place.

The monster knocked V to the ground in its rush to get away. Unlike the last time it had fled the librarian, it was rather limited in where it could go. One long straight line until wherever the canal ended. Eventually, it came to the opening of a small alleyway. It dived in.

A dead end.

The brick wall couldn't be seen from the mouth of the alley. The monster had trapped itself. Unless it disappeared again. Irene braced herself.

Footsteps behind them. The sound of someone trying to catch their breath. They turned around to see Mae leaning over and resting her hands on her thighs.

The monster took a step towards her. Irene screamed out with every fibre of her being.

Mae straightened up and looked at her. At *her*, Irene was sure.

"Irene?"

There was a sensation like when you're half asleep and think you're falling, that peculiar quirk left over from evolution. The monster stumbled backwards, bowled over in pain. Its screams filled Irene's consciousness.

For a moment, she saw it as it truly was: a cowering, skeletal figure. She felt the briefest pang of pity, but that was replaced almost immediately by victory. Then she felt something she had never expected to experience again.

Peace.

17

KATHARINE HEPBURN

V wasn't there when I woke up the next day. I would have assumed he had done a runner, but his guitar was still in his room. That was pretty much the one thing he was guaranteed not to leave behind. I might just have envied that beat-up old noisemaker.

It was well into the afternoon when he returned, straining under the weight of several of my Bags for Life. He startled slightly when he caught sight of me sitting on the sofa staring at him. He tried to cover it with an awkward smile. He nodded towards one of the bags, the Border Collie one I had stolen in a wave of grief.

"Had some stuff I needed to get. Hope it was okay that I took the key?"

I shrugged. "You live here now, dude. I'll get you one cut at some point."

V went to drop his stuff in his room. I followed him.

"What did you get?"

He shoved the bags into a corner, making no move to empty them. "Just went round some charity shops in town for clothes. I can't keep wearing your stuff forever."

That thought had not occurred to me. Maybe I should have offered to buy him something. It was hard to know what was appropriate or inappropriate to suggest. Reimbursing him for what he had already purchased was definitely a step too far.

We stood awkwardly facing each other for a moment. I scrambled for something to say before remembering I needed to talk to him about last night.

"Listen, when you're settled and whatever, do you think we could have a chat?"

His face was perfectly impassive. "What about?"

"About when you first met The Nothing."

"Not a lot to tell there, but whatever." He nodded towards the bags. "I'd best get started putting stuff away."

I left him to it.

An hour later, V took a visibly reluctant seat next to me on the sofa.

"What exactly did you want to know?"

I had made an list of the things I needed to ask him, but it would appear too crazy to consult it in front of him.

"Who was Gail?"

"No one, turns out." There was a distant look in his eyes. "I thought she was my one and only friend on the streets, but it was all bullshit."

"Why didn't you tell me about her before?"

V shrugged, picking at the tattered Pride bracelet on his wrist. "Didn't want to talk about her. It wasn't fun, you know?" He looked up at me. "How did you feel when you found out about Doris?"

"Terrified, mostly."

We shared an unhappy smile.

"But, yeah. It was a pretty miserable time. How come I haven't seen Gail?"

"She's gone."

"What does that mean?"

"I don't know exactly. That's just what The Nothing said."

That was puzzling. Was she gone as in dead? Gone as in The Nothing no longer had her? Or could she possibly have been saved? A glimmer of hope attempted to form within me. I crushed it beneath my heel.

"What happened the last time you saw her?"

He shrugged. "She was chased by a librarian."

"She was chased by a what now?"

"There was this librarian who knew her from before. The Nothing acted like it was scared of her; it ran when she showed up. The next thing I knew, Gail was gone and had been replaced by this old man. I could barely get any sense out of the librarian when I talked to her afterwards. She saw something, though – I'm sure of it."

"Something we could use?"

"Maybe?"

"Do you know which library she works at?"

*

The library was pretty much dead by the time we got there. No one on reception and barely any patrons present, bar the odd person sat at a computer. We did several little circuits of the place before we spotted what must have been the librarian.

Black hair run through with grey on top, bright red underneath, pulled up into a messy bun. She was perched on a tiny stool in a position unlikely to be comfortable. From the looks of it, she was tidying and organising the books. That must be what librarians got up to when it was quiet. I could see little of her face when she turned as she wore a facemask and glasses that were attached by a chain. She got out of her crouching position on the stool with about as much grace as could be expected under the circumstances.

"Hi," the librarian said. "Do you need me?"

I looked to V, since he was the one who apparently knew her. He cleared his throat.

"Hi, yeah, do you remember me at all?"

She gave him a once-over. "Sorry, no. I see a lot of people in here every day."

"Gail's friend?"

She drew her brows together, chin dropping slightly.

"That wasn't her real name," I prompted V.

"Right, yeah, I think you said her name was Iris or..."

"Irene! Have you seen her?" The poor thing looked distraught.

"No, sorry. We just wanted to know what happened the day she disappeared."

"Why?"

V was dumbstruck by the question, so I spoke up. "We have a friend who's in a similar situation. Maybe it'll help."

Their name is Mask, and you're likely their last fucking hope.

The librarian raised an eyebrow. She looked beyond us for a second before motioning us to sit at a table.

"First of all: I don't know how much sense any of this is going to make to you, but it's exactly what happened as far as I can piece together."

"What do you mean, piece together?" I asked.

"Well, I was knocked down and possibly out. Actually, the whole thing only makes sense if I was unconscious for part of it. So Irene used to come in regularly and then she suddenly stopped. Naturally, I was worried about her. I tried to tell myself she'd had a stroke of luck and moved on. I guess I would have forgot all about it eventually, but I happened to see her one day sitting with a busker. When I went over, she ran from me. I guessed she was homeless and embarrassed about it. Was I right?"

V sat up, startled. He obviously hadn't been expecting to do anything more than listen. "Erm, yeah."

Mae nodded and then carried on. "So after weeks of searching on and off, I finally found Irene. I chased her – I know that makes me sound like a crazy stalker, but I was worried about her. If she had told me to leave her alone, I would have, no question, but I needed to hear that from her directly.

"So we're face to face, and I can't tell if she's angry or scared or both. She takes a couple of steps towards me, and I call out to her. Then she doubles over in pain. I try to help her and she shoves me to the ground – that's when I must have been knocked out. There was a scream, I think, but like several people screaming in harmony and then these awful crunching sounds. I must have been hallucinating because I'm sure I heard Irene laughing. When I stood up again, there was an old man standing where Irene had been. I asked him who he was, and he just barged right past me. Then this guy… oh, was that you? I spoke to you, didn't I?" She nodded at V.

He nodded back. "Yeah, that was me. I saw the old man running away. Then I couldn't get much sense out of you. The bit I understood was that Gail's name was Irene and she had just disappeared. Then I asked you why you'd been looking for her and you said…"

"Because I'm a librarian." Her eyes were sad, and I fancied I could see an equally sad smile under her mask. Her gaze was a thousand miles away. Or maybe just a few years. It seemed a shame to interrupt, but I needed to know something.

"You said you called out to her – what exactly did you say?"

The librarian slipped out of her reverie. She frowned slightly. "Her name."

"That's it?"

"Yes. I just looked her in the eye and said her name. She reacted like I'd stabbed her."

I tried to catch V's eye, but he was also lost in his thoughts. Either he hadn't heard what she said, or the implication had not registered. I tapped on the table to wake him.

"Well, we've probably taken up enough of your time; I'm sure you're busy."

There was complete silence in the library. If a tumbleweed had rolled past, no one would have batted an eye. I stood and signalled to V to do the same.

The librarian sat forward. "If you do see Irene…"

V turned to walk away. There was an incredibly awkward couple of seconds before he stopped, shook his head and turned back.

"Look, I wasn't sure whether to tell you this, but she passed away." When her face fell, he hastened to add, "It was really peaceful! No more pain. She told me to thank you if I ever saw you again."

The librarian nodded slowly for far too long. Her eyes welled up with tears. I took hold of V's arm to make a speedy exit. Turned out there was no need; someone sat at a computer called over to the librarian for help with printing. I saw her wipe her eyes and zip her feelings back up. She stood, giving us a quick nod.

"Thanks for letting me know. Take care, guys."

She went off to continue being a librarian.

As soon as we were outside, I was frantically slapping V on the arm. "Did you hear what she said?"

He didn't appear to share my excitement. "Which part?"

"She said that calling The Nothing by Irene's real name hurt it."

He looked away and back again in a gesture that wasn't quite an eye roll, but was definitely in the vicinity. "That's a bit of a reach, Mask."

"No, it makes sense! The false names, hiding those movies. It doesn't want us to know the names of its victims because that hurts it. That has to be the way to defeat it!"

"Who says there's even a way to defeat it? There doesn't need to be. Maybe the second it lays eyes on you, you're fucked."

"You weren't!"

"Wasn't I?"

We stood staring at each other in the library car park.

"What harm could it do to try?"

V wiped his face. "Trying won't hurt you, it's getting your hopes up and having them dashed that hurts. And maybe, when you're trying to chat to it about Katharine Hepburn, it gets just close enough to you to claw your face off. Maybe we're both doomed and should accept it sooner rather than later."

"Not even trying is just letting it win."

"We don't need to *let* it win! It's so much more powerful than us that it's not even sporting. The best we can hope for is keeping away from it for as long as we possibly can. Maybe it'll get bored and move on to someone else."

The library door opened behind us. The man who had needed printing came out. We both shut up and looked away until he had passed.

V reached out and squeezed my arm. "Look, why don't we just go home? We can talk about it in the morning; maybe things'll be clearer after a decent night's sleep."

*

I ruminated on the situation for the rest of the evening.

V was obviously just upset about his friend. If he had been thinking clearly, he would have seen the wisdom in what I was saying. Definitely wisdom, not frantic grasping at hope at all.

It was up to me to find out which one of us was right. I waited until well after dark and let myself into the house next door.

It was just as I had left it the night before. Perhaps it smelled slightly better for having had an airing. Perhaps I had just got used to it during my brief but enlightening visit.

"You in here, you piece of shit?" No point beating about the bush.

I poked my head into each room, finishing with the bedroom. I tried for the light switch, only to find that it wasn't in the same place as it was in my room. A hideous lamp next to the bed came on without much fumbling on my part. The whole room was a mess. Drawers half open, contents all over the place. Had V done this when we were playing detective? It was hard to imagine the man who had been almost compulsively cleaning my house from the moment he moved in leaving a mess like this. Maybe The Nothing had done it when it was in its Terrifying the Victim phase.

I tutted loudly. "You really should be taking better care of Doris' place."

No reply. No Nothing.

I sank onto the bed. I continued to sink for a moment or two. How could she have possibly slept on this monstrosity? Rather than attempt to dig myself out, I lay there staring up at the pristine ceiling.

"Moved on, have you? Found some other poor cunt? I was about to cave, you know. Say the magic words." The ceiling gave me no answer. I muttered under my breath, "I wish the Goblin King really would come and take me away."

The mattress seemed to shift beneath me. It was so unstable that I barely registered it at first. But then my body rose and fell in a sickening wave. Before I could scramble off, my elbows were fixed in a death grip. I looked down to see two wrinkled hands sticking out of the mattress. A pair of pale, veiny legs shot out of the bed on either side of me. They wrapped around my own legs, locking me in place. My elbows were released, but only so cardiganed arms could trap me in an embrace.

My only coherent thought was that I was going to be pulled down into the mattress where I would be crushed between the springs. Unless The Nothing was set on dragging me all the way down to Hell.

Instead, it began to rock me. Once, twice, then it flipped our positions, crushing my face into the mattress. There was a weight on my back. The Nothing leaned down to speak directly into my ear.

"You little idiot," it growled at me. "Looking in the mirror and calling for the monster on a dare. You know what happens next, don't you? You get ripped to shreds and everyone realises that the old legends are true after all." Keeping a grip on my head, it slid down to lie by my side. Its Doris face scowled at me.

It definitely had a point about my bravado being idiotic. Luckily, said bravado failed immediately. Instead of dragging it out further, I looked into its stolen eyes and said,

"Katharine Hepburn."

Shock registered across the face, then it crumpled up in anguish. The hand in my hair tightened and I was thrown backwards. I hit the floor hard. On the other side of the bed, The Nothing screeched and then crashed out of the room.

Still in a daze, I scrambled up and after it, following a trail of destruction that led to the kitchen. And to V.

He was turned away, leaning against the side. One arm was round his middle. I could hear him gasping for breath.

"V?"

He spun around, wincing in pain.

"What's going on?"

With difficulty, he straightened up. His breathing calmed down enough to let him speak.

"The Nothing just crashed into me on its way out. I take it you did it, then?"

I nodded. "I definitely did something to it. Why were you here, anyway?"

He paused. "You weren't in your room, so I thought you might've come here on your own like a little idiot."

I froze. "That's what The Nothing called me."

"It had a point." He looked furious. "Help me get home, would you?"

"Are you really that bad?"

V stared at me for a beat. Then his face softened. "Just bruised, I think. Should be all right after a couple days."

I got his arm around my shoulders, and we stumbled home like we were in a three-legged race. He protested at my entering his bedroom, but winced again when he tried to separate himself. Thus, I was permitted to get him inside and lower him onto his nest. He wisely turned down my offer of some of Nan's out-of-date anti-inflammatories.

On my way out of V's room, I noticed he had a holdall packed and ready to go.

18

R

Something had changed, but Ray couldn't tell what.

It had started with him suddenly being in an alleyway confronted by a girl with trashy dyed hair. He charged out of there, only to almost run into a Black youth who looked extremely surprised to see him. Then his body hurled itself over a bridge and fled.

After that, he found himself spending way more time conscious than usual. He had even been outside a few times. That was new for him; he usually spent all his time at home, insides churning as he was digested. Sadly, the change in scenery only served to make him feel worse. He was out in lovely weather, his body sturdier than it had been in decades, but it wasn't really him. He was reduced to being a passenger inside his own spry corpse.

One night, Ray found himself in an area of town that appeared to be riddled with the homeless. All ages, all colours. Swarming around him as though they were going to attack at any second. Part of him would like to see them try. Whatever he was now, he could hardly be threatened by pathetic street trash.

Seriously, why were there so many of them? What was wrong with this country? They should have brought back national service, that would have sorted these lot out. Tyler, too; he wouldn't have been such an aimless, ungrateful little sod once the army had been through with him.

One of the tramps was looking at him. Staring, actually. His heart would have stopped beating if he had been connected to it. He watched himself approach the vagrant youth. Only when he was practically upon him did he realise it was the same lad he'd seen as he ran from the alley. Maybe that was why he was staring – he recognised Ray from then.

"Hi there, V."

Ray was pretty sure he didn't know this young man. Was V his name? Or was it some kind of street slang? V for Vagrant, that kind of thing?

The vagrant's eyes were wide. "Who are you, exactly?"

"I'm a friend of Gail's. She wanted me to bring you to her."

Oh, that it explained it. Some part of it, at least. The lad must have also had an encounter with Gail.

The boy looked him up and down as he mulled this over. "Bullshit."

Ray's own laugh had never sounded like the one that came out of him then. Come to think of it, he couldn't remember the last time he had laughed.

"If I'm lying, V, then what is really going on?"

V shrugged. "I don't know, but you're definitely full of shit. Gail was backed into a dead end with no escape and then you walked out instead of her."

"There must be countless rational explanations for that."

"And then there was the way you ran away. You're not a doddering old man, you're something else. Are you even fucking human?"

Ray's corpse unleashed more awful laughter. "Several times over."

"Just what the fuck are you?" His voice failed halfway through the sentence, becoming higher and meeker. For all he was standing his ground, the boy was terrified of the thing in front of him.

Said thing leaned forward, head tilted to the side. "Nothing you have ever seen before. Nothing you could even imagine in that tiny, human brain of yours."

Tears welled in the lad's eyes. He cast a quick glance around. "Where is Gail?"

"She's gone to a better place. Better for her, anyway. It's pretty much fucked me over, to be honest."

V took a few breaths to steady himself. "She was my friend."

"You never even met her, not really. I think you probably would have got on with the real one, though, if that makes you feel any better."

"What did you do to her?" There was some fire there, Ray could tell, a bit of rage behind the tears and the terror.

"Not 'to', but 'for'. The same thing I could do for you: take you away from this miserable existence."

V stared at the ground for a moment, then slowly started to nod. "You kill people who don't want to live? And then you, like, wear their face?"

"Think of it as recycling. I never take anyone who doesn't come willingly. Usually I'm a lot more subtle about it, but I'm in something of a bind now. How about the two of us go somewhere a bit more private?"

The boy was still not looking at him when he started to speak. "Here's the thing, though: I don't hate being alive. It's not exactly ideal, but it can continue for as long as fucking possible as far as I'm concerned." By the end of the statement, he was staring right into Ray's stolen eyes.

Ray's mouth sneered. "Well, aren't you a brave little thing? Living in denial is still living, eh? I'll tell you what, though, V for Victim." He stepped closer. "I may not be a terrific friend to have, but I am so much worse as an enemy and you really wouldn't like me when I'm hungry."

V's face was calm. He stared over their shoulder. "Check that ginger guy behind you."

Ray assumed it obeyed him more out of surprise than

anything else. There was indeed a pencil-thin ginger lad leaning against a wall some distance from them. Another homeless, at a guess. Probably a junkie too, from the way he was twitching.

"You want someone with a death wish, yeah? Someone whose life is not worth living? Look no further."

"What's his name?"

"Dunno, everyone just calls him Ginger. He hates it apparently, but no one cares because he's a massive cunt."

The language on that little thug was disgusting! Ray had no time to contemplate it though; as he watched, a second person approached the twitching junkie. He leaned in and said something. Their hands met. The man left and the junkie disappeared down an alley. It took Ray a moment to realise what he'd just witnessed. Practically out in the open, too. Surely this was a more worthy victim than he had ever been.

He turned back to V.

"Well then, my lad, looks as though you get a reprieve. Don't rest too easy, though. I'll be seeing you when I wake up."

With that, he stalked off in the direction of the alley. Ray was going to witness the thing do to the junkie what had been done to him. He couldn't help feeling just a small tinge of excitement.

This was how it should have been, Ray thought. If this thing needed to feed on people, then it should have been cleaning up the streets as it did. Maybe it could even work with the government to sort out the homeless problem. It didn't even need to stop at the homeless: there were refugees and migrants; there were people like his daughter, choosing to not only live that way, but to involve innocent children too; that Debbie's grandchild who could have been anything under those shapeless, baggy clothes; then there were petty criminals and violent youths and the myriad other little oxygen thieves infesting this once-great country.

It could have freed the world from vermin instead of picking on harmless old men like him. It was all so typical, really.

That was what you got for being a decent, hard-working person these days.

19

JIM HENSON

You're lonely. You know that, don't you? It's almost as though it's your default setting. Frankly, it gets a bit depressing to watch sometimes. All that clambering for attention while being mortally terrified of being perceived. The desperate yearning for intimacy while instinctively rejecting any offer of it. It gets so boring to see the same patterns play out in different people across different settings over the centuries. But then, that's mortals for you.

I would devour every last one of you if I could, be done with your nonsense for ever. But, alas, I am cursed to subsist on you miserable morsels. Honestly, humans have no idea how lucky they are that their main food source isn't really fucking annoying. And you never change – not at your core – no matter how much everything else changes around you.

So-called ruined maids always used to be a favourite of mine. Young women shunned by their communities as a result of being seduced or even attacked. This is not a moral judgement. Well, actually, it is, isn't it? But I'm not the one doing the judging. People make other people into perfect prey for me. If you make someone too ashamed to show their face, you don't question it when they no longer do. By the time that same face pops up again, no one remembers it.

In a similar vein, sex workers always tended to be easy targets. That was one thing that never really changed over the years: mostly women, fending for themselves or a few looking out for each other. Undesirable enough that society didn't care for them, but desirable enough to keep themselves in business. They were usually missed by friends and loved ones – or even customers – but they all eventually accepted the disappearances as something that came with the job.

Poverty is pretty consistent too. It manifests in different ways, obviously, but it's always the same basic principle: the haves having too much at the expense of the have-nots. There has always been a steady stream of the homeless or the soon-to-be homeless stumbling right into my gaping maw. Austerity Britain brought me my beloved Irene. Plus V and Grant.

It's rare, but I do sometimes get a shot at someone wealthy. Obviously, I go all in for it. It's a mixture of novelty and professional pride. Convincing someone who has everything they want (and naturally assumes that they're entitled to every last bit of it) that their life is not worth living is no mean feat. They have to be desperate to vanish in order to fall for any of my tricks. But, of course, rich people always have hangers-on, so there's no hanging around for me afterwards.

Crude science and medical practices led to them locking people away in asylums not fit for human habitation. I set them free. Sometimes, I genuinely do people a favour in taking them. Don't know why no one else seems to see it that way. Now the asylums are gone and replaced with years-long waiting lists and serious underfunding. So many sad little souls slipping into my arms.

War sustains me; I barely even have to tempt anyone away from it. No one questions when someone disappears, either. It's just a shame that there hasn't been one on British soil for so long. I couldn't even tell you if I was at the last one. A lot of my more distant past is just a blur these days. I don't even know how old I am; perhaps I'm ageless.

Since they all went overseas, it's been the after-effects of war that interest me. I'm ever such a big fan of what they used to call shell shock. That was a real treat. People returning home with new disabilities that they were ill equipped to handle. Having lost loved ones and seen countless others die in front of them. Being left somewhere to quietly slip away, only to decide to dive instead. A million mouthless dead churning in my gut.

One would think, given the nature of pandemics, that I would do quite well during them. All that isolation, people being encouraged to cut contact with others down to a minimum and stay indoors. They are lonely times for even the most gregarious. It certainly sounds like a situation in which I would thrive, but, alas, I have to be careful. I can never be certain what consuming someone with a serious ailment will do to me. My once-robust body has taken quite a few hits over the centuries. The Spanish flu came fairly close to taking me out completely. I slept through the height of the AIDS crisis, thanks to a lithe teenage runaway back in the '70s. If this is insensitive, I do beg your forgiveness, but I absolutely could have cleaned up back then. So many people forsaken by family, friends and strangers alike. All suffering enough that they would have taken me up on my offer to end it before I had even finished speaking. But, as I said, unhealthy people take a toll on me. Though I will take anyone if I'm hungry enough.

My actual, true form does not really heal. It's a big part of why I need a steady supply of livestock.

The very young are ideal morsels in a lot of ways. They're so easy to manipulate for one; all their negative emotions feel like the end of the world to them. They also last me a good long while; that lad in the '70s had me in hibernation for the better part of twenty years. It's always long enough that anyone who could recognise them would not possibly believe it was actually them, which is certainly handy. The main drawback comes afterwards: people have a lot of questions for an unaccompanied minor. Plus, I never inherit any resources from them. With older people who own their own houses, I can usually hang around for a while once I have awoken. It's just nice to have somewhere to lay my various hats, you know?

I cannot say I enjoy hunting people. Elements of it are fun, obviously, the mind games and the satisfaction that comes with breaking someone down over time. It is ultimately pretty tedious, though. Anything becomes boring if you do it for long enough. And what's a jaded monster to do except just keep on being monstrous? To be fair, something interesting does happen every now and again.

My options had been limited in the '90s due to my wariness of HIV. I had to adopt something similar to the blood transfusion rules: no sex workers, drug users or queer people. It took a huge chunk out of my hunting pool. By the time that seemed to be under some semblance of control, my teenage runaway had started to go bad. It always happens eventually. Temperature does not affect me, so I can get away with wearing clothes that cover every inch of my body. I was fucked when it reached my face, though. I had to stick to the shadows until the boy had been completely used up. Then I was down to my true form which usually somehow tips people off as to the fact that I'm a monster.

Irene was a gift, wrapped up by kismet in pretty silk bows, just for me. I followed her home from the job centre one day. Unwittingly, she led an invisible stalker into her cold and lonely bedroom where the bills were starting to pile up. The first time I appeared in her dreams, she asked me if I was Death. So that's who I became for her. She never once questioned my presence in her subconscious. By the time we met in the waking world, she had accepted me as an inevitability. I did like being with Irene. It was infuriating to have her ripped away from me by some meddlesome librarian. I have always intended to go back for Mae one day. People do not get away with crossing me.

Hey, I've got a good one for you! Whatever happened to Mask's neighbour who kept interfering? No one nose! Did you get it? I hope you got it.

Don't blame me for that joke, I'm older than you can possibly comprehend.

Now Ray was a cantankerous old bastard. I quite enjoyed the fact that he could have been with his daughter any time he chose. He inflicted his isolation on himself because he was so focused on bigotry. Honestly, it was delicious. And I got the house in the bargain as well. The only problem with Ray was that he started rotting so quickly – always a downside with the elderly. Facemasks becoming something of a common sight extended his shelf life, but he was still pretty useless. He has yet to win me a single victim on his own merit. I do so hate freeloaders.

As for Grant, that weaselly mess, he was merely convenient. Bless V for pointing him out to me. It's just in his nature to be helpful, I guess. I am really not a fan of taking someone without the usual build-up, firstly because it seldom works and secondly because I am an artist. Still, needs must. There are some juicy memories in here of an unhappy childhood and an adulthood that could not really be called an improvement. It passes the time. Never thought I would get much use out of Grant, but he worked a treat on old Kathy.

Katharine Hepburn. All the effort I went to in order to keep Mask from finding out her name only for them to go and dredge it from their memory. Another one taken from me before her time, and I had so loved playing with her. Once you added up our waking moments, we barely had a few months together. It was all so unfair. At least she got me in good with Mask before they went and ruined it all.

Mask is going to pay for that, obviously. They are going to pay for a lot of things.

Just call me an anti-masker.

I will say this for them: they have reinvigorated me. I have not felt this eager to break someone in decades, not even my one true love, Irene. It's an entirely novel experience for me: no one has ever known what I was and come to me anyway. This is my greatest test and will surely end in my greatest achievement. I have so many ideas already! Plenty of cards up my sleeves to aim at Mask: dead Mommy, dead Nanny, dead doggy. And, of course, V. We have so many fun times ahead of us. The main thing I have learned from all my time among humanity is how to truly torture someone.

I have tasted the bitter depths of the human soul. Seen every inch of you. No form of malice or cruelty shocks me. There is still goodness in the world, of course; a lot of my meals have some wonderful memories of kindness. It's just never enough to save them in the end. And there's been so many of them! Countless lifetimes' worth of history folded together, layer upon layer, until the individual pieces become lost in the mix. Sometimes, I'll be convinced a memory is mine, only to have it become apparent that it is not. It would be easier to distinguish them if I could remember all my victims more clearly. When you watch a thousand people crumble into dust, returning to the nothing they once were, eventually the dust is all you see. And yet, certain things shine through so clearly.

Cholera took my entire family, but somehow spared me. I made it through the war alive, but I lost the use of my legs. I'm trapped in a facility that has no idea how to treat me and doesn't care to figure it out. My ex outed me as trans and now I need to get out of here fast. It's been three weeks since the night my boyfriend didn't make it home from work and the police don't care about my missing 'flatmate'. Fresh from serving decades at Her Majesty's Pleasure, the world is barely recognisable and everyone I once knew has now moved on. Running away was the biggest mistake of my life, but I don't know what my parents would do to me if I went back now. I fled to a country where I don't speak the language and I have yet to see a single friendly face.

I'm a small child playing in the rubble of a bombed-out house until my mother calls me home. I'm a young girl crying ostensibly because I can't have a cat, but really it's because no one will acknowledge that I'm a girl. I'm a small boy cowering in my neighbour's greenhouse, praying that no one will find me. I'm a bigoted old man raging at the changing world around me.

I'm convinced the illness that took my sister is about to consume me too. I'm starving in a house from which I'm soon to be evicted. I'm shaking and vomiting through withdrawal from street drugs. I'm naked and immobile on my cold bathroom floor.

A thousand lives all at once, overlapping. Layer upon layer until it all becomes mulch. So much noise. That is the issue: you tiresome people grating at my very being with your incessant whining. The only way to stop it – the only thing that gives me any relief – is to grind you down one by one until there's nothing left to irritate me. Not a single atom. Eviscerated. Annihilated. Benothinged.

20

LEOPOLDO FREGOLI

I was wearing a beautiful, puffy, white gown that looked familiar, but was certainly not anything I'd ever owned. That was the first clue I was in a dream. The second was that I appeared to be in some kind of enormous glass dome. My hair reflected in the glass was much longer and darker than in real life. The whole picture was definitely something I'd seen before, but I just couldn't put it together.

I could see a pair of large oak doors behind me. I went through them and stepped into a ballroom where it all became immediately clear. I descended a marble staircase into a fantastic masquerade ball. Full of gaudy chandeliers barely above head height, fat cushions lining the edge of the room for the orgy that was undoubtedly going to take place once the music stopped. The jeering, obnoxious crowd around me wore beautiful Venetian masks. All that was missing was David Bowie.

Whether this was a Nothing dream or simply my subconscious tossing me a well-earned break, I elected to enjoy myself. Presumably, there was a goblin prince waiting for me somewhere in the mix. In the daintiest shoes imaginable, I made my way through the crowd in search of anyone who stood out.

As it turned out, several people didn't appear to belong in the crowd. I kept getting odd glimpses of black, white and grey between the masquerade dancers. I couldn't figure out what exactly they were until I pushed through a couple of braying masked men and came face to face with Audrey Hepburn. There she was: famous little black dress and beehive, holding one of those fancy fag holders that probably has a proper name. An actual, living woman in black and white. She winked at me before taking the hand of a technicolour dancer and spinning away.

After Audrey came Katharine Hepburn. I watched her share a toast with Jimmy Stewart. Peter Lorre crept around the edges of the ballroom after a striding Raymond Massey. Out on the dance floor, Irene Dunne was struggling to keep up with Ralph Bellamy.

I turned away from the scene and bumped into the man I'd been looking for. Taller than me – even more so given the height of his hair – and clad almost entirely in black. Holding a mask over his face. Then the mask came down and there was V, somehow pulling off that ridiculous Bowie wig. He would definitely get a kick out of this when I told him: *Labyrinth* being just about the only movie on my list of favourites he would admit to enjoying.

V dipped into a slight bow and offered me his hand. When I reached out to take it, the puffy sleeves of my gown had been replaced by a perfectly tailored black suit. My own hand was the pale grey of black-and-white movies.

I was Cary Grant, of course; who else would I be?

V twirled me to the centre of the dance floor and led me in a perfect waltz. Somehow, dream-me knew how to dance. As we turned around the room, I allowed myself to sink into the scene. Frankly, I could have stayed in there for ever. With no baby brother to rescue, I could just gobble down peaches and waltz for all eternity.

Suddenly, I caught sight of something awful at the edge of the room. My stomach sank. It was Peter Lorre again, but this time it was the neighbour I'd named after the actor. His rotten jowls shook as he came dancing towards me. Beyond him, there was Ginger, looking more out of place than the black-and-white Hollywood stars. Then there was Doris. Not Kathy Hepburn, but Doris, dragging her leg behind her. All three of them made their way towards me at the centre of the room.

That was not all. Masks were coming off all over the dance floor. Unfortunately, the wearers' skin was coming with them, flesh tearing away from skulls in long gruesome strips. The mutilated dancers continued to move, unbothered by their missing faces. Finally, V ceased dancing and took a step back from me.

He brought the mask up to his face and held it there for a moment. I opened my mouth and screamed for him to stop. No sound came out.

Doris and company caught up to me, seizing my arms. Their fingers pierced my flesh. My Cary Grant layer was ripped off to the Jennifer Connelly one beneath. They kept going until I was just myself. Desperately, I hoped they would stop there.

Once again, V brought his mask down. The Nightmare Creature stood before me. Then it was everywhere. Every single person in the crowded ballroom became a version of the creature, including those still tearing at my skin.

Claws sank into my body. My mouth was forced open and a dozen fingers entered. I felt myself being torn to pieces.

The glass dome shattered around me as a thousand Nothings roared with laughter.

I woke to the sound of the television coming from the living room. The normality of that was a welcome relief. It was even more of a relief to examine my body and find it still perfectly intact. I settled in bed to wait for my pulse to calm down. At least the dancing had been fun.

When I entered the living room, V scrambled for the remote. As the screen went dark, he gave me a smile so over the top I could not even pretend to think it was genuine.

"Morning!" he called with painfully forced cheer.

"Morning. What were you watching?"

"Just daytime garbage, you know how it is."

I let it go, giving him a quick little nod. When I took the seat next to him, he immediately sprang up, clapping his hands.

"Right, I'm off out; got a lot to do today."

"Like what?" I called after him.

"Busking," he shouted before disappearing through the back door.

I have never really got music. Listening to it is enjoyable enough, but anything to do with composition just goes straight over my head. Almost nothing about musical instruments makes sense to me, all those boxes and sticks and strings. But even I know that in order to play your guitar, you need to have it with you.

Of course, V didn't need to account for his every movement; he could come and go as he pleased. But the blatant, pointless lie aroused my suspicions.

I switched the TV on just in time to catch the end credits of *Central News*. V hadn't wanted me to see the local news for some reason. I flicked through the other terrestrial channels in case one of their local shows was just beginning. None were, so I gave up and checked my phone.

Scrolling through the headlines, I couldn't fathom what V would possibly want to keep from me. There were stabbings and car accidents and people fundraising for good causes. Then there was a photo of a building I vaguely recognised. It didn't click until I read the headline underneath it.

Wolverhampton library burns down in suspected arson attack.

I skimmed the article in case I was mistaken. I was not. It was the library in Mount Pleasant, the one we'd been to. Luckily, the fire had been in the middle of the night, so no one was hurt. There were quotes from someone at the council and a few people who lived nearby. No one saw anything. CCTV had proved unhelpful. It would do, really, when the culprit was an invisible monster.

I couldn't see the point in The Nothing burning down a library. But then again, what had been the point of it slaughtering my neighbour? It was just pissed off. It probably happened right after I hurt it. But how did it know we'd been to the library? We would have noticed Doris or Ginger or Peter following us, assuming that those were the only disguises at its disposal. It could easily have kept some back, not shown its entire hand. That would have been the smart move.

Then again, it liked tormenting us with the knowledge that it was watching, that we were powerless to do anything to stop it. There was no point in hiding your cards when your opponent had no idea how to play.

It occurred to me then to search for news about the woman on the end of the row. Realistically speaking, her death must have made something of a splash in local headlines, but I generally avoided those even when I wasn't scared of being eaten.

Sure enough, there were numerous articles about her. The latest one I found informed me that the police were now treating it as an animal attack. They didn't speculate on the kind of animal that could do that to a person. In the comments underneath, some people were ranting about dangerous dogs with irresponsible owners while others linked to blurry images supposedly showing jaguars and other big cats roaming the Staffordshire countryside. Then one person brightened the mood considerably by detailing how a pair of polar bears had apparently once escaped from Dudley Zoo and gone on a jolly. Neither the article nor the comments told me whether or not the police were still investigating.

In my bedroom, I stuck my head out of the window as nonchalantly as I could. Fortunately, there was no one there to bear witness. No police around, no one going in and out of the house on the end. My viewpoint was not the greatest, but it looked as though they had also removed the crime-scene tape. The front door was still boarded up, but that would probably remain so until the son or the landlord or whoever turned up to do something with the house.

A shadow appeared in the corner of my eye. I turned to find a middle-aged man staring straight at me. Not just staring, either; he looked furious.

The Nothing. It had to be. Wearing someone completely new. Or old, I supposed. At any rate, it was a face I hadn't seen before. Our eyes remained locked, neither of us moving. I waited to see just what it had in store for me. A foul smell rose up from somewhere below my window. I looked down to see a French Bulldog mid-shit. The owner grumbled as he retrieved a baggy from his pocket and got to work. Embarrassed, I closed the window.

Just a dog-walker. One who would have got away with not cleaning up after the dog had I not been watching. As he walked away, I listened out for my letterbox just in case.

The next few hours were spent hanging around in my bedroom, jumping up every time someone passed the window. Finally, I decided to stop winding myself up and started a book in the hope of distracting myself. Inevitably, the doorbell went.

I tried to peer through the window first, but the angle was too bad. I could see someone there – a man from the looks of things – but that was it. Opening the window would let him know I was home and I wanted to avoid that for the time being.

Standing in the hallway watching his outline through the frosted glass, I ran through a mental list of everyone it could be. The police were gone, and they had pretty much told me they no longer needed me; Jehovah's Witnesses tended to go around in pairs; I was not expecting a delivery and I very much doubted V was either. A locked door was usually no obstacle to The Nothing, but if it were pretending to be another person, it would not give the game away that easily.

I stood there long enough that whoever it was gave up and left. I breathed a sigh of relief.

V had better hurry up and return. I was obviously not going to relax until then. Plus, I didn't have a single thing to do today. How had I occupied my time before this mess? Taking care of Sam had probably been the main thing. That was obviously out. Job hunting was best left until if and when I got rid of my saboteur. I had already given up on a book that morning. The only thing left to try was television.

I had just sat down with the remote when a man leaned against my living room window and peered in. He stumbled back when he saw me. Hopefully, he missed me utterly shitting myself. I was up and out the back door before my brain could catch up with me.

It was a lad roughly in his mid-twenties, wearing a tracksuit that could have been fashionable for all I knew. He held his hands up and took his cap off as he approached.

"Sorry! I thought it was empty. I tried the front door first."

So it had been him at the door. Why the fuck would he come round the back? As much as I shouldn't have, I felt the need to explain why I hadn't answered earlier.

"Yeah, you woke me up." Whether this was The Nothing or just some random guy, I didn't give a shit what he thought about me still being in bed at this hour.

"Shit, sorry. I'm Asif." He pointed to Peter's house. "My dad owns that place. The police told him they thought it was empty, so he wanted me to come have a look. Have you seen the old guy who lives there?"

I shook my head. "Never. And I moved in three years ago. What about his rent?"

"The daughter pays it straight to us every month. They've been estranged for ages; none of us would've known anything was up if the police hadn't said."

It was certainly plausible enough. Plus, this Asif didn't appear to be an obvious example of The Nothing's type (which, as far as I knew, was old or homeless or me).

"Do you not have a key?"

"Dad has, but he didn't want me just barging in there. He said he'd come down with it later if I couldn't get an answer. Then I thought of trying all the neighbours, but no one seems to be in."

Again, that was all perfectly logical. If he were the real deal, he could even be helpful.

"Do you know the old guy's name?"

His eyes flittered to the left for a second. "Dad did say, you know, but I can't remember now."

No help there then, and no proof that he was who he said he was. The final test would be if I got to walk away from this conversation and never saw him again.

"Sorry I couldn't be more help." I stepped back to go inside.

He stepped forward. "Have you noticed any weird smells?"

An image of the dog from earlier flashed through my brain. "No, why?"

"Just thinking that he might've been lying there dead this whole time. The place would really start to stink, you know?"

Suddenly, I was cold all over. Asif's placid smile now read as a smirk to me. I ran back inside and slammed the door, collapsing against it.

A coincidence, I told myself as I slid down to the floor. If an elderly person hadn't been seen for years, anyone would guess they'd passed away. But it was also exactly what The Nothing would have said to upset me. Evidentially, it would have worked. Just what the fuck would Asif think of me if he was a real person? Perhaps he was on the other side of the door concocting wild theories about how I'd murdered Peter and was now terrified of being found out. Maybe he was scared of me. I barked out a crazy little laugh that I really hoped Asif didn't hear.

It finally occurred to me that he could still be lying even if he wasn't The Nothing. He could have been scoping out the houses on this row for burglaries. Good job I'd presented myself as an unstable, paranoid mess. I certainly wouldn't want to rob me. Quite when I had become the kind of person who suspected every Youth in a Tracksuit of being a potential burglar was beyond me. I suppose if you live as an elderly shut-in for long enough, you become one.

Lost in my stupid brain that hated me, I must have spent ages leaning against the back door. I was only awoken from my stupefied slumber by someone trying the handle. I scrambled away into the centre of the room.

The only sign that V was surprised to see me on the floor was a raised eyebrow.

"Alright?"

"Alright," I replied, feigning nonchalance from my kitchen floor.

We moved into the living room and I explained the day's happenings.

"You're a paranoid mess, Mask," he said. He was completely correct, but it was still pretty annoying. His face screwed up in thought for a moment. "Does that guy's dad own the house next door as well?"

I shrugged. "Doubt it, or he would've said. I think Doris owned her house. Katharine, I mean." I wondered vaguely if Doris counted as a deadname. Or the opposite, really, given it was a false name I'd given her after she died. Maybe that made it even more like a deadname. Either way, it would probably be best to erase it from my vocabulary. "Does it matter?"

"Just wondering," V said without looking at me. He was definitely being weird lately.

The rest of the day passed uneventfully. I kept trying to get V to do something with me, but he seemed distracted, wanting to spend all evening in his room by himself. Eventually, I got bored and went to bed early.

When I awoke to darkness, my first thought was that it was another Nothing dream. I lay looking up at my ruined ceiling and waiting for something awful to happen. Then my bladder complained and I realised that I was just awake.

I noticed on the way to the bathroom that V's bedroom door was open, but I had more pressing matters to attend to. Afterwards, I stuck my head inside and tried to make out his sleeping body in the gloom.

Once I was certain it wasn't there, I turned on the light.

The nest had been replaced by what appeared to be a brand-new sleeping bag. The guitar – or the case, at least – was leaning in the corner as usual. The to-go bag was still there. So where the fuck was V?

The boxroom really was tiny. I didn't see how it was meant to be used as a bedroom. It might have been better for the builders to have forgone it and just made the bathroom bigger. I wondered briefly what the late Katharine Hepburn had used her adjacent boxroom for. And because I just happened to be thinking about it, I knew exactly where the noises were coming from when they started a moment later.

I had heard them before, I was sure. The very first time I met 'Doris', there had been a weird noise after she left. It was like something was rubbing against our joint wall. I'd heard the same noise just before it trashed my living room. That was how this noise started out. Then it shifted to bangs and other movements that I couldn't identify.

I now had two mysteries to solve, or three depending on how you looked at it.

Where was V?

What was happening next door?

And were the two things connected?

21

GRANT

It was a hot night, but that was not why Grant was sweating. He was sweating for the same reason that all his joints ached and why he had puked in a bin an hour or so earlier. He leaned against the wall, shivering, his arms around his tiny slip of a waist. The money he had got from V was burning a hole in his pocket.

Where the fuck was Sketch? Meeting at this time had been his idea and he was nowhere to be seen. Probably keeping him waiting as a power trip, the sick fuck. Because there was a hierarchy here that needed to be respected: some bigshot dealer leaned on his underling, Sketch then leaned on Grant, Grant in turn leaned on shitty little buskers who thought they were special.

He could see V from where he was standing. Talking to some old cunt. Maybe he had given up on the guitar in favour of – the far less irritating to Grant – sex work. He should have, really, it was a more respectable profession than bothering people trying to go about their day with shit covers of 'Wonderwall'. At least it was an actual job. Unfortunately, it didn't look as though a transaction was taking place, they just seemed to be chatting shit. Grant got the distinct impression that they were talking about him. He watched them for a moment more before writing it off as paranoia. He certainly had that in spades.

Finally, he saw Sketch approaching. From the corner of his eye, he thought he spied V and the old man looking at him. They could look as much as they wanted, he had far more important things to deal with.

Sketch was not one of those chatty drug dealers who thought he needed to connect with all the junkies under his dubious wing, thank fuck. He stealthily handed the shit over like a professional before walking away without a word. He didn't even check the cash.

Grant darted into the alley. He was immediately hit with the stench of old and recent piss. There was no time for anywhere nicer; an end to his suffering was in sight.

Fumbling through his pockets, he managed to drop the stuff. He swore at himself under his breath and bent down into a crouch to search for it, hoping it hadn't landed in anything too disgusting. He spotted it a moment later. In his haste to grab it, he caught himself on the broken glass next to it. As he got to his feet, he strained to see how bad the cut was. It needed wrapping up from the looks of things. Whatever. It would have to wait.

There was a sound of movement behind him, and he braced himself to either be robbed or arrested. Or both. His first thought on turning round to see V's old man was that the little shit had turned him down and pointed him in Grant's direction. Some poorly thought-out revenge scheme, probably. Quite what he thought this old bastard could do to him was beyond Grant's imagination.

"You want something, grandad?"

Grant had lived with his own grandad for stretches of his childhood, every now and then, whenever things with his parents got too much. He had been a tough old fucker in his late fifties, far removed from the frail creature currently shuffling towards him.

The old cunt grinned. "My boy V tells me your name is Ginger."

"Fucking isn't," he hissed. "It's Grant."

It pissed him off no end that all those unimaginative little shits had taken to calling him Ginger. Unfortunately, he was nowhere near enough of a threat to most of them to get them to stop. There was only one person that Grant could boss around, and what would be the point of telling V his real name?

The old man tilted his head. "Grant. Grant, Grant, Grant. We can help each other out with a few things, Grant."

"Fucking doubt that." Nausea overtook him again. He fell back against the wall, eyes screwed shut to fight the dizziness. His fist tightened around the packet in his hand. "You really need to fuck off now, old man."

When he opened his eyes, he was alone.

Grant pushed away from the wall, looking to the mouth of the alley. There was no sign of the old man. He must have been far quicker and quieter than he looked.

All the hairs on the back of Grant's neck stood on end. He turned and swung on instinct. His wrist was caught in the old man's painful grip. He swung again with his other hand, but that one was caught too. The old fucker laughed at him.

Grant's eyes welled with tears from the pain. "What the fuck do you want?" he roared.

The old man tilted his head to look back up the alley. Either no one had heard Grant's plea, or they'd chosen to ignore it. The only person likely to respond to his calls for help would be a stranger who didn't know how much of a cunt he was. Even then, most people would probably not bother to stop.

Grant's stomach lurched again. He needed relief fast, but he couldn't shake the old man off.

"What do you want?"

"I want you, you poor little thing."

Of course. He had been right the first time about him being a regular old pervert. He was going to fucking kill V next time he saw him. At least he had a way out now: convince the bastard that he was willing for long enough to get him to release him. He just needed to gamble that whatever spark of adrenaline that was making this guy so strong didn't extend to making him fast enough to catch him if he ran.

"Ok, ok, we ca-ah!"

The old man's grip tightened on Grant's wrists. His fist was forced open until he dropped the packet. Two pairs of eyes followed it as it tumbled to the floor. The old man hummed. Then he hurled Grant into the wall.

By the time Grant gathered his wits and sat up, the old man had the drugs in his hand.

He hummed again as he held it up to his face. "Doesn't look like much to me. Don't see what all the fuss is about." He bit into the packet, tearing it with his teeth.

Grant watched in horror as the contents scattered everywhere. What the fuck could he do now? Slather his tongue all over the floor in a desperate hope to feel something? A laugh bubbled up his throat at the absurdity of the situation. He slammed back against the brick wall, smacking his head. The pain was nothing to him. He had no money and no strength left to even get to his feet.

The old man's feet shuffled forwards. Grant kept his eyes on them.

"Oh dear, Grant. Oh dear, oh dear, oh dear. Quite a mess we've made here."

Another laugh threatened to come up. Grant shook his head to dispel it. He peered up at the old man. Calm now, he asked, "Seriously, what do you want?"

The bastard smirked down at him. "I want to take you away from this miserable excuse for a life. Don't you want that too?"

Grant was crumpled on the floor of a piss-drenched alleyway with bruised and bleeding hands. His skin was on fire and his guts were eating themselves. All hope of relief was gone, taken by an evil old man for reasons Grant couldn't hope to guess. He turned his head in the direction of town. There must have been dozens of people milling around just a few feet away. Grant could take a desperate chance on sprinting to safety. But what was the point? What was the fucking point?

"Yes," he said, a tiny child answering his terrifying Grandad. "I want that too."

22

JOAN FONTAINE

V tumbled backwards, tripping over his guitar case. My arms were still outstretched from when I'd shoved him. Luckily, they were visibly not my arms. 'I' had pulled them back and shoved my hands in my pockets by the time V struggled to his feet. As he stood, he grabbed his guitar and raised it up like a baseball bat.

Not-me sneered at him. "What the fuck are you going to do with that?"

"Smash your face in!" V's voice wavered unmistakably as he said it.

"You wouldn't fucking dare – you're shitting yourself."

V kept the guitar up, but made no move to swing it. Poor thing was clearly terrified.

"Pack it in, lads," a bored voice called from nearby.

Ginger – for surely I was Ginger in this dream – spun menacingly in the voice's direction. He backed down when he saw it belonged to a PCSO. Then he made an irritated noise and stomped away.

I opened my eyes to the familiar darkness of another Nothing dream. I supposed I was overdue. A moment passed without anything popping up into my field of vision. Then the noises began. It was a bizarre mixture of wet, sucking sounds and crunches. Ignoring it was impossible, so I pushed myself up to look. The wretched thing was perched on the end of my bed, facing away from me.

It was wearing Peter today – what was left of him, at least. His head was moving back and forth. As I watched, he turned and spat a chunk of something white onto the floor. Then he twisted around on my bed to face me, his hands clutching something white and spherical.

The wig head. Oh, how I'd missed her. She no longer contained any of my neighbour's facial features. In fact, she was now missing a few more of her own. I looked up to Peter's face.

The lack of skin around his mouth made his face look unfinished. Bits of polystyrene stuck to the loose flaps of flesh. A set of perfect false teeth sat in the middle of the hole in his face. The teeth parted and he bit into the wig head again, the sucking and crunching noises now making sense.

It took an age for the creature to work the remains of Peter's mouth around the wig head. Finally, it pulled off a lump of polystyrene, chewed it a while, then spat it out again.

"Nasty stuff. How did you used to eat that as a child?" The messed-up mouth opened, but otherwise didn't move, like a toy playing recorded speech. I realised with a shudder that The Nothing was compensating for Peter's lack of lips. Poor Peter.

And poor Mask. "I never actually ate it; I only chewed it. Just one of those weird compulsions that everyone gets in childhood."

"If you say so." The thing appeared to grin at me. "Where's your little friend, by the way? Tucked up safe and sound in his brand-new sleeping bag?"

"Where's Katharine Hepburn?" My voice shook as I said it, but I could see the hit still landed.

Peter sneered at me, tossing the wig head to the floor. "He's up to something, you know. Out all the time, bags packed and ready to go. What will you do when he leaves, I wonder?"

I shuffled forward slightly, testing my ability to move. It seemed to increase with each dream.

"I imagine I'd get a cheap laugh out of the fact that someone would rather be homeless than live with me."

"Or maybe he'll outlive you. He's done it before. His good friend Gail and his not-so-good friend, Ginger. Nasty habit of surviving, that one. Sometimes at someone else's expense."

"Hardly."

That rotting face darkened. "You're forgetting I know him better than you do. I've seen the little fucker at his absolute worst. You wouldn't catch me blindly trusting someone who won't even tell me his name."

"He hasn't picked one yet."

Peter tilted his head, his eyebrows going up. "Oh, little Piglet, how likely do you think that is? How long have you had yours picked out? Do you think he got as far as the first letter and then just gave up? If you ask me, it's V. suspicious."

"I didn't ask you."

"That's the spirit!" He began to crawl along the bed towards me. "You let him into your house, told him everything about yourself, and he's barely told you anything. You barely know each other."

The Nothing was right, loathe as I was to admit it. At least I didn't have to admit anything to its face. I let it get close enough that one of its hands rested against the side of my leg under the blanket.

Then I poked it straight in the eye.

It shrieked, diving for the window. It splattered through the glass, and that was the last I saw of it for the night.

With a deep sense of satisfaction, I snuggled down to sleep.

*

I woke up facedown, barely aware it was daylight. Pushing myself up, I cast my eyes around in search of the wig head. It wasn't there. My carpet was still covered with polystyrene from the ceiling, though. If V found out I hadn't cleaned that up yet, I would never hear the end of it.

I looked up to see a shadow through my still-nasty, still-old curtains. There was something weirdly familiar about it. It gave me a sinking feeling in my gut. Nevertheless, it turned out to be nothing more sinister than V cleaning the windows.

I was greeted with a nice cool breeze when I stuck my head out to speak to him.

"What are you doing?"

He paused, gesturing to the sudsy glass and the cloth in his hand. He blinked at me for added punctuation.

I rolled my eyes. "Okay, but why are you doing it?"

"Because your windows are filthy?"

He had me there. I watched him for a moment, finding something satisfying in it. Then he turned and I noticed one of his eyes was bloodshot.

"What happened to your eye?"

His hand rose to the relevant side of his face. He shrugged. "Got a bit of window cleaner in it."

That didn't sound healthy. "Don't you need medical attention? What does the bottle say?"

He made a show of pretending to read the bottle. "It says you're a fucking nerd."

"V..."

V rolled both his regular and his bloodshot eye at me. "I'm fine, it just stung like an almighty bitch. Let me get on with this, will you? I'm nearly done."

I left him to it, but not because he told me to.

It was only after I shut the window I remembered I needed to ask him about the night before. But how could I phrase it in a way that didn't sound like I'd gone snooping round his room? Of course, he might have just been out for the night and the noise from next door was something else entirely. I decided that sneaking round there for a look would shed some light on things.

At first glance, our Kathy's home was just as I had left it: not a thing out of place except the photo I'd moved the first time.

Then I noticed something off about the furniture. It was not glaringly obvious, but the sofa cushions were slightly askew, as though they'd been moved and then carelessly replaced. It was entirely feasible that I had missed their positions last time but, still, it unsettled me. I carried on into the bedroom.

It had been completely trashed. The bed I'd been pinned to was now ruined. The sheets and covers had been thrown to the floor in a heap, the mattress overturned and slit along the side. Not a million miles away from what The Nothing had done to the airbed. Had it just been blowing off steam?

At least that settled the matter of who had been here last night. I stuck my head into the boxroom just to see. Of course, I hadn't been in there before, so I had no idea if it was a mess because it always was – as mine had been before it became V's room – or if The Nothing had blown off some steam in there as well. It must have done, really, I had definitely heard it in there the night before.

I ran into V on the way out. He was poking his head out the back door as I locked up at Katharine's. His mouth dropped open when he saw me, then he folded his arms and leaned back against the doorframe.

"What's up?"

It was so strained that I stared blankly at him for a moment. "Nothing."

He nodded slightly, not meeting my eye. Then he turned and stepped back inside. "Tea?" he called over his shoulder.

"Yeah, sure." I followed him into the kitchen, dropping Kathy's keys back in the drawer.

V busied himself with the kettle. He hummed a random tune that went all over the place. Finally, he asked me.

"What were you doing next door?" He was obviously aiming for nonchalance, but his voice betrayed him, the inflection straying just a touch too high.

"Heard some weird noises coming from there last night, thought I should investigate."

V scoffed. "Sounds like a good way to get your face bit off by The Nothing. At least you weren't stupid enough to charge round there in the middle of the night."

"I came to get you first. Your new sleeping bag was empty." I saw him freeze for a second at my partial truth. "Where were you last night?"

"Out. Sorry I didn't wake you to tell you first." The cup in his hand hit the surface of the counter a little too hard.

"Out on your own in the middle of the night? Sounds like a good way to get your face bit off by The Nothing."

"Wasn't on my own, went to see some old friends. Wouldn't expect you to understand."

Fucker.

A second cup never materialised. I assumed I was now being denied tea. Then V fetched my milk from the fridge before turning and finally making eye contact with me.

"Oat milk and three sugars, right?"

"Erm… yeah."

He turned and got on with it.

"You didn't have to make me a cup if you weren't making yourself one."

"Yeah, but I'm just that nice a guy." He handed me my tea. "The windows are all done – inside and out – except for your room, obviously. Didn't feel right to barge into your bedroom and nose around."

V flashed me a passive-aggressive smile before stomping off to his own room and slamming the door.

That was me told.

With nothing better to do (and a housemate who was in a mood with me), I cleaned myself up and went for a walk. I didn't aim for anywhere in particular, just picked a direction and walked. It was fifty-fifty to avoid V and to get my thoughts in order. Some twenty minutes later, I found myself on the long road that led to the library. I wasn't sure whether this was a coincidence or down to my subconscious. Once I knew where

I was, my steps became more focused.

There were no fire engines outside, just some yellow caution tape and a futile line of traffic cones. The library looked worse than the picture online. From where I stood, it looked as though the roof was now completely gone. Perhaps it had collapsed after the photo had been taken. There was also no glass left in any of the visible windows. The bricks above each one were burnt black in rough triangles. The tiny car park in front was full of debris. I had stood arguing with V in that same car park such a short time ago.

Moving V in had seemed like a great idea when I'd been sleep-deprived and having a crisis over the fact that the monster from his story really existed. Reality had set in since then. That said, we'd had fun initially. Obviously, it was awkward at first, but that had passed and it seemed like we really got on. Something had changed in the last couple of weeks, and I had no idea what.

There was a noise to my left. A woman with a pushchair was waiting for me to notice and shift out of her way. I pressed myself up against the caution tape to let her past. Then I turned and headed for home before I could get in anyone else's way.

As I walked, I put together a mental list of V's questionable behaviour: disappearing on me; never telling me where he'd been; generally avoiding any of my questions; obvious, awkward lies; hiding the library arson from me.

I didn't include the obsessive cleaning, as that made sense in its own way: V obviously felt like he owed me one for letting him stay no matter how many times I told him he didn't. There was maybe some sort of control issue there as well; he hadn't had any kind of living space for so long and rearranging it probably made it feel more real. Plus, it had to be said that my house had been an absolute shit tip ever since my nan died. I definitely hadn't cleaned my windows since I moved in. I hadn't even thought about cleaning them before or after Doris mentioned how filthy they were.

Doris.

Doris standing at my window, a sinister shadow. Then telling me it needed cleaning. V doing the same thing with a bloodshot eye. The same eye in which I had just poked The Nothing to end my dream. It had jumped through the window immediately after that.

It had to be a coincidence. Just like how Kathy's house being trashed while V's bedroom stood empty was a coincidence. Like V's behaviour suddenly changing for no obvious reason. Like V coming and going from my house at all hours when I hadn't got round to giving him a key.

It had to all be a coincidence. There needed to be a simple, innocent explanation for everything. Because the only other option was that V was The Nothing.

23

KATHY

Her diary was missing. In all the years she'd been keeping one – ever since the dreadful day Audrey was first diagnosed – it had remained in the same spot next to the phone. This was specifically so she wouldn't lose it. She checked underneath the table and down the side of the chair, just in case she'd knocked it off without noticing. Nothing. The only thing she could think of was that Fred had moved it for some reason, not realising this would cause her any distress.

Young Fred had been a godsend. It must have been fate that he arrived so soon after Deborah had been taken to the hospital. He'd seen her struggling home with her shopping one day and come running out of the house next door to help. He'd come round to see her pretty much every day since then. He was always stopping by to check she was okay and ask if she needed anything. Now once a week she gave him a list and some cash and he did the shopping for her.

Kathy had never really spoken to Fred's grandad. His name escaped her. She hadn't even seen him for ages; she probably should have guessed he'd passed away. She mentioned to Fred once that she would have gone to the funeral if she'd known. Fred gave her the funniest look and told her that she had been at the funeral. That hadn't sounded right, but trying to argue about it would have upset them both. Kathy scoured her diary after Fred left, but could find no mention of a funeral. Perhaps it had been the year before. All her previous diaries were in a box somewhere in the cupboard; it hadn't seemed worth the effort of digging them out.

Kathy took note of her forgetting the funeral, but tried not to dwell on it. Still, she renewed her efforts to make sure that not a single relevant detail of her day was omitted from her diary.

Until it went missing.

Now she thought about it, she could recall Fred asking questions about the diary. Despite her best efforts at subtlety, he had caught her jotting down a reminder of his name and who he was for future reference. Naturally, he wanted to know why. At first, she'd made a flippant remark about her age and changed the subject. Fred didn't let up. Then, slowly but surely, the whole sorry tale seeped out.

Audrey had been four years younger than her sister, but the first of them to go. Not only that, but her mind had gone years before. There was no telling how long it went unnoticed; once you got to pension-drawing age you were always forgetting little things here and there. Then it escalated to the point where it was obvious to both sisters. Audrey had been terrified she would end up a shell of her former self. She made Kathy promise to stay by her side until the end. For the last twelve months of her life, she'd had no idea as to the identity of the sad, old woman who kept on visiting her.

Kathy's single greatest fear was to follow in Audrey's footsteps. Hence the diary. Hence all her sudokus and crossword puzzles, and the books she took out from the library (that nice girl with the pink hair had been very helpful). Her second greatest fear was currently happening to Deborah Whitehurst, her only friend. You didn't get to Kathy's advanced age without having to watch people you loved fade away.

Kathy tried to banish her gloomy thoughts the same way she

always did: with a nice cup of tea. She nearly spilled it all down herself when she returned from the kitchen to find Fred sitting in her armchair.

"Oh... when did you get here, love?"

The boy frowned at her. "About an hour ago. We were talking about your diary, remember?"

Kathy took a long sip of her tea in an attempt to calm herself. She plastered on a smile. "Of course we were. Did I tell you it's missing?"

Fred's eyes darted over to the table by the phone. The diary lay in its usual place. Just like always.

Kathy returned to her seat by the table, avoiding Fred's gaze. She picked her diary up and flicked to the last page with writing on. One week ago. She had described a disturbing dream about Fred's poor grandad. The man's flesh had been rotting. He showed it to her gleefully. It was the one thing she wished she could forget.

"Eating grass, apparently."

Kathy started. She was sure neither of them had been speaking. "What was that, love?"

Smiling kindly, Fred leaned forward and raised his voice. "We were talking about next door's dog. It was sick all over the path outside."

"Right. Did Deborah clean it up?" She realised her mistake instantly. "Sorry, no, she's still in hospital. I know she is."

Fred opened his mouth to say something, then changed his mind. He stopped meeting Kathy's eye. The room turned suddenly cold.

"She is in hospital, isn't she?"

Fred looked up. "It's best not to upset yourself, Kathy."

That could only mean one thing, couldn't it? Kathy's eyes filled with tears.

"Please, Fred, tell me what's going on."

She saw him brace himself. "Deborah passed away a while back. You just keep forgetting."

Kathy shook her head so forcefully it sent her glasses sliding down her nose. When she pushed them back up, Fred was kneeling on the floor in front of her. Her diary was in his hands.

"You wrote it down at the time. Here look, 21st of February 'Deborah died'."

Kathy squinted at the page. It didn't look like her handwriting, but how could she expect to recognise that when she could barely recognise herself?

Deborah was gone. How often had she needed to be told? Had it hurt this much every single time? Her mind filled with the memory of her new next door neighbour popping round to introduce herself. She had reminded Kathy so much of Audrey back when she had still been Audrey. Then Deborah and her sister blended together in Kathy's mind until she had to shake her head again.

"I just want it all to stop," she whispered, hardly aware she'd spoken.

Fred dropped the diary and took her hands in his. Their lack of warmth was odd, but the sunshine in his smile made up for it. Such a nice young man.

"Oh, Kathy, my sweet." His fingers slid over her wrists in an unsettling manner. "I can make it all stop."

24

JOSEPH CAPGRAS

It was a long walk back to the house I might have been sharing with The Nothing.

I kept telling myself it didn't make sense. But I also could not shake off the certainty that this was exactly the sort of stunt The Nothing would pull. One designed to finish me off completely. It would be worse than Doris, even. I had pinned so much of my weird little hopes onto V in a way that couldn't possibly be healthy. He was not only going to save me from the monster that wanted my head, but fix my broken life as well. A friend, finally. It was my old childish desire for a companion, someone to go on adventures with, care about, sacrifice myself for.

Fuck, I was pathetic.

Whether or not V was The Nothing, I needed to come up with a plan. Confronting him was out: I would either hurt an innocent man or give a monster the excuse it needed to stop playing nice. Realistically, the only other option was observation. It had to slip up eventually. Or just get bored with the ruse. It was just a matter of biding my time. Sitting down and twiddling my thumbs while in a state of complete – but possibly justified – paranoia.

At least I had plenty of practice at that.

An unwanted memory popped up, then: sitting on a bench outside the hospice just after my nan had died. I had been in the room with her, bundled up in all my protective gear, but she had been barely conscious the entire time. I had walked out once it was over, unsure as to the rules on whether I was allowed to be in there once I technically was no longer a visitor. On the way out, I noticed a Christmas tree in reception that I hadn't seen on the way in. We were barely halfway through November, but I conceded that Last Christmases could come as early as they wanted. Then I sat in the crisp air in silence, my head filled with frantic screams.

When I reached home, my back door was locked and Kathy's was wide open. I found V in her kitchen, rummaging through the drawers.

"What's this?"

V leapt about a foot in the air. He turned, gasping, with a hand pressed to his chest. It was rather theatrical. Possibly even over the top.

"You scared the shit out of me!"

I said nothing. He was the one who needed to explain himself.

He shuffled awkwardly. Cleared his throat. "I came over here to tidy up. You mentioned the place had been trashed."

"Did I?"

"Then it occurred to me that maybe Dor… Katharine would have a spare key for the old guy's house like your nan did with her."

"Why would you even want to get into his house?"

He gestured feebly at me. "You know… clues, like you said."

I had said that, couldn't fault him there. "I think we're past all that by now."

"If you say so."

I looked around at the state of the kitchen: V had obviously not started with his cleaning.

"You want me to help tidy up?"

"You can if you want." A big, friendly grin. "You'd probably just get in my way, though."

I nodded in lieu of a more appropriate reaction. "Shouldn't I stay with you in case The Nothing shows up?"

"What're you gonna do, bite its face off?"

Had I told him about biting The Nothing's face in that one dream? I couldn't remember. Then I realised he was making a callback to what he'd said earlier. Of course, he could have been alluding to the dream when he said it. I was in for a long day of tying myself in knots.

"I'll make a start on the bedroom," I announced, leaving a confused V in the kitchen.

The first thing I did was drag the mattress back into place. It tired me out so much that I lay down on it. If The Nothing crawled out of it again, it would be an answer to the question that plagued me.

Okay, so, if V was The Nothing then what was the point of it being in Kathy's house? Had it left behind something it didn't want me to find? It knew I had been in there multiple times and still very much had a key. In that case, hiding the key from me would have been the easier and more logical thing to do. Whereas V's compulsive cleaning habit leading to him wanting to fix the place up was perfectly logical. I supposed it all came down to whether or not The Nothing would tidy an entire house just to keep its secret safe. It was certainly patient enough.

Sitting up on the bed caused enough of a wobble that I nearly fell off. It was here I had last seen The Nothing outside of a dream. Where I had last knowingly seen it, anyway. I peered around the empty room.

"Are you here? You sure you don't want to pop out for a quick torment? Maybe we could have our first non-dream fight."

Silence. Then V calling from the other room. "Are you talking to me, Mask?"

"No!" I shouted. "I hope not," I added in a whisper.

"You hope what?"

For shit's sake, was he a bat?

"Nothing!"

At that point, I decided to get off my arse and actually sort the bedroom out. It seemed the respectful thing to do. Plus, there wouldn't be any awkward questions when V – hopefully V – came in and found that I had not done anything.

As I went about cleaning, I thought back to the night I'd dared The Nothing to show itself and then seriously hurt it when it did. I'd chased after it and ran into V. Or had I? The librarian said it turned into Peter when she said Irene's name. It could have taken V's form before I caught up to it. He had been visibly in pain. Then he went and quoted The Nothing at me.

For argument's sake, say V had been The Nothing at that point. When, exactly, had it taken him? I was fairly certain he had not been The Nothing the entire time; I had seen the two of them together when we first met. There had been no evidence of The Nothing being able to be two people at once. The second time we met, V ate and drank in front of me – the third time, he explained The Nothing couldn't do that – and then he had been the one to introduce me to the whole concept of The Nothing in the first place.

Did it know V had warned me? Not then, probably, but I told Doris about it later. It was entirely conceivable that dear Doris had then gone and eliminated the threat. That would mean the person who agreed to move in with me – arguably too easily, given I was essentially a stranger – was actually The Nothing. It probably couldn't believe its luck. Or how lonely and gullible and desperate I was. Again.

I really had made things easy for it. No one can walk all over you if you don't lie down for them first, as my old nan used to say.

"You're doing better than I thought."

I didn't jump half as badly as V had earlier. It just made me even more convinced that his had only been a performance.

I cleared my throat, fighting against my thunderous heartbeat. "Yeah, turns out I'm not completely useless."

"Never said you were, I just thought it loudly." V winked.

I tried to figure out if V would have winked just then. It was hard to work out if someone had been replaced when you barely knew them.

"Are you my friend?" I blurted out, immediately wanting to die.

V blinked a few times. "Yes?" He came closer and patted me on the arm. "I know I was pissed off this morning, but I'm over it now. Stay out of my room, though, will you? It's called boundaries."

His smile seemed so genuine. I wanted to believe in it more than I had ever wanted anything.

There had to be some way of testing him. I could ask him something only V would know, but I had no idea what that would be. Plus, wouldn't The Nothing know about it as well? It certainly seemed to know a lot about Kathy's friendship with Nan. It was too bad I couldn't just chuck a cup of tea over him. Something occurred to me then.

"Hey, did you ever hurt The Nothing?"

V blinked, no doubt thrown by the rapid conversational changes. "No. I didn't think it could be hurt."

"I've hurt it a couple of times when it's entered my dream. But I scalded it with tea in real life and it didn't so much as flinch."

V's head tilted as he processed that. "Well, maybe it can only be hurt in dreams for whatever reason. Makes as much sense as anything else."

I nodded at that. I could hear any random rule about how The Nothing worked now and just roll with it. Once monsters existed, you didn't really get to question the logic surrounding them.

We finished getting the house in order in a silence that was only moderately awkward. My idiot brain was swirling with paranoid thoughts the entire time. I kept trying to watch V for signs of Nothingness, but he always either caught me looking or was doing something entirely innocuous.

When we got home a couple of hours later, V stopped me in the kitchen.

"We're all right, aren't we?"

I wanted us to be all right. I nodded, not really trusting myself to speak. Then I went to walk away, only to turn back immediately and attack him with a hug.

His body was warm and his arms were strong when they wrapped around me. I told myself The Nothing would never hug me, but of course it would. It would do anything that set me up for complete and utter devastation once the truth came out.

V patted me on the back. I wanted to ignore the signal and stay in the hug, but I managed to step back like a normal person.

"I'm sorry for snooping round your room. I'm sorry if it sounded like I was accusing you of something." It was all I could think of to explain my behaviour.

He smiled down at me. "Hey, it's okay. Don't upset yourself. I still like you."

From somewhere in the deep, dark recesses of my mind, I heard my mom saying the single most devastating thing I had ever heard at seven years old:

"No one really likes you, you know?"

The woman had been troubled and – it went without saying, really – not a great mother. Unfortunately, that didn't mean she was wrong. Now or then or ever.

I looked up to where he was still smiling at me. "Have you eaten? I feel like splurging on a takeaway."

He frowned. "We have plenty of food here."

Eat some of it in front of me, then.

"Honestly, whatever you want. My treat."

"I'm fine, I had a sandwich earlier. If you want to get yourself something, though, go ahead."

He went off into the living room and I desperately looked around for any sign that he had made himself a sandwich. I found nothing. But then, he wasn't me and actually tidied up after himself so that was inconclusive.

I told V I wasn't feeling well and went to bed early. Then I lay in the dark staring at my Benothinged ceiling and feeling nauseated. It was a good few hours before I fell asleep.

I dreamt of V cradling me as we lay in bed. I was trembling with some sort of fever. He brushed away the hair sticking to my sweaty forehead as he sang softy. It started out as 'Vincent' but morphed into 'The Flight of Dragons' about halfway through. It was soothing, but I knew I needed to get away from him. As he crushed me to his chest, I bit into the flesh just above his collarbone. V's voice wavered as my mouth filled with his blood, but he continued to sing. The dream ended with him hugging me tighter and tighter until I could no longer breathe.

There was someone standing at the foot of my bed when I woke up. In the blackness, all I could see was their rough outline. As soon as they realised I was awake, they fled through my still-closed – and locked – bedroom door. I got up, unbolted and peered into the hallway after The Nothing.

The door to V's room was wide open. I couldn't see anything in there until I tiptoed up to the doorway. V appeared to be fast asleep in his sleeping bag. Was it just for appearances? I stayed watching him in silence for as long as I could stand. Then I went into the kitchen for water.

When I got in there, I changed my mind and boiled the kettle for a cup of tea. If it woke V, it woke V. If he was even asleep. If he was even V.

The dream had been an odd one, somewhat different from the usual Nothing dreams. I had no idea if that meant it was just a regular dream or not. It was all a bit too coincidental that it was so like a Nothing dream. Then again, it made sense to dream about things that were on your mind, especially to this extent. I hated that I couldn't arrive at a decent conclusion.

I put way too much sugar in my tea. I always did. Why bother giving a fuck about your teeth when you were likely to have your soul sucked out any day now? If anything, I should probably destroy them so The Nothing couldn't make use of them. That was a thought. If I ever did decide to give in, I could fuck my body up so much beforehand that it would regret ever taking me. Like when you know you're about to be evicted so you trash the place on your way out. My blurry-eyed, half-awake state also had me adding way too much oat milk. It gushed right up to the brim and I had to lean down and slurp up enough that it wouldn't immediately spill. It was still too hot for my delicate little mouth, so I added some more milk and repeated the whole process. By the time I got sick of that and carried it back into the hall, it was still almost sloshing over the top, but at least it was cool enough to drink.

Pausing outside V's room, I strained to see if he was still asleep. As far as I could tell, he was. I stepped inside, creeping towards his sleeping bag. I knelt down next to his head.

The tea might have been okay to drink by then, but the cup was still too hot to hold in my hands continuously. I forced myself to keep hold of it. In just a few seconds, I could know for sure. Then maybe I could finally be rid of the wretched thing.

The heat in my hands switched over from uncomfortable to straight-up painful, so I set the cup down while I thought.

Tea burns weren't a serious threat to adults, were they? Not healthy ones, at least. When you saw people who'd been scarred for life by it, it had always happened when they were little kids. V would be fine, just in a lot of pain. When he woke up demanding to know what was going on, I could make up a lie about coming into his room for some reason and tripping.

I looked down at my red palms. They were still stinging from the cup I had been holding minutes ago. Christ, what was I thinking? I'd almost talked myself into scalding someone. I scrambled to my feet and rushed for the door.

A noise stopped me.

It was the unmistakable sound of something unzipping. My first thought was the sleeping bag, but I turned to find V hadn't moved. I looked around the room until I caught sight of the holdall in the corner. It was now lying completely open.

Knowing damn well I shouldn't, I went over and looked.

I could see some clothes and things poking through from underneath, but the top layer consisted entirely of an enormous pile of cash. Various notes, some bundled together, some not. I didn't know how much money was in there, but it was definitely a shitload.

There was another noise behind me.

"Mask?"

I went cold.

"What are you doing in here?" The sleeping bag rustled as he got out of it. There was a soft *thunk* as he presumably knocked my tea over. "The fuck? Mask, what is going on?"

Finally, I turned. "Where did all this money come from?"

V's body language completely changed, stiffening and straightening. I couldn't see his face in the darkness.

"None of your business." His voice was ice cold. "I can't believe you're in here again a couple of hours after apologising for going through my stuff. And why the fuck was there a cup of tea on the floor?"

Despite not being able to see his expression, I could tell when it clicked into place for him.

"You were going to…"

I turned and ran from the room. V followed up to the threshold, but stayed inside. He loomed in the doorway.

"Come in here again, touch any of my stuff again and I will fucking hurt you." He slammed the door in my face.

I cried quietly in the hallway until my legs went numb.

25

GRAN

Kathy was a sweet old dear. She reminded Grant of the lady who lived next door when he was a kid. She had always been nice to him, talking to him over the low fence in the garden, giving him sweets. On a few occasions, he had hopped the fence to hide from his parents in her greenhouse. Once she discovered this, she began to leave her back door unlocked so Grant always had a warm, safe place to hide. She ended up having to move out after calling the police on Grant's parents for threatening her when she complained about the noise. The little boy she left behind cried his eyes out for days on end. For the life of him, Grant could not remember that old woman's name.

That had been the better part of thirty years ago. She must have been dead by now. Hopefully, it was quick. The thought of her getting older and weaker and being aware of it the whole time was unbearable. She deserved a pleasant last few years and a peaceful death. So of course, had poor old Kathy.

It was hell watching her fret over losing her mind. Being convinced that 'Fred' was a nice young man who wanted to help her out while he was secretly tormenting her. He cursed the thing out when it took her diary and wrote lies in it, when it made shit up to get her to doubt herself. It broke his heart, but he was unable to do anything for her. It was almost a relief when the thing finally put an end to it by doing to her whatever it had done to Grant. Of course, that now meant she was trapped like he was. At least his part in it was over.

The next thing he was aware of was taking up residence in Kathy's empty house. It was a cosy bungalow. Grant would have skinned someone alive for the chance of living in a place like this. Some people had no idea how lucky they were. He watched the thing snoop around in Kathy's belongings until it stumbled on a stash of cash in the bedroom. Fuck, Grant wished he'd found this place himself. He could have befriended the lonely old woman for real. A mutually beneficial relationship where they traded companionship for food and shelter. She was old enough that he wouldn't even have had to fuck her. It was depressing to think of what might have been.

Grant wasn't sure how much time had passed since he'd last been conscious and aware, but things were definitely different now. That Debbie woman next door had never returned. Instead, there was someone young living there. The same dog was still there, so it had to be a relative. He didn't usually take much notice of what Kathy said to the thing pretending to be him, but he thought he remembered her mentioning Debbie had a grandkid she'd raised herself. It must have been them.

When he started stalking someone, it took him a while to realise that it was the next door neighbour. He hadn't even twigged he was following someone at first, being outside in a bustling crowd again was far too distracting. People still avoided him, thinking he was a typical homeless junkie. If only they knew. Then the person in front had stepped in something, turned and looked right at him. He'd stopped and looked away awkwardly, but Grant had finally seen who it was. Then they moved on and he trailed behind.

So the thing was following Debbie's grandkid from next door. Setting itself up for a new victim. Poor fucker. At least it wasn't an old lady this time.

Grant lost interest for a while, tuning out until he realised they'd stopped again. When he peered through his own eyes, he was shocked to see V. There he was with his poxy guitar, looking like he was fucking shitting himself. It was a familiar sight for Grant.

He felt the happiest he'd been in years as he watched the thing get in V's face. It was a massive disappointment when the neighbour interrupted and they had to back off. He was even more disappointed when he realised that the thing had no interest in pursuing V. Surely that piece of shit had it coming. No one could possibly deserve it more.

Bizarrely, V moved in with the neighbour. Grant couldn't fathom it. Maybe they were fucking; a grand love story stemming from the thing inadvertently bringing them together. It twisted his guts to think of V getting a happy ending after throwing him under the bus. But the thing was still going after the neighbour. There was no happy ending there; V was still very much in harm's way. It gave Grant a measure of peace.

That peace lasted right up until he watched the thing rip an old woman to shreds using his own two (formerly) human hands.

It was the same woman Grant had threatened a short while before. The neighbour's nosy neighbour. If she had just kept her nose out of things like he told her, it might have remained attached to her face instead of between Grant's teeth. For one awful moment, Grant had thought that they were going to swallow it. Instead, it spat it out where the woman could still see it. Then it moved on to her eyes. And Grant had thought Kathy's death was horrific.

After that, Grant saw nothing until he suddenly found himself back in Kathy's kitchen. The thing was convulsing like it was going through withdrawal. V was in front of it, scared out of his mind again. Had that snivelling little wuss done something to it and then lost his nerve? He really was pathetic. When the thing slammed into him, possibly cracking his ribs, it was almost like Grant had control over his body again. It ran after one hit, though, probably because it was injured. Shame.

Grant never did figure out what had hurt the thing. He hoped V was the cause of it. That would mean the cunt's days were numbered. And if anyone had that coming to him, it was V. Grant just hoped he got to see it.

26

RAYMOND MASSEY

I didn't go back to sleep. I didn't even try. I just wrapped a blanket around myself for warmth and sat there until sunrise. The headache from crying and lack of sleep felt like a form of penance.

How could I have been so fucking stupid? Of course it made no sense for V to be The Nothing. I had let my paranoia fuck up my entire life. It was fortunate that The Nothing didn't make an appearance that night. I would have gone with it in a heartbeat. Fucker missed a trick. Probably wanted me to wallow in my own misery for a little while first.

To my surprise and relief, V didn't attempt to sneak out in the middle of the night. That hopefully meant he wanted to stay. As soon as it got to an acceptable time to be awake, I sat in the living room to wait for him to rise. I automatically went to make myself a cup of tea before realising it was probably best not to be holding a mug the next time V saw me. So I sat there cold and miserable for two hours.

Around nine in the morning, I heard movement in V's room and braced myself. The door opened, light footsteps sounded on the hall carpet, then the bathroom door closed. It was another twenty or so minutes before I heard all the same sounds in reverse.

I sat patiently. The penitent did not rush those whom they had wronged. Even when said wronged party finally emerged from his bedroom to head into the kitchen ignoring someone's perfectly good penance.

When V finally took a seat on the opposite sofa, he had a cup of tea in his hands. It was pretty well played. He raised the cup slightly in my general direction. "Thought better of making you one."

I remained silent, watching V take a few long drinks of a beverage he didn't even like just to make a point.

"Am I right in thinking you were going to scald me last night?"

I shrugged. "I thought about it. Decided against it, for what it's worth."

"Wow, I'm truly grateful. How could you think I was The Nothing?"

It probably wasn't a real question, but I went ahead and answered as though it was.

"There were some things that didn't add up. Then I had a dream. Plus, it's exactly the sort of thing it would do."

V made a gesture just shy of a nod, conceding the point.

I hoped that meant I was winning him round.

"It must have opened your bedroom door, if you closed it last night. It definitely unzipped your bag, so I'd look inside."

The silence hung thick in the air until we stepped over each other to fill it.

"You don't have to..." I said.

At the same time, he said, "I've had it for ages."

That didn't exactly make sense, but I couldn't really question him after the shit I'd pulled the previous night.

When I didn't challenge him, he continued. "It's just what I've managed to put together over the years. Can't exactly take it to a bank."

That was plausible. If you really wanted it to be. If you applied enough pressure to it to forcibly change its shape. I gave him a big smile.

"Just The Nothing trying to shit stir."

"Exactly!" His smile was just as fake as mine.

I really wished I had a cup to hide behind. Trying to take V's would probably make him think he was under attack again.

"I'm sorry about..." I tried to mime throwing a drink at someone. He seemed to get it.

"I mean, you did change your mind in the end."

"Exactly." I traced the word exactly onto my leg with my finger over and over again. "Plans for the day?"

He shrugged.

Between us, the clock on top of the fireplace ticked louder and louder.

"I might..." As soon as I started, I realised I had no ending for the sentence.

The clock reached Big Ben decibels.

"There's probably something I could be cleaning." V got up and left, putting us both out of our misery.

I breathed a sigh of relief and went to make myself some breakfast.

When I found The Nothing in my bedroom, I nearly dropped my toast.

It was wearing Ginger – the lesser of two utter horrors – and sprawled on his side across my bed in what presumably was meant to be a seductive pose.

"Can't tempt you, can I?" he said, waving a flowing hand across his body. He gave up at my disgusted look. "Oh well, worth a try. Not my fault you're asexual."

That threw me. "I didn't tell you that, did I?"

Ginger placed a palm on his chest, closing his eyes serenely. "I'm an empath."

"Fuck off!" I hissed.

"Or what?"

"Or I'll poke you in the face and bite your eye!" The words probably wouldn't have been that threatening, even if I hadn't fucked them up.

Ginger rolled his eyes at me as he sat up. "Are you really going to let V lie to you about the money?"

"I don't need to know where it's from."

"I do know where it's from and, even if I didn't, it's pathetically obvious."

I wasn't taking the bait, no matter what shit it pulled. I finished my toast as slowly as possible. Unfortunately, he didn't take the hint and skedaddle.

"Come on, Mask, play detectives with me. V – who's been acting weird enough that you thought he was me – has an unexplained pile of money. And he cleaned Doris' house top to bottom yesterday."

"Why did you trash Dor… Kathy's house?"

He smiled. The conversation was obviously heading in the direction he wanted. "I didn't. Why would I?"

"Because you're a spiteful little bitch? Her mattress was shredded just like V's air mattress."

"Well, thank goodness he had the cash to get a brand-new sleeping bag. And everything else he bought. Ridiculous, really: if he'd robbed a bank, he would have been caught by now."

I huffed, crossing my arms. "Look, whatever this is, I'm not getting it. Either come out with it or fuck off back into the ether."

He sauntered over to me on long, borrowed legs. "Tell me, Mask, why would someone cut open an old person's mattress? What could they possibly be hoping to find?"

Like I needed The Nothing to tell me the money had come from Kathy's house. It was exactly as obvious as the fucker had said. The hard part had been not working it out.

"Why should I care about that?"

"Well, it doesn't show terrific moral character, does it? Stealing from the dead."

"You can't steal from the dead; they don't own shit."

He rolled his eyes again. "Wow, you two are perfect for each other. Too bad he's going to fuck you over in the end. That lad doesn't do friends."

That one landed. I glanced vaguely in the direction of V's bedroom. Not that I could see him through two closed doors.

"He won't."

"Ah, but he's got form. Just ask poor Ginger here."

I turned back to look The Nothing in his eyes. "V and Ginger weren't friends; he was his enemy."

This seemed to please it. "Exactly! Isn't it a bit convenient that I took him out of the picture?"

It couldn't possibly be implying what I thought it was. V might not have been a gallant hero, but there was no way he would...

When I shook myself out of my treacherous thoughts, The Nothing was gone. I turned and marched into V's room.

He was on all fours, attempting to scrub the tea stain from the carpet. He sat back on his heels when he saw me.

"Alright?"

I gestured vaguely behind my back. "The Nothing..."

V scrambled to his feet and rushed towards me. "Are you okay? Did it do anything to you?"

"Just trying to shit stir again."

"What did it say?"

Involuntarily, I glanced at the money bag in the corner. V stepped back slightly.

"It told you where I got the money?"

I let the question hang in the air between us. I didn't give a fuck about the money, but I was avoiding the thing I did give a fuck about. I just stood there, stupidly, unable to even look at him.

"It was shitty of me to mess up her house, that's why I fixed everything. But the money... it's not like she needs it. You can't rob the dead."

I snorted. "That's what I said."

"So you're not upset about that?"

Obviously, the next question would be what had actually upset me. I reached out desperately for a subject change.

"I tried to get you to eat first, you know?" I could see he didn't understand. "When I thought you were The Nothing, like you did with me that time."

He nodded slowly, eyes unfocused. "Yeah, I haven't been eating much."

"What would you have done then, if the situation were reversed?"

He focused on me, raised an eyebrow. "What? Why?"

I shrugged. "Thought exercise."

"Well, not being you, I would have used logic and reason."

I smiled. This was better, nice and familiar. I could pretend we were really close friends instead of two people who didn't trust each other.

V continued. "See, I know your name, and it knows that I know your name. So it wouldn't hang round waiting for me to say your name and fuck up its shit. Plus, I'm pretty sure it hibernates or something after it takes someone."

That was completely new information as far as I was concerned. "It does?"

"It said something like that when it went to get Ginger, and then I didn't see it again until the day we met."

Cold flooded my chest. "It talked to you before it went to get Ginger? It told you that's what it was doing?"

V looked everywhere but at my face. "I… no, it…"

The Nothing was right. It never lied when telling the truth would be more devastating.

"Did you give Ginger up?"

V stared at me for a long time before answering. "It wasn't like that. I just pointed it in his direction."

I stumbled backwards. V fell forwards, catching me.

"You don't understand what a piece of shit he was, Mask. He made my life hell and it wasn't exactly fantastic to begin with. The Nothing was on my heels and I gave it an alternative. It was him or me."

"And what if it came down to you or me?"

His mouth dropped open. He let me slip from his arms. "It wouldn't. It won't happen, so don't worry about it."

I looked past V to the room that was barely more than a cupboard, where I'd insisted on keeping him so we could both be safe.

"I think this was a mistake."

Without another word, I turned from him and shut myself in my bedroom. I burrowed into the bed and listened as V clattered around, obviously packing.

I could have stopped him. I could've rushed out and told him not to leave, that we needed to present a united front against The Nothing. But there was no unity between us. I had been trying to force something with V that was obviously not there. Best to just let it end. Stay in my little blanket cocoon forever. Breathing in stale air, but being warm and safe.

Cotton rubbed against the bare parts of my skin as the blanket shifted. I knew what was coming, but it was still horrifying when Peter appeared inches away from my face. His greying pearly whites were at my eye level. There was an awful smell when they parted.

"I won't say 'I told you so'," came his haunted-music-box voice. "Just that I'm here for you. When you're done crying it out, I'll be waiting to make it all better."

I kicked him in the shin. It earned me a satisfying grunt and a hiss. Then I tossed away the blankets and ran out to find V.

He was packed and ready to go, seconds away from stepping through the front door and out of my life for ever. He flashed me an awkward smile.

"The rest of the money is in a box in my… in that room."

"You should keep it."

"I can't be walking around with that kind of cash on me."

"Don't go," I pleaded.

He opened his arms. For a moment, I thought he was inviting me in for a reconciliatory hug. But he was just gesturing.

"This was always a crazy idea, Mask. It was doomed from the start."

"But The Nothing..." My voice was tiny, pathetic.

"It would end up killing one of us to get to the other. The only reason it hasn't yet is because it was waiting for this, the inevitable fallout of me moving in."

Big, ugly tears were threatening to spill. "So we're just giving it what it wants?"

"More like we're not giving it a reason to murder us. Despite everything, we probably stand a better chance alone."

"You mean you stand a better chance away from me?"

V's expression told me there was an element of truth to that. He sighed. "Take care of yourself, Mask." Then he left.

I was alone again. Except for Peter who was standing behind me when I turned around.

He opened his arms out to me. This time, the invitation was unmistakable. I took a few steps forward. Then I launched myself at him, a tornado of claws and fists and teeth and weird, pointy elbows. It sent me flying, of course, but not before I got some licks in. Then I was straight back on my feet and going for the face.

Without thinking – none of this shit had involved thinking – my fingers shot into the vast cavity of Peter's face. I pushed upwards into his cheeks until I could see the movement beneath his skin.

The Nothing gargled, stumbling backwards into the living room. I was pulled along with it initially, then my fingers ripped through his skin and we were separated. Pulling back, I lifted a leg and slammed my bare foot into his stomach. It gave way beneath my sole. My foot carried on until it met what I was certain was Peter's spine.

Stuck up to the shin, I could do nothing but wait until it grabbed my leg and shoved me backwards. I landed on the sofa with a thump. The Nothing swooped down and wrapped a hand around my throat. I scrabbled for its face again as it began to choke me.

Peter's jaw unhinged. "You can knock that shit off or I can start breaking all the parts of your body that I won't be needing later."

I knocked that shit off, becoming still beneath its touch. The hand on my throat eased up just enough that I was no longer in danger of passing out.

"The trouble with you, young Mask, is that you've become too comfortable. You think that because I want you I won't physically hurt you. You're wrong. If it came down to it, I'd skin you literally instead of figuratively and then just move on to the next sucker. Do not ever fall into the trap of thinking you're special. You…" It suddenly seemed to lose its breath.

The hand vanished from my neck. Peter stumbled backwards, making the worst sounds I'd ever heard. He bent forward, clutching his non-existent stomach. Then his body collapsed in on itself. His flesh disintegrated, sinking into the black hole that was his torso. As Peter was peeled away, the nightmare creature was revealed underneath.

It looked frailer now, withered and somehow… drier? I couldn't see any of the colourful viscera layer I'd seen before. Instead, there was a lot more bone. The cracks in its skull were deeper and wider. It stood swaying slightly as it looked down at its own claws. Its hollow chest lurched and for a horrible moment I thought I was going to find out if The Nothing could vomit. Thankfully, it emitted nothing.

"What was that?" It was stupid to bring its attention back to me, but I wasn't capable of being rational.

It looked at me, still a bit dazed. "That was the end of our Raymond. Used him all up."

"What?"

It grinned its wretched grin. "You're finite resources, you little sacks of meat. Nothing lasts forever." It paused and then laughed to itself. "Nothing lasts forever."

I watched as it walked out through my windows. There was still something off about it, as though it were in shock. Perhaps it was.

I remained in place on the sofa for a long time trying to process the morning's events. V was gone. The Nothing had used up one of its victims. It was all so overwhelming that it didn't occur to me until hours later that I had hurt The Nothing for the first time outside of a dream.

27

KAT

The most difficult thing to get her head around was the fact that Fred was not a sweet young man who wanted to help her out. Kathy had no idea what he actually was.

It had taken her some time to figure out this was something Fred had done to her. When she'd woken up with no control over her body, her first thought was that it was just the next stage of the disease. She spent a day or so watching herself wandering around the house, thinking she was bound to return to normal at any moment. It would pass and she would be lucid once more. That was generally what happened to people suffering from dementia. She just had to wait it out.

Then she watched herself go over to Deborah's house and knock on the back door. For a moment, she got her hopes up that Deborah would answer, alive and well and raring to save her friend from whatever was happening to her. Instead, a young person answered the door and informed them that Deborah was dead. Kathy had already been told, of course, and she could even remember it this time, but it had not stopped her hoping there was some sort of mistake.

"She was my nan."

Kathy's attention returned to the person in front of her. Little Piglet, of course! Who else would Deborah have left the house to? She was an only child and that wayward daughter of hers was long dead now. Hopefully Piglet would be able to tell that something was wrong, perhaps even call an ambulance. But then, the child had not even recognised her.

Deborah's home had changed precious little. Still, it somehow felt far emptier without her. As Kathy watched herself flit around the living room asking all sorts of questions, she became more and more convinced that she was not merely experiencing dementia. In all her reading on the subject, she had never heard of anything like this as a symptom. It could be that anyone who felt it could not explain it to someone else, but people observed these things, didn't they? All that research would have turned up something by now. And, if it wasn't that…

The last thing she could remember before this was that strange encounter with Fred. When he'd said all that stuff about making her pain stop or words to that effect. Then he had done… something. She couldn't properly articulate what he had done to her. At the time, she'd written it off as some sort of hallucination, her senses failing her. It was hard to trust her recollection of mundane things, but she gradually became certain that this had actually happened.

So Fred had control over her body; he was making her do things. And from the way he was snooping around Piglet – now called Mask, it transpired – she deduced that he was after another victim. She had to do something. Warn them. Warn everyone who came into contact with him. But how?

In the end, all she could do was sit back and watch as 'Doris' and Mask became something like friends. So many chats over cups of tea that just got colder; Mask trying to help whenever it looked as though she was having an episode. Deborah would have been pleased to see the two of them like this, if only any of it had been real.

And then poor Mask was there on the doorstep, skinned knees exposed to the breeze. Going on about antidepressants and how they never worked. How life was just one crushing disappointment after another. Kathy desperately wanted to offer some comfort, but it was impossible. What could she have said even if she were capable of speech? She had nothing to offer.

Finally, the day came when Fred made a mistake. Kathy couldn't feel the tea that had been spilled over her, but it gave her a shock just the same. That shock doubled when she looked down to see the hot liquid immediately evaporating, leaving her stone dry.

Mask saw and asked for an explanation. Fred tried to run. Mask, bless them, had not given up. Kathy was rooting for Fred to be exposed as whatever he was. And then, unfortunately, he was.

Backed into a corner, it had shown its true colours. Kathy had had no idea it could be like that. It had always been so gentle and sweet with her; possibly because she was an easier person for it to win over. That had cost her in the end. It clearly terrified poor Mask, twisting her leg around unnaturally, switching between several faces, giving birth to itself. If it had done any part of that to Kathy, she would have died from a cardiac arrest.

When it didn't kill Mask, Kathy began to hope this was the start of something big. Young people generally had the energy and the inclination to fight for their lives, didn't they? Maybe now the poor thing knew she wasn't Doris, Mask's life would be spared. Surely it had no chance of succeeding now it had been exposed. Why would someone so young willingly give up on their life?

Fred had gone straight from Mask's house to the town centre. He stormed over to a young lad who looked homeless. The lad must have known something was up, as he grabbed his stuff and made a run for it.

What must people have thought seeing an elderly woman chasing after a homeless boy? Not only that, but catching up to him and grabbing hold of his arm. No one seemed willing to interfere. No one even seemed willing to look at them.

"You've been telling tales about me, V." Kathy had never heard her own voice sound so cold.

The boy looked as though he might cry. "Please, I just wanted to warn them; they didn't even believe me!"

"Oh, they believe you now." From the look on V's face, Kathy could tell Fred was tightening his grip. "Let me tell you something, V for Victim, you are going to stay away from Mask. Do not go anywhere near them."

"I didn't in the first place, they came and found me."

"Then you need to be somewhere they can't find you. If you happen to bump into them, you turn and walk the other way. Understood?"

V nodded frantically.

"Try to help Mask, interfere in any way, and I'll make you wish you'd said yes to me all those years ago."

Fred dropped the poor boy and walked away.

Kathy was pleasantly surprised when she found out that V had not listened. He'd gone and helped Mask. Perhaps the two of them could save each other.

Maybe, then, something could be done for Kathy. That awful thing could be stopped and countless other people would be saved in the future. So long as the two of them worked together.

28

MX BRILL

I was alone again. It was my natural state, really. Nothing I couldn't handle. Probably.

Even The Nothing had left me for now. I assumed it needed to regroup after Peter – Raymond, I guess – was 'used up'. That must be another way to hurt it, getting it to deplete its resources. What did that mean for the victim, though? Hopefully an end to their suffering. Hopefully.

After several days of bittersweet isolation, I was done wallowing. I had grieved the friendship that had been about seventy percent in my head, self-flagellated over all my stupid mistakes, and freaked out about what The Nothing was getting up to. My emotions exhausted, now I was merely bored.

My entire Saturday night was spent flicking through the Freeview channels, but finding nothing worth staying on for more than a minute. When the glorious Sunday morning rolled around, I found myself desperate to do something outside. The only productive thing would be a shopping trip, but it was a few hours before any supermarkets would be open. And I didn't really need anything; my grocery needs had just been halved, after all. So maybe I didn't need a valid reason to go out, I could just go. But where?

Back when Sam had been alive and capable of it, I had occasionally taken him to a small park down the road. It was pretty decent – just the odd bit of broken glass here and there, but almost no dog waste or needles. Going for a dogless walk there seemed like a perfectly normal thing to do.

Sitting up in bed, I dug into the drawer of my bedside cabinet. I pulled out the framed picture of Sam I'd hidden so I wouldn't keep catching sight of it and bursting into tears. I preferred to plan my crying sessions rather than have them sprung on me.

It had been taken in the park on a lovely, sunny day. Sam was squinting in the sun, but still smiling (I know dogs aren't really smiling when they do that, but let me talk about my dead dog however I fucking please). My Samuel had been a good boy. He may have become moody and snappy as he got older, but he was still an absolute sweetheart underneath. My little irritable angel. Currently in Heaven haranguing Nan to give up whatever she was eating while my mom wondered who either of them were. I thought about taking the picture to the park with me. There was a lot of back and forth before I ultimately decided it would be too pathetic.

It felt good being outside in the nice weather. One of life's simple pleasures. National levels of depression would nosedive if it were like this all year round. Either that, or we would all just find something else to cry about.

The park was just the right level of busyness: a few people dotted around so it wasn't empty, but nothing even approaching a crowd. I had successfully managed to keep my distance from everyone without having to look like a weirdo. I did about three laps before finding a nice bench to sit on by the pond.

I perched, enjoying the armrests to either side of me before I remembered why the bench had them. Certain people just could not be happy unless they were actively making someone else's life worse. And the group selected were always one already having an awful time. The homeless, the disabled, trans people who just wanted to piss in peace. It really made you despair of humanity. I slammed the brakes on that train of thought and banished it, determined not to let shitty reality ruin my mood.

All sorts of birds were tweeting (don't ask me which ones; unless it's a seagull, I'm stuck). Beautiful butterflies flittered around. A squirrel ran past going about its business. Everyone in the park could have burst into song and I wouldn't have batted an eye.

There were a couple of old women sitting on the opposite side of the pond feeding the ducks. I wondered what their relationship was: friends, sisters, a couple. They had probably known each other for decades. How nice that must have been for them.

Some youths (when the fuck did I get old enough to start calling them that?) were playing an unstructured game of football. It had to be, really, as there were only three players. They mostly passed the ball between each other until one got bored and raced off with it, the other two giving chase.

It was nice to sit and observe. I didn't need to be a part of things.

We all have double standards when it comes to people-watching, don't we? It's hard not to look when something interesting is happening. Or, conversely, when nothing interesting is happening and you just need something to look at. No harm in it, as long as no one notices. If you caught someone doing it to you, though, it would be an enormous violation. It was like talking to yourself: completely understandable when you did it, but anyone else who did it was a fucking weirdo to be avoided at all costs.

Out of fucking nowhere, an Old English Sheepdog bounded up to me, no owner in sight. For one horrible moment, I worried that The Nothing had branched out. I'd been traumatised by the huskies in *The Thing* at a young age (did I mention that Grace Kelly was not a fantastic mother?).

The unaccompanied pup was gorgeous and very friendly. He let me rearrange the fur on his face to get a look at his beautiful little eyes. My wrist was thoroughly sniffed and then quickly licked. I was giving his owner exactly thirty seconds to show up and then he was coming home with me.

Just then, a complete and utter bastard came running up.

"God, I'm sorry! He's usually so good that I'm all right to let him off the lead a bit. He's not slobbered all over you, has he?"

"No, he's not." He very much had. "He's a perfect angel." He very much was.

"Yeah, he's a good boy. Come on, Rufus, say bye to the nice lady."

I waved goodbye to Rufus, pretending his dad hadn't just punched me in the gut. Was it the cooing over the dog that did it? Dudes could coo over dogs too. Not that I was a dude.

It seemed a shame to let the casual misgendering spoil the nice morning, so I just pretended it hadn't happened. In fact, the guy hadn't even been there. Just Rufus, all alone and abandoned. I had searched thoroughly for the owner, of course. But, when it came down to it, anyone careless enough to lose such a precious baby didn't deserve to find him again. So I had no choice but to take Rufus home with me to start a new life together.

You were supposed to get a new dog when the old one passed away, weren't you? Fill the void. Use up all the leftover dog food. Repeat the whole cycle. It was both a distraction from your current pain and an investment in future pain that you elected not to think about.

A new dog would have been just the thing. It would drag me out of my funk and give me a reason to live. But it would also give The Nothing a pretty big target. I definitely couldn't rule out it hurting a dog. Once this shit was over – and it would be, hopefully soon – I was going to get a dog. A rescue, probably. Old enough that it didn't need constant attention, but young enough that my future pain would be a good while away.

It was nice to have a plan, even an inconsequential one. It had certainly been a while.

A few minutes later, a couple of teenage girls walked past. I had an awkward moment of eye contact with one. She turned to her friend and commented loudly enough for me to hear it, "That old bloke was checking you out."

I supposed it balanced out the earlier misgendering in a double negative kind of way. Still, I could have done without the implication that I was hanging round the park perving on schoolgirls; surely it was too early for that crowd. I got up and walked away. Apparently, that just made me look suspicious. One of the girls shouted, "Perv!" after me and the two of them collapsed into giggles.

I sped up, subtly looking around for witnesses. Thankfully, there seemed to be no one within hearing range. Still, it was time to get out of the park. Perhaps I could stop at Asda on the way home and get a nice little cupcake or something. Treat myself.

Glancing up, I moved over onto the grass for a straight couple holding hands and taking up ninety percent of the pavement. I looked at them on the off chance they would offer some acknowledgement, either a nod or a muttered apology. Instead, I got the strangest look from the guy. I glanced back after we'd passed. I could see him gesturing to his throat as he talked to his girlfriend. He looked back at me without shame or embarrassment at having been caught.

I had forgot about the bruises on my neck. The light hoodie I was wearing covered them when I zipped all the way up. But, of course, it had got too warm. I zipped it right to the very top. I walked even faster, trying to get home before I sweated to death.

Someone fell into step beside me. Just what I fucking needed. I set my eyes on the pavement and did my best to pretend I hadn't noticed anything.

"I can't really feel it, but it certainly looks too hot for a hoodie."

I stopped in my tracks. Ginger stepped around to stand in front of me.

"Miss me?"

He had cleaned up. An old-fashioned suit that looked ridiculous on a Sunday morning in the park. His hair was washed and neatly combed back, stuck down with enough gel that it spoilt the wash. Ridiculously, the image that came to mind was Rik Mayall in *Drop Dead Fred*, the bit where he was dressed up for the posh party. Wish I had pills to take that would make The Nothing go away.

"Why are you dressed like that?"

"Ginge is the last one left and if I have to be him all the time, I'm gonna look good doing it. Besides, it's not like I need to hide who I am around you. You know exactly what I am and yet you love me anyway."

I started walking again. Of course, he skipped after me.

"I did so hate being away from you, Mask, but I needed to lick my wounds."

That reminded me. "What happened to him when you used him up?"

He shrugged. "Just dead, I think. Good for him."

I side-eyed The Nothing.

"Well, it's an end to his suffering, isn't it? But, boy, there sure was a lot of it!"

"You know I'll never agree to go with you in a million years, right?"

"I don't know that. And neither do you."

I pulled my hood up so I didn't have to look at him.

"I'm okay with walking in silence, I just want to be near you. Your companionable shadow. Constantly at your heels, waiting for you to get tired of living."

"I don't think that's what companionable means."

"It means I'm here for you. For the rest of your life, if necessary. Background noise you'll eventually have no choice but to dive into. We are going to have some fun together."

We came to the end of the path. I stopped and turned to him. "So I'll be living my life, going about my business, but there'll be a little voice there the whole time telling me to give up, saying that I would be better off dead?"

"I wouldn't phrase it so crassly, but yes."

I laughed, loud and ugly. "The fuck do you think I've been doing for the last thirty years?"

Drop Dead Ginger raised his eyebrows, but gave no answer.

I turned and looked at the road ahead. I could either cross over, go to Asda and get myself the treat I had planned, or I could stay on this side of the road, go home and have nothing.

I stomped off in the direction of my sad little house.

When I got home, I pulled Sam's photo from the back pocket of my jeans. I had gone back one final time before leaving and taken it out of the frame. There was my boy, squinting in the sun. His mouth hanging open as though he were smiling.

But, of course, dogs don't really smile. It's all just projection.

29

GR

When Grant woke up in an alleyway, he had a moment of pure bliss. The whole thing – from the old man onwards – had just been an awful, drug-induced dream. The shit in his system must have really done a number on him. Still, he'd never known a sense of relief like this. It lasted right up until the moment his body stood and started walking without him having to instruct it.

Not a dream, then. Just more of the same ceaseless nightmare. He had to wonder if the thing had deliberately tricked him by bringing him to the same alley where it had picked him up. He had no doubts as to the depths of its cruelty. Then again, it was just as likely that it never even thought about Grant. He was unsure which was the more depressing option.

Grant's best guess as to why the thing had come into town in the middle of the night was that it wanted to find someone to take. Did that mean it had given up on V's friend Mask? Or was it after something to tide it over while it waited? He had no idea how often it needed to take someone.

He was extremely surprised when it plonked itself down on a bench next to V. What was he doing here? Hadn't he got his feet well and truly under the table with that Mask person? Maybe this was a pre-arranged meeting and V was about to hand someone over to the thing yet a-fucking-gain. Treacherous fucking snake. It was even shittier of him to be screwing Mask over, given they'd put a roof over his head. Some people wouldn't know loyalty if it cornered them in a dark alley.

V barely looked up. "Took you long enough."

"Well, I had some healing to do. Imagine you did, too."

That got his attention. "Mask hurt you?"

"No, just fingered my face crevices. The energy expenditure cost me. Now I'm down to just the one outfit."

Grant watched V process this; it didn't help him understand it any better. Once it had sunk in, V looked around the square.

"Far too many people around for you to kill me."

"I know."

"And that's not changing any time soon."

"I know."

"So what are you here for? Warn me off again?"

"Try to listen this time, will you? Mask is a lost cause. Walk away."

V leaned forward, eyes on the floor. He rested his elbows on his thighs. "Would you even let me walk away? Don't I know too much?"

"Frankly, my dear, you don't know shit. Except for Mask's name. And since you know that's an issue for me now, I'm best off staying out of your way."

Grant was not following this at all. What did Mask's name matter?

V sat up, twisting in his seat to face them. "You're right: I do know their name. If I ever catch a glimpse of them anywhere, I'll be running up and screaming it at the top of my lungs. How about you be the one to give up on Mask? There must be plenty of time for you to find someone else."

"I want them, though. More importantly, they want me. Who are you to stand in the way of true love?"

V's lip curled in disgust. He sat back, saying nothing. To all appearances, he had given up.

Grant wasn't having that. He'd just sat there and listened to a backstabbing coward face down a monster to defend his friend. He willed V to fight on, piled up all his psychic energy and fucking threw it at him. Do not back down, you piece of shit!

He was rooting for him. His own murderer. Grant had always been of the opinion that people didn't change. Not for the better, anyway. Just this once, though, he wanted to be wrong.

The thing cleared Grant's throat. "Are you familiar with the phrase 'mutually assured destruction'? Once I get Mask, you'll have a way to hurt me. And you know I have all sorts of ways to hurt you right back. It's best we stay out of each other's way."

V said nothing. He stared blankly ahead.

"I'm giving you quite the opportunity, you know? No one has ever walked away from me knowing what I am. You're one in a million, Vincent Val Vittorio the fifth. Take my gift and be grateful for it."

The thing stood and walked away, only looking back for a moment.

In the dim glow from the streetlights, V's unfocused eyes were shining.

Grant didn't question it when he found himself at the creepy old guy's bungalow. He'd given up on questioning things these days. He watched impassively (not that he had a choice) as the thing emptied the wardrobes until it found a decent suit. As it stripped him, Grant noticed a few patches on his torso had crumpled and turned black, as though burnt. The suit was both too short and too baggy on Grant. There was nothing to be done about the length of the trousers, but braces were added and that seemed to keep them up at least. The thing stood in front of a mirror to inspect its handiwork. As far as Grant was concerned, he looked like an ageing extra in *Bugsy Malone*. Still, the thing seemed pleased.

When it found Mask in the park, a few things became clearer. Grant was the last remaining victim. The last man standing. For all the good it did him. Poor Kathy, poor creepy old dude, poor countless others. No wonder he'd been 'awake' for so long. It had previously only ever been for a few hours maximum, now it had been somewhere in the region of forty-eight. A long, sleepless future stretched out before him. All he could do was wait for it to be his turn to go.

Mask got right in the thing's face, challenging it before storming off; good for them. Grant felt the same grudging respect as he had for V the other night. He recalled that conversation now with interest. There was a way to hurt the thing – V knew it, Mask probably knew it. For a moment, V had clearly thought Mask had hurt it. That had to mean there was a realistic chance that they could.

As unlikely as it seemed, that short-arse depressive was probably Grant's last hope.

30

BARBARA CARTLAND

I dreamed about my trip to the park – because why would my brain let me have a little bit of peace? It was none too clear, but I had the sense I'd been sitting on the bench while everyone stared at me. At one point I had been naked from the waist down. That hadn't helped with the staring. Not a pleasant dream by any stretch of the imagination, but its one key selling point was an absence of The Nothing. I was relieved when I woke up in my bed, but only until I realised I wasn't actually awake. The darkness had that weird, grainy texture apparently unique to my Nothing dreams.

An anxiety dream within an existential nightmare. My subconscious tag-teaming me with The Nothing. Honestly, if it hated me so much, why didn't it just fuck off and leave me alone?

I stared up at my Benothinged ceiling, making the most of the time before it appeared. It was a blissful five seconds or so. Then the nightmare creature floated into view above me.

"How're you coping without V, poppet?"

"Fine. I knew him for a couple of weeks; I'm over it."

It pouted, I think. It definitely did a sympathetic head tilt. Long, awful fingers reached down to brush my cheek.

"Look at you putting on a brave face. It's all very endearing. I will miss you when you're gone, you know?"

"I'd be inside you."

"Lucky you. It's not the same, though. I'll miss our little double act, this charming back and forth."

"I hope you fucking choke on me."

It smiled without lips. Then it floated down to an inch away from my face. "I can hardly wait."

Thankfully, my eyes opened for real that time. Relief washed over me. Then I rolled over in bed and came face to tit with Ginger in his ill-fitting suit. My head rest against his chest. I left it there, beyond tired. His arm slipped around me. We were cuddling, for fuck's sake. I hated myself for how good it felt.

"Did you sleep well, beloved? Did you dream of me?"

I should have bitten it or something when we were still in the dream, that usually made it stay away for a while.

"It's still early, if you want to go back to sleep. Don't worry about me; I'll be here when you wake up. I'm never going to leave your side again."

I placed a hand on his chest to lean up and see the clock. Not even six in the morning. I settled back down on his bosom and, somehow, went back to sleep.

The Nothing was as good as its word. For the next week, it trailed me everywhere. It was in every dream, no matter how many times I physically hurt it. I made no attempt in real life where it was more likely to hurt me right back. It was just a way of venting my frustration. For its part, The Nothing kept letting me get away with it; I think it found the whole thing amusing.

It followed me around shops, loudly commenting on my propensity for shoplifting; it gave a running commentary on any show I dared attempt to watch; it reached over and switched the laptop off in the middle of half-hearted job applications. My phone never had any charge in it because The Nothing always slyly unplugged it the second I looked away. Apparently, it was attempting to annoy me to death. There was a very real chance it would succeed.

One afternoon as I lay on the sofa flicking through TV

channels, The Nothing decided it was going to read aloud from one of Nan's old romance books. It kept pausing to either comment or ask me what a particularly rude or euphemistic term meant.

"Mask, what's a love cavern? Is it made of rock? If so how can it tremble?"

Sighing, I turned the telly off and dropped the remote on the floor. I rolled onto my side to face the cushions. Behind me, The Nothing went back to reading.

"*With every powerful thrust within her, he brought her closer and closer to her peak.* It's honestly quite good, this. I suppose it does nothing for you, with you being asexual and what not."

"It does nothing for me because it's badly written heterosexual nonsense for old ladies."

"I'm sure Nanny wouldn't like to hear you slag off her taste in erotica like that."

"I'm sure she wouldn't want me fucking hearing about her erotica."

Generally, I tried not to engage with The Nothing on its nonsense, but it was hard to resist the constant barrage. Talking back always encouraged it; I ended up regretting it every time.

There was movement behind me. Gentle fingers began to stroke my hair.

"I just don't want to upset you with this talk about all the things you're missing out on. You know, the perfectly natural and disgusting things all normal human beings do to each other."

Don't engage. Don't engage. Don't engage.

It leaned in, apparently unperturbed by my lack of response. "And, obviously, I'm not just talking about the sexual side. Don't you people all get it hammered into you from a very young age that the single most important thing in the world is having someone who loves you? Even if it's just the one? And that a person with no one to love them is sad and pathetic and ultimately doesn't matter?"

For my part, I was exceedingly fucking perturbed.

A finger stroked the shell of my ear. "You know, you're nothing if nobody loves you. I could love you, Mask. I could make you matter."

When it appeared in my peripheral vision, I knew it was checking for a reaction. My face remained blank, no matter how much I was crumbling inside. The Nothing made a small noise of annoyance and switched tactics.

"I bet the most frustrating part of being nonbinary is that whether strangers read you as a man or a woman, you're still going to get misgendered. No one's likely to guess they/them on the first try, are they? To be honest, you could put more effort into looking the part. A little androgyny never hurt anybody."

"No, but transphobic hate crimes did."

"Finally, they speaks!"

I turned over to face it. He was closer than I anticipated. Our noses brushed.

"You're not getting anywhere with this shit, you know? I'm far too used to it."

He smiled. "Darling, you look seconds away from tears."

"I always am. It's my default. I'm either seconds away from tears or shedding them. You have no power over me."

It grinned. "Oh, I know that movie, Irene loved it. Ginger said it was stupid, but he secretly liked it." I went to speak again, but it cut me off. "Yes, I know, everyone loves it, it's barely a cult film anymore, blah blah blah."

When had I said that? When I was watching movies with V? That was certainly confirmation that the fucker had been watching us all along.

"By the way," The Nothing went on, "did you have a confusing crush on Jareth as a kid? Irene and Ginger both did and neither of them were particularly attracted to men."

Of course I had. That wasn't something I wanted to share with The Nothing, though. Instead, I went for a subject change.

"Ginger?"

The Nothing frowned at me in confusion.

"I was calling you Ginger, just in case."

There was a beat before it understood. Then it grinned. "Nuh-uh, doesn't count. Not his name, just what everyone else called him."

I hadn't really expected that to work, but it would have been nice. "That's how it works then? Legal names? Would someone have to call me by my old name to save me, or would Mask work?"

The Nothing huffed, looking bored as hell. "Is Mask your name?"

"Yes."

"Then Mask would work. If Ginger had called himself Ginger, then I'd be in trouble now."

That was interesting.

"This is boring! I'm going back to the old-lady porn." When that failed to elicit a reaction, it added, "Or I can play Jareth for you." It must have read something in my face because its eyes narrowed and it gave a sly smile. In its best Bowie impression, it quoted, "Just let me rule you." The emphasis it put on *rule* dripped with yearning.

I stretched up and kissed The Nothing. I had no idea where the impulse came from – maybe it was something imprinted on anyone who watched *Labyrinth* at a young age – but I felt it, so I did it.

The Nothing stumbled backwards. It stared blankly at me as I slid down onto the floor. It remained motionless as I crawled forwards on my knees until I was in his lap.

My fingers sunk into ginger hair. I pulled his head back sharply, making him hiss.

"Ooooh, did that hurt? Poor little thing." I punctuated this with a light slap on either cheek. "Why didn't the tea hurt you? Why can I hurt you?"

His eyes were wide. I could tell he hadn't the slightest clue what I was doing. That made two of us. He forced a chuckle and covered his face with a smile.

"You always hurt the one you love."

I pulled his hair again. "Do you love me, Gingie?"

The smile faded into something more sinister as he stared up at me. "I'm the closest thing to love you'll ever get."

I stared right back. "Why don't you show me what I've been missing?"

There was a lengthy, silent staring match. Slowly, we crept closer and closer until our lips met.

What makes a good kiss? That's not a rhetorical question, I genuinely have no idea. I've never really understood the concept. Just two people gobbing into each other's mouths. And that's supposed to be the most romantic thing in the world. Still, when it came to the components of the perfect kiss, there were definitely a few things I could rule out. Firstly, only one of the parties being human. Secondly, both of them hating every moment of it, but neither being willing to back down.

And so The Nothing and I kissed passionately for all the wrong reasons. It seemed to have more clue about what it was doing than I did; if it had memories from its victims, presumably several were snogging aficionados. Still, what we lacked in technique we made up for in unenthusiasm. With its tongue still in my mouth, The Nothing leaned forward, cradling me as it dipped me. My back was placed gently on the floor.

The tongue slipped from mine. The Nothing pushed itself up and hung over me. I was hit with the revelation that I had very likely fucked up. I was laid out on my nan's best rug seconds away from losing my virginity in a game of chicken with a monster that would kill me afterwards. Something for the obituary, I guess.

Ginger's hand caressed the side of my face. He looked down at me in something akin to wonder.

"You are full of surprises, Mask Whitehurst. I've never known anyone I was chasing sink to such pathetic depths."

A beat.

Then I thrust my fist up into the empty air where his face had just been.

I sat up, relieved that my foray into monster fucking had ended when it did. After a moment of consideration, I was further relieved to find that I was in no way aroused by the experience.

At least I had finally lost my shadow. The black dog that constantly followed me around, mostly just calling me a dickhead. There was no telling how long it was going to leave me in peace. I made the most of it by watching several hours of television uninterrupted. It was the most normal I'd felt in weeks.

By the time I eventually stumbled into my bedroom, I had almost forgotten The Nothing existed. I was getting the hang of dealing with it. You just needed to ignore it when it was dripping poison and assert yourself when it really started to take the piss. It was likely the two of us were in this for the long haul, but I was certain I could take anything it would throw at me.

When I reached my bed, I saw there was an envelope on my pillow. Small, and old from the look of it. As I was opening it, I remembered the missing letter from my mother. The photo inside confirmed it was her. Several years older than when I had last seen her, but most likely not several years wiser. I unfolded her letter. Oh, this was going to be good.

To my little star,

She had literally never called me that. And, at the time of writing, I would have been way too old to be called something like that.

How've you been? I just know you turned out great.

And therefore, it doesn't matter that I left you.

Did you end up going to uni? I hope so, you were always so bright as a child.

Maybe tell me that one single fucking time.

I don't know if Nan told you, but I'm probably getting married soon. I'm just waiting for him to set a date.

Doesn't sound good, Ma.

I haven't told him about you yet. I just told him I was writing to my mom to tell her about us. He told me not to bother so I've had to do it quickly while he's down the pub.

That actually really didn't sound good.

He's said it'll just be the two of us in a registry office, if it even happens. I want you and your nan there, though. Maybe we can keep it a secret until the special day. If he's not happy about it, we can always say you turned up uninvited to surprise me.

Alarm bells rang.

You'll like him, everyone always does. He's such a charmer! I can't wait for you all to meet.

I better wrap this up as he'll be home soon. I've included our address, but it's best you don't write me there. I'll write you again soon, though, I promise. In the meantime, I want you to have an updated photo of me. Hopefully, I'll have one of you too soon.

Love always and forever,

Your one and only Mom.

At the very bottom of the page was a drawing of a little star with the name she had given me written in the middle. A tear dripped onto the letter, leaving a big wet splodge on the paper. I tossed it away before I could ruin it.

I'd known from Nan's letter that she wanted to get in touch with me. But this… fuck. She loved me and she wanted a photo of me and she wanted me to be at her wedding. She wanted to be my mom again. Instead, she had rotted in a fucking bedsit alone and unloved.

Tears streamed down my face. My mouth dropped open and I fucking howled.

I wanted V back. I wanted The Nothing to make an appearance so I could fight it or fuck it or finally let it have me.

I wanted my mom.

More than I had ever done in the many years since she'd left me, I wanted my mommy.

I cried long enough and hard enough that I gave myself a splitting headache. I only got to sleep because I still had a stash of the knockout cold medicine. I necked way too much of it and passed out with the letter from my mom crushed against my chest.

31

MIKA

I was in a wheelchair. A pretty old-fashioned wheelchair at that. One leg stuck out in front of me in an enormous cast. Apart from that, I was in some rather fetching pyjamas. A camera hung from my neck, an uncomfortable weight on my chest. I was in a shabby little flat, parked at a window overlooking my neighbour's house. It was unmistakably *Rear Window*. And I was James Stewart for whatever bloody reason.

Okay, so how did this one thematically fit into my life? Was I trapped in a room watching The Nothing murder people? That was true enough. Frankly, I didn't remember enough about the movie to speculate. I just knew who the two main stars were.

Oh, *fuck*.

I heard the door open and shut behind me. Heels clacked on the floorboards as she entered. She came up close enough that I could see her reflection in the window. This Grace Kelly was not blonde. When she spoke, it was in The Nothing's best guess at a voice that I barely remembered myself. It went for an approximation of my accent, but comically high-pitched.

"Oh dear, it's really not good for you to stay cooped up inside, you know?"

I snorted. "I have a broken leg in this one, there's not a fat lot I can do about that."

The reflection set her hands firmly on her hips. "Well, not with that attitude, my little star!"

I peered down at the giant camera and wondered if I could bring myself to smash it into an imitation of my mother's face. Soft hands began to play with my hair.

"I just worry so much about you, darling. If only you would stop shutting yourself away from the people who want to help you."

I had to laugh at that. "That's you, is it?" I shook its hands off. "Anyway, these characters were lovers: this is all a bit Oedipal, isn't it?"

The Nothing bent over me and grabbed my jaw, its hands supernaturally strong. "If you don't like it, son, perhaps you should pluck your eyes out. It's only going to get worse from this point." It licked a stripe along the side of my face, then released me as I gagged.

Suddenly, it straightened up and stumbled backwards. It pressed a hand to its forehead in a swoon. "Oh dear, I'm really feeling ever so unwell." It collapsed onto the sofa.

Dread crept into my bones. I knew exactly what trick The Nothing was going to pull on me next. I kept my eyes firmly forward on the window, on the too-clear reflection of my mother passed out on the sofa.

Her body began to decompose. I'd spent so many sleepless nights reading about decomposition, over and over. Now I was forced to bear witness to a speed run of the process.

I watched the body go stiff as blisters appeared across the skin, then it bloated to almost twice its size as it filled with gas. The skin turned red, then black from the blood pooling beneath it. An ochre liquid gushed from the mouth and nose; I could smell it from across the room. Then the body began to lose mass as the internal organs liquefied. The nails and teeth fell out. Tiny holes appeared in the skin as insects began to eat it away. The holes spread to huge gaps across the corpse. Bone appeared beneath.

Finally, Grace Kelly Whitehurst, my one and only mom, began to resemble the monster that haunted her one and only child.

Through momentum – and sheer force of will – I managed to jump up onto my unbroken leg. I rested against the window for a moment, then reared back and sent myself hurtling through the glass. I tumbled to the ground.

As soon as I woke up, I vehemently wished I hadn't. My mouth was like a desert and my eyes were sandpaper raw. My brain throbbed inside my skull, desperately attempting to fight its way out.

The letter was stuck to my bare midriff via sweat. I could feel it. I wondered if her words would be printed on my skin until I scrubbed them away. The ink was probably too old to run.

I lay spread-eagled staring up at my massacred ceiling. I should have replaced the tiles years earlier; they were yellowed with a mixture of age and Nan's thirty-a-day habit before she cut down and started smoking outdoors.

Perhaps she smoked to deal with the guilt of hiding my mom's letter from me, or from effectively leaving her to die. Deborah had known where her daughter was for years and still let the police kick down the door of a stinking bedsit to find a mummified corpse. It was disgusting to view cancer as a punishment, but I fixated on the fact she was diagnosed within months of the news about Mom. Guilt metastasised. Had she tormented herself with thoughts of storming round to Grace Kelly's flat to bring her home within an hour of reading the letter? She must have done. Lord knows I'd had similar thoughts over the years, and I hadn't even known where to find her.

Of course, the other thought that had plagued me was: what exactly happened to her? Knowing she had a controlling boyfriend suggested one very upsetting conclusion. My mother's murderer could be sauntering around the Black Country hurting numerous other women, never to be punished for his crimes. Then again, perhaps he was not controlling but just disinterested in marrying her. Her death could have been a suicide due to the heartbreak. And, of course, my almost-step-dad might have been completely irrelevant. I had no idea of either when she wrote the letter or the date of her death, so the two events could have been days or years apart.

The most information I'd had about her in years still solved nothing. Realistically, Grace Kelly Whitehurst's death would always remain a mystery.

If some fucker made a podcast about it, I'd claw their eyes out.

The woman herself had been something of an enigma. Telling me how adorable I was one day, then insisting my hair was stupidly long the next. The hatchet job she did on my silken locks had surely been deliberate. When my nan asked about it, Mom told her I did it myself. Nan just laughed at me and ruffled what remained of my hair.

Her behaviour improved somewhat when we moved in with Nan. Less stressed, she had nothing to take out on me. Some of my absolute fondest memories were from that period. The three of us under a blanket on the sofa watching animated movies taped from the telly. Mom seeming genuinely pleased when I snuggled up against her and started to fall asleep. Sometimes I faked it just for the contact. In those moments, I was absolutely sure of her love for me. But when it came down to it, she just couldn't hack it. She left for good just after dawn one morning without saying goodbye to either of us. Me, shouting at my nan through rivers of tears to call the police. Nan, calmly and patiently explaining that Mom had packed up and left of her own free will.

The letter threatened to rip as I peeled it from my skin. Luckily, it remained intact. I permitted myself a fleeting glance at my mother's handwriting, at her crudely drawn star, and tossed it away. No point in preserving it. No point in preserving any of this.

I padded into the kitchen on my bare, dirty feet and took a sensible amount of painkillers to mend my tender head. Then

I had some toast for the nausea. I ate it sitting on the side next to the cooker, taking in what I could see of my sad little home.

My depressing kitchen led to a depressing living room. After that was a depressing hall and a boxroom where the only friend I'd ever really had lived for exactly five minutes before deciding he was better off homeless. Then there was the bedroom, with filthy net curtains and yellowed polystyrene crumbled all over the floor, stinking of sweat from nights spent either sleepless or filled with nightmares. Finally, there was the bathroom with all its bars and poles around the bath because my nan had expected to live out her last few decades here. Instead, I was the one who was going to die in this house.

Eating started to get on my nerves, so I balled up the rest of the bread and shoved the whole thing into my gob. I barely managed to swallow it. I had to slap a palm onto my chest to force it down. Then I sat there feeling unpleasantly full. Fuck, I hated eating. The list of things I didn't hate grew smaller every day.

Keeping as still as possible, I sat and listened to the silence. There was no old woman cackling at a classic sitcom before being interrupted by her hacking smoker's cough. No ageing dog shuffling around before collapsing on the floor with a grunt. No formerly homeless man tuning his guitar or running the hoover round as he loudly expressed his disgust at my lifestyle choices. No nothing.

Where was that shapeshifting piece of shit? It had to be watching me. There was no way it would launch the grenade of Mommy's letter at me and not stick around to watch the explosion.

"You here, Ginge? Got any pearls of wisdom for me? Some insights into my character you think I somehow never stumbled across in thirty years of self-obsessed introspection?"

I watched the door to the living room, expecting the monster to jumpscare into view at any moment. Not a single thing happened. I was hit with the very depressing thought that it might have moved on to someone else. That it had thoroughly destroyed me as a human being and then not even stuck around to feast on my corpse. The final cruelty.

"I'm not gonna try to have my way with you, if that's what you're worried about."

Not a peep.

The silence was getting to me.

Shuffling along on my arse, I made it to the fridge and reached up to grab Nan's old radio from the top. It hadn't been used for years, but the batteries were still in it and there was no obvious reason why it should have broken.

I found something insufferably cheerful that I bopped along to until I realised it was 'Lollipop' by Mika. I very quickly switched the station to one that only played oldies. Ridiculous, really, it wasn't even the bad Mika song.

There was a fun couple of months during secondary school where it seemed as though just about everyone was constantly singing a song about the mother who abandoned me. Imagine you'd grown up in the '70s and your deadbeat mom's name just happened to be Rasputin.

I had successfully avoided all Grace Kelly films since the ones Mom and/or Nan had made me watch during childhood (including *Rear Window,* obviously). Thankfully, Nan lost her taste for them when her namesake daughter dumped her child on her and didn't leave a forwarding address. Not until much later, anyway.

The only child of the only child of an only child.

It seemed appropriate that this particular branch of the Whitehurst family tree should wither and die with me. Our genes were not exactly outstanding. We just seemed to get crazier and crazier.

The oldie I didn't recognise ended and was replaced with the intro to 'A Whiter Shade of Pale': the perfect song for the mood I was in. I slipped down from the side.

There was a moment of awful, perfect clarity and I knew what

I had to do. The Nothing was right: all this suffering was unnecessary. It was just wrong about there being only one way to end it. I wasn't sad, I wouldn't even really say I was depressed. It just felt peaceful, like something had finally clicked into place and I knew it was going to be all right. All of this was finally going to end.

At first, I could feel one half of my brain trying to talk me out of it. It brought up all the usual things: TV shows I was looking forward to; all the crap on my bucket list; the idea that maybe I was just about to turn a corner. Then it stopped, accepting the reality that this was The Right Thing To Do. That it was something I should have done for myself a long time ago. Self-care King.

The radio had a handle on. I swung it like a tiny child carrying a bucket and spade. As I skipped, I sang a rough approximation of the lyrics in an even rougher approximation of the tune. It's a cracking song, 'A Whiter Shade of Pale'. Wish I heard it more often.

From my depressing kitchen, I entered my depressing living room. After that, the depressing hall. I stood a moment in the boxroom where the only friend I'd ever really had lived for exactly five minutes before deciding he was better off homeless. Then into the bedroom with its filthy nets and crumbled tiles trod into the carpet. I breathed in the stench of my own sweat. Finally, there was the bathroom with all its bars and poles around the bath.

I set the radio on the windowsill and began to fill the bath. Hot and cold taps both turned up full blast.

Procol Harum had never done another song, had they? Not a really famous one, at least. There was something to be said for doing one great thing and then bowing out. Most of us never even managed the first part. At least we all got to bow out eventually.

I have never had much patience for baths. They take way too long to fill up and then even longer to cool down enough to get in. I don't even find them all that relaxing. The only time I ever have one is when some part of this rusty old meat sack is giving me trouble. I got sick of waiting and turned the taps off. The water looked far too shallow, but it would obviously rise when I got in.

'A Whiter Shade of Pale' ended. An irritating DJ began to prattle on. I got into the bath in my shorts and T-shirt.

The water level rose more than I was expecting. Long legs appeared either side of me, still clad in too-short trousers and even shoes. Arms wrapped around my waist. Ginger's pointy chin came to rest on my shoulder.

"Please tell me you're just being thrifty and washing your clothes and body at the same time."

I leaned back against him. "Why, what else could I possibly be planning?"

"The stupidest fucking thing you've ever done."

"Doesn't feel stupid. Feels like the smart option, seeing as the alternative is you."

"You really want someone to find your rotting, bloated body several years from now? Think it through. I thought ending up like her was your worst fear."

I swallowed down my rage. "I thought so too. Then you gave me a brand spanking new worst fear. It's over, Ginger. Find some other miserable cunt and torture them."

"You could live with that, could you?"

"I literally won't have to."

The Nothing had no response to that. I could feel the fury radiating from it.

The prattling DJ announced that the next song would be Don McLean. I prayed for 'American Pie', or even 'The Flight of Dragons'. My prayers are seldom ever answered. The intro to 'Vincent' kicked in and I scrambled to get to the radio before the singing could start but The Nothing held me tight. Its grip tightened painfully around my waist.

"Now, Mask, I could have sworn you liked this song. Why on earth are you finding it so upsetting right now?"

I thrashed around, sending water flying everywhere. Sadly, it didn't reach the radio.

"Oh, of course! Silly me, I forgot. This is what that charming young man was singing the first time you met him, wasn't it? And you obviously don't want to think about V at a time like this."

I gave up fighting; the damage was already done. I let myself go limp against The Nothing.

"What would V say if he knew you planned to end it all?"

"He'd say, 'Good for you, Mx Mask,' and then he'd high-five me."

It chuckled. "Probably. But it would be very short-sighted of him, given he's next on my list."

I stiffened.

"Oh, had that not occurred to you either? Why would I start from scratch when I still have one I prepared earlier?"

Mr McLean hit the line V had been singing when The Nothing interrupted him that day. It was strange I remembered it so clearly.

"You're trying to bargain with me?"

It shrugged. "If you want to put it like that. I was merely pointing out that your death would doom V. Whereas giving yourself to me would guarantee his safety."

I snorted. "Bullshit. You'd tear him to pieces the first chance you got."

"Except you know I avoid anyone who knows the names of one of my little treats. As much as I'd like to make that boy eat his own skin, it would be far too risky to go near him. Plus, I sleep after I've eaten; he could be a million miles away by the time I wake up. This is the right thing to do, Mask. The only truly selfless thing."

It was right and both of us knew it. My options were either: kill myself and be free but condemn V, or sacrifice myself for the first person to apparently give two shits about me since my nan died.

My chance to do one great thing and then bow out.

Still, I was not naïve enough to automatically trust The Nothing. I mentally sifted through everything it said in search of loopholes. There was potentially an enormous one: it could have killed V the second he left my house.

"I want to see V one last time."

The Nothing leaned forward, its grip on me loosening. "And then you'll do it?"

"If I'm satisfied that he's okay and that you're not going to screw us over. Then, yes, I'll do it."

There was a pause, then the monster crushed me in a hug, rocking me from side to side. Yet more water sloshed out of the bath.

"You won't regret this, Mask, I swear!"

"I already do," I grumbled.

Ginger's laugh was way over the top. "Oh, you're so funny! I really am going to miss you."

Sitting up, I looked down at my clothed and submerged body. I looked and felt ridiculous.

The Nothing must have picked up on my thoughts. It placed a delicate hand on my shoulder.

"Might as well have an actual bath now. Do you want me to bathe you?"

I was fairly certain that this was a joke, but I nodded anyway. Then I let the monster peel off my wet clothes and toss them aside.

As good as his word, he stayed in the water in his daft suit and washed me head to toe. He hummed a song to himself. It took me a few minutes to realise it was 'Lollipop' by Mika.

32

K

Cut off from her own body as well as the world around her, all Kathy could do with her time was think about the past.

Most of her earliest memories were of playing in the rubble. Growing up in Coventry in the '40s, there had been plenty of that going spare. Seemed like madness to her now, that someone would let their little girl wander off and play in a bombed-out house, but it had been a different time back then. Her mother would just lean out the front door and shout "Kathy, come home" once her tea was done.

Decades later, there was an afternoon play called *Cathy Come Home*. She had watched it over at Audrey's house. Despite it being an incredibly sad play, Audrey had taken to calling her Kathy-Come-Home for years afterwards.

At some point towards the end, there had been an afternoon with Audrey in the hospice. Kathy was a regular visitor there, despite not knowing if Audrey got anything out of it. Audrey didn't recognise her, she never did. Kathy just liked to sit there with her for an hour or two. Out of nowhere, Audrey had looked up at her and said, clear as day, "Kathy come home." Just for a moment, she knew who she was. It passed in seconds. Kathy came home sobbing that day.

She never visited Deborah in the hospital, she couldn't face it. She told herself that she'd go in if Deborah asked to see her, but she never did. Little Piglet never passed it on, anyway. When Fred lied to her about Deborah being dead, in among all the sorrow was a touch of relief that she would never be called upon to make that awful trip.

Poor Deborah, the last couple of years of her life blighted first by the revelation about her daughter and then by her cancer diagnosis.

The very last time Deborah came round for a coffee, she all but collapsed on Kathy's sofa in tears. She had just received a letter from the hospital giving her an appointment for a biopsy. They hadn't even known at that stage, but Deborah was devastated.

"I'm not telling Piglet until it becomes unavoidable. It's all way too soon after finding out about Gracie. I mean, how much shit can happen to a family at once?"

Purely from force of habit, Kathy raised an eyebrow at the swearing. Then she schooled her face and wrapped an arm around Deborah.

"I know, love. It's all so unfair. All these wretched things we can't possibly stop."

Deborah snorted, pulling away from her. "I could've stopped plenty."

Kathy had no idea how to respond to that, so she waited for Deborah to go on.

"I knew where she was. She wrote to us – both of us – a few years ago with her address. I could have gone over there at any point."

"Why didn't you?"

Deborah wiped her eye with the palm of her hand. "She abandoned her child! Not to mention her mother. We were probably both better off without her, but that doesn't make it okay." She wrapped her cardigan tighter around herself. "It was too easy, just one letter. She said she'd write again so I thought maybe I'd respond the next time. Another letter never came. She was probably already dead."

The last sentence was punctuated with sobs. By the end of it, she was hysterical. Kathy let her friend cry it all out until the sobs turned to awful, hacking coughs. She slapped Deborah on the back with her frail, bony hand until it cleared.

Back then, Kathy wondered if the guilt and grief were what led to Deborah going downhill so fast. She had no idea about the science, but they said older people died of broken hearts all the time. It was a wonder she'd survived Audrey.

Years later, Kathy heard the thing possessing her bringing up the whole sorry business to taunt Mask. She'd never wanted someone to get what was coming to them so badly. She cheered when Mask attacked it, even though it was her flesh being bitten into.

For some time after that, everything was a blur. Kathy caught the occasional glimpse of her home in an increasingly messy state. The photograph of her and Deborah disappeared from the mantel. Mask was the only person likely to have taken it; they were welcome to it. It was the same with the money someone had ripped from the mattress. Kathy had no use for it and no one left to inherit it; it might as well go to someone who could have done with it.

If Kathy had ever got round to writing a will, she would have left everything to Deborah. And Deborah would have left all her possessions to Mask, so it made sense that her things belonged to Mask in a roundabout sort of way.

Plus, despite them not recognising her, Kathy found that she quite liked Mask. They were clearly very unhappy, but they ploughed on. They still managed to be kind to an old lady they thought was suffering. And then there was that sense of humour, unmistakably inherited from Deborah and able to survive just about anything. You had to admire that kind of resilience.

Finally, Kathy got to see Mask one last time. It was in the ruins of her bedroom. The poor thing was pinned beneath them on her bed. Kathy was worried that this was it, Mask would be killed by her hands. Instead – and clearly, shaking with terror – Mask had looked right into her eyes and shouted out her name. Her actual name. After old Katharine Hepburn, her mother's favourite actress.

Kathy felt dizzy somehow. Then she seemed to separate from her body. Her last coherent thought was a merging of memories of Audrey and their mother. The same words in completely different tones.

Kathy, come home.

33

DICK CAVETT

There seemed to be so much to plan. I found myself regretting not just ending it all in the bath there and then.

I made my bed for some reason. It felt like something that needed to be done. Then I pottered around tidying until it occurred to me there was something I needed to find. Unfortunately, that meant messing up a lot of things again. The Nothing shadowed me the entire time in its now-dry suit.

"You're definitely not going to change your mind, right?"

I was on my knees rummaging through the bottom of my wardrobe. I didn't bother stopping. "I might if you don't shut up."

I heard it throw itself onto the bed I'd just spent ten minutes making.

"This is boring, though. Shall I go find V?"

"Not yet. There's some stuff I need to do first."

Behind a pair of boots I hadn't worn for a decade, I finally found the box I'd been searching for. An old stationery set of my nan's. Possibly the single most lavender thing in creation. Mom had owned the same one – that was what her two letters had been written on. I turned and sat back, dropping the box into my lap.

The Nothing perked up, shuffling to the edge of my bed and leaning over. "What's that for?"

"I'm gonna write a letter for V." I took the little pen out of the box along with one of the sheets of paper. "You don't mind explaining a few things for me now it's already over, do you?"

It raised an eyebrow. "Like a villainous monologue?"

I snorted. "I'm sure you'd love that, but I meant more like an interview. There's just some things I want to clear up."

The Nothing didn't look impressed, but it waved a hand for me to proceed.

I decided to go the route of quickfire questions, not giving it time to decide to lie.

"Where did you come from?"

"Where did you come from?" It snapped back. "Presumably, like you, I was once nothing and will be nothing again one day."

"So you're not immortal? How long have you existed?"

It shrugged. "A fair few centuries, I reckon. As for immortality: I will most likely continue to exist as long as I have people to feed me."

I nodded, scribbling parts of that down. "How many people have you taken?"

"I couldn't possibly begin to answer that."

Which meant it was an absolute shitload. And I was going to add to the total. I reminded myself who I was doing this for.

"You said you sleep afterwards – for how long?"

"Depends on the person: age, health, strength. I've had an unfortunate run of biddies and drug addicts lately; you would put me out of action for a good, long while."

"Put a number on it."

"It might stretch to a decade, maybe even more."

Ten whole years of safety for V; ten years of no one else being harmed by this monster. Surely my sad little life was worth that. Maybe there was a way to warn potential victims of the future, let them know how to beat The Nothing.

"Why do names hurt you?"

It shrugged. "Why does carbon dioxide hurt you? It just does. If you really need to come up with an explanation for it, the best I can do is this: I don't just take isolated people for practical reasons. I feed on loneliness and despair as much as your actual flesh. Plus, the lonely tend to fade away before I even get to them. Observation is existence. Taking notice of someone, calling their name, it makes a person real. And so, I lose my grip on them."

That was arguably deep. It was definitely deeply uncomfortable.

"I'm pretty sure I'm a real person whether or not there's someone around to watch me being one."

"If you say so."

A new question occurred to me that I hadn't preplanned. "Hey, is the nightmare creature your true form?"

It blinked several times. I tried to remember if it normally did that. "The what now?"

"You know, that messed-up skeleton thing? I don't know how else to describe it. Besides fucking creepy."

"Yes, that's me."

"Can you not just stay like that?"

"That would make it rather difficult to go about now, wouldn't it? Plus, that body is weak."

Perhaps that meant it could be killed in that form. Or, at least, that it couldn't last in the long term. That was worth filing away for later.

"Is that it yet? This is boring."

"Just one more thing: how come the tea didn't hurt you, but I've been able to hurt you."

It eyed me, its mouth becoming a straight line. It crossed one leg over the other. If it made the same stupid joke as last time, I was going to tear it limb from limb.

"First of all, child, you have never really hurt me. Sure, being pummelled by a tiny ball of fury is hardly fun, but less than a minute later I'm completely healed."

"So why can I do it at all?"

It shrugged again. I could have snapped my pen in half. A long silence stretched between us before it deigned to answer me.

"You weren't trying to hurt Doris when you spilled the tea."

Obviously. A moment of confusion, then it clicked into place.

"It has to do with intent?"

"Something like that. Though it only really works once we have a connection."

"We very much do not have a connection."

It did its creepy, slow, Grinch grin that always seemed to be the same no matter whose face it wore.

"Darling, I'm in your dreams. You've spent more time with me than with any living creature on Earth. Of course we're connected."

I fought back a shudder. The Nothing carried on.

"But I must reiterate just how little good physically hurting me would do you. Has it got you anywhere thus far?"

The most it had ever got me was a temporary reprieve. Still, I was glad of every single time I'd hurt it. I may have been about to willingly surrender the war, but at least I won several tiny, inconsequential battles. I could hold my head up high right until the point where the monster entered it with my explicit permission and destroyed every aspect of my being.

I dropped pen and paper back into the box. "No further questions, The Nothing."

It frowned. "I still don't like that name, you know?"

"Then come up with a new one."

"I just might. I'm going to find V now. What do you want me to do: bring him back here?"

"No, I don't know when I'll be ready. Just come and tell me where he is. Leave it as long as possible, though. I need some alone time."

"Whatever. You do you." It vanished.

Finally, a breather.

I wanted to crawl back into bed, but I needed to get on with my letter for V before The Nothing came back.

When is a suicide note not a suicide note? When you're technically not killing yourself, but merely inviting a parasite into your system. And when the person you're leaving it for is maybe one step above a stranger to you, but still somehow the most significant person in your life.

I know that's somewhat of a depressing way to look at things, but, hey, I wouldn't be in this mess if I weren't a tragic, self-pitying fuck.

Counting through the remaining sheets of Nan's old lady stationery told me that I had seven attempts at writing this letter. I took a few deep breaths and then dived in.

Dear V,
Please don't think less of me for doing this. I have measured my shitty little life against yours and all the people that The Nothing would get in my absence.

Was that too pathetic? Whatever, I'd read it through at the end and make up my mind.

There was always a strong chance this would happen eventually, so I might as well do it on my own terms.

I am leaving happy in the knowledge that my death will save others.

I switched out 'happy' first with 'relieved' before settling on 'content'.

The Nothing told me it could sleep for as long as ten years after me, possibly more. It also pointed out that it will avoid you in the future, as you know my name. If you do ever see me again after today, please fucking chase after me and tell me who I am.

I considered taking that out, not wanting him to put himself in danger. Then again, if anyone had an opportunity to hurt The Nothing, it would be in everyone's best interest for them to pull the trigger.

I've enclosed my house keys. If you feel safe enough, I would be honoured if you stayed here.

I changed the latter half of the last sentence to 'feel free to stay here'. Then I spent several minutes worrying about having 'feel safe' and 'feel free' in the same sentence, because I was unquestionably worrying about the right things at that moment.

No idea how long you'd be able to pull it off, but the two houses next door were empty for years without anyone noticing. Hopefully, it should last at least long enough for you to sort out something more permanent.

Did that sound like I was making a bunch of decisions on his behalf and telling him how to live his life? To be fair, I was already dying for him; what was one more enormous overstep?

The rest of the money from K.H. is still where you left it. You're the only person left, so you might as well have it.

I'm sure I'm preaching to the choir here, but it's probably best you don't go after The Nothing. You were right when you told me we couldn't beat it. The best any of us can hope for is to avoid it for just long enough. I wish you a long, happy life filled to the brim with people who care about you.

Live long and prosper.

Where the fuck had that come from? Neither of us were even particularly into *Star Trek*. I crossed it out.

And, hey, if you want to change your name to Vask to honour my memory, that would be a nice gesture. Just saying.

Your friend (hopefully),

Mask Whitehurst

I got rid of the part in brackets; it looked too pathetic.

I read through the scribbled letter a few times before deciding I was happy with it. Then I wrote it all out again on clean paper and put it in the accompanying fancy little envelope.

So that was it. I'd done everything I needed to. I took a slow walk through every room in the house, then sat down on the sofa to await The Nothing's return.

The smiling Sam picture, the updated photo of my mother and the one of Kathy and Nan at Christmas now sat on the table in front of me. How was I supposed to say goodbye to them again? I wasn't, was the answer; they had all beaten me to it. I was most likely letting Nan down by giving up, but given the recent revelations about her behaviour, I couldn't bring myself to care. Kathy probably wouldn't appreciate me giving myself to her murderer either, but I'd saved her from it; my debt to her was clear. Mom wouldn't have a fucking clue what was going on, bless her. And I didn't know her well enough to guess how she would respond if she did. Sam, were he still alive, would not give a single solitary fuck as to what was inhabiting my body, so long as it still fed him and let him out to piss. He'd give his paw to a soul-swallowing monster in the hope of a biscuit.

The thought made me chuckle. Then I burst into awful, hysterical tears.

A long time ago, there was a child with a troubled mother they nevertheless loved with all their heart. The mother abandoned them, but they still had their grandmother who doted on them. Then they got the most beautiful Border Collie puppy in the world. Then, of course, they learned the mother had died years before. Then the grandmother was diagnosed with a terminal illness. Finally, the Border Collie died of old age. The child just got unhappier and unhappier. And they had been utterly miserable to start with.

Frankly, it was ridiculous I'd stuck around for as long as I had.

Despite telling it to give me some time, I was still annoyed when it took over an hour for The Nothing to return. It's just cruel to leave me alone with my own thoughts for that length of time.

"Found him?" I didn't look up, not wanting it to see my undoubtably fucked-up face.

"Daft twat's busking in his usual place. Must be hoping you'll come and find him. Lucky him, eh?"

I gave it no answer. It slid into the space beside me and put an arm over my shoulders.

"You're doing the right thing, you know. Giving your life for others is really something special."

"Kill yourself, then, you'll save countless others."

There was a pause. Then The Nothing laughed uproariously. It wiped away an imaginary tear.

"Oh, Mask, as much as I can't wait to be inside you, I'm really going to miss you."

With those sickening words, it jumped up and skipped out of the house, expecting me to follow. I took one final look at the photos of everyone I'd lost. Then I got up and followed The Nothing.

34

G

This was wrong. This was all so fucking wrong.

Mask – Grant's last fucking hope – had just handed themselves to the thing on a silver bastard platter. His dreams of escape crumbled to dust. Story of his fucking life.

To be fair to Mask, Grant could understand why they'd given up. He'd been present for the entire time the thing had gradually worn them down. As for Mask trying to fuck him... Grant had forced himself through many depressing sexual encounters over the years, so he'd been relieved not to add to it. Quite what Mask had been hoping to achieve with that behaviour was beyond him. Maybe just to scare the thing off for a while. It had worked, after all. Until it hadn't.

While he had no context for the letter that had apparently been the final straw, it was clear enough that it was a huge emotional blow. Then finding himself in the bath, holding them still so they couldn't kill themselves. He had never felt so frustrated with someone and sorry for them at the same time.

What was really getting to him was the fact that they were sacrificing their life to save V. The same person who had sacrificed Grant's life to save his own. It was just so fucking typical. V had screwed him over again without even being aware of it. Maybe if he were, he could talk some sense into Mask before they went through with it. One or both of them was supposed to save him. Now it seemed that his only hope was V figuring out a way to get revenge for Mask afterwards. Good luck to him with that.

A long, dreary future stretched before Grant in his mind's eye. A lifetime – several, in fact – of watching as the thing lured more and more people in with promises of companionship only to turn on them when they reached their lowest point. Watching countless poor souls tormented into making the worst mistake of their lives.

Grant liked to think he had at least a measure of self-awareness; he knew he had been awful to plenty of people in his time. School bullying to take out his frustrations about home became violent muggings for the thrill of it became stealing to support a drug habit. All three of them combined when he finally ended up homeless.

It had always seemed fair enough to him: the world fucked him over, he fucked someone else over. The circle of fucking life. He wasn't about to have some kind of revelation that he should have been a good little boy who always helped others and ate all his vegetables. Still, being trapped inside this thing, watching it hurt people over and over seemed like an ironic punishment. If he believed in lessons from above, this would definitely be one of them.

His grandad had been vaguely religious, nominally Church of England. Grant had heard plenty of times growing up that bad people all ended up in Hell. Grandad's views on just who made up the bad people in the world were rather colourful. Specifically, those colours were: black, brown and rainbow. Despite constantly being told that he would go to Hell when he was being naughty, Grant had never really believed in it. Why would there need to be somewhere out there worse than this?

Grant had hoped Mask's weird little interview thing had been their way of stalling for time while also digging for information. A lot of it had been news to him: Mask could physically hurt it, but not for long; calling someone by their name freed them; it was going to sleep for ten years after it ate Mask.

What would those ten years mean for Grant? A complete switch-off? Would it continue to use him up so that, when it finally awoke, he would be ten years closer to death? It was frustrating that he couldn't communicate to Mask that those were the questions he wanted answering.

Most crushing of all was the fact that he could have been saved ages ago if only V or Mask knew his real name. If only he could regain control of a small part of his body for a minute or two, he could scribble it down somewhere, move the fridge magnets around or even attempt to blink it at them in Morse code. Grant doubted either of them knew Morse code, he certainly didn't.

There was a blur. Then Grant found himself back in town. Somewhere in the distance he could hear V. He was busking again, not a care in the world as far as anyone could see. Apart from the obvious one of being homeless. There was something vaguely sad about it: all the shit V had been through – a lot of it caused by Grant himself before the thing had even made an appearance – and there he was singing boring covers of shit songs so more fortunate people would toss him the odd quid. It was weird how Grant had never seen it like that before; to him, V's busking had always been some irritating shit that he forced on the general public, as well as something to separate himself from the normal beggars. V had seemed to him like a man with ideas above his station. Naturally, that had really boiled his piss.

Grant waited for the thing to approach him, but it just stayed and watched a moment. There would be no attempting to communicate with him. The time for telling V his real name had long since passed. Grant had no idea if V would bother to save him even if he did know it. He had to admit to himself that he didn't really deserve it. All he wanted to do was scream at V that Mask was going to give themselves up and plead with him to save them. That cause was so lost it was in fucking Narnia.

Later, as the thing walked alongside Mask like it was leading them to their execution, they told it about their plan to let V have the house and everything inside it. The thing did not appear to be listening. That was all well enough, really, as Mask didn't seem to be talking to it. It was more like they just wanted to say it all aloud. They went on to say how glad they were that they were finally doing something that would benefit others.

The stab of bitterness Grant had been expecting to feel never materialised. V landing on his feet yet again didn't bother him as it should. So what if someone else got the break he felt he was owed? V had suffered enough to earn it. As for Mask, it was a relief to see they'd made their peace with the whole sorry mess. Grant wished them both well.

Somehow, realising that gave him a sense of peace.

35

GORBASH

The evening was cool, but not so much that it made me uncomfortable. The light touch of the breeze on my skin felt pretty good. The sun was just about setting. Most of the shops in town were starting to close. Presumably, V would pack up himself once the crowd thinned out. I was surprised he was still busking as late as this; perhaps The Nothing was right about him waiting for me to find him. Disappointing him was going to haunt me. At least it would be the last time I would ever disappoint anyone.

The Nothing and I were squeezed onto a bench within view of V's spot. We weren't in his immediate eyeline, but there was a chance he would look over and see us at any moment. I couldn't make up my mind whether I wanted him to. The walk from my house had been spent trying to decide how I wanted this to go. After running through several scenarios, I decided against talking to V. There was no way he wouldn't try to talk me out of it, and that would lead to a nasty argument. I thought about attempting to sneak the letter to him without him seeing me – maybe even getting The Nothing to do it – then he'd find it however long afterwards and open it with no idea what it was. I could practically see the journey his face would go on as he read it. I pictured him shedding a tear for me; I liked to hope I'd be missed by someone at least.

"Was he really my friend?" I stared straight ahead as I said it, not talking to The Nothing so much as asking myself, or perhaps the universe. Figuring out relationships had never come easily to me.

I felt The Nothing shrug next to me. "Probably. The fuck do I know about friendship? He tried to talk me out of taking you, if that helps. Never offered himself in your place, mind. I think that means you win the friendship."

I smiled at that despite myself. It was exactly the sort of thing I used to think about back in school when I'd actually had friendships: scoreboards and running totals and who was getting the most out of whom. Just this constant obsession with things and people being even. All part of my complete inability to relax, I'm sure. Fuck knows where that came from. Probably the whole abandonment thing, that tended to be the source of all my personality flaws. Makes you wonder where any of the good stuff came from.

V started on a bit of Cat Stevens for the evening crowd. 'Wild World'. I wanted to sit and listen for as long as possible, but The Nothing was getting restless.

"Right, you can see he's okay; can we go now? If you're not gonna bother talking to him, then just toss that letter and get a move on. I haven't got all night."

"You're immortal, dickhead."

"Still."

It slid its arm around my shoulders. I contemplated shrugging it off for a moment, then remembered I'd let it bathe every inch of my body several hours earlier. What a weird last day alive this was turning out to be.

"I know you like to wallow in your own misery – obviously, I would usually be all for that – but what's the point of dragging this out? You'll only make it harder on yourself to leave him."

On some level, that was probably what I wanted. To be revitalised upon sight of V and decide my life was worth living after all.

Or perhaps, for V to come bounding up to me, excited to reveal his intricate new plan for finally defeating The Nothing. Maybe V could sing a song so beautiful that The Nothing wept, repented its misdeeds and promptly disintegrated by way of penance. Honestly, weirder shit had happened over the last few weeks.

I sank into The Nothing's side for a moment. "I'll go over in a minute; I just need to build up to it."

I didn't look, but I suspected it was rolling its eyes at me. "Okay, but having stalked young V before, I must warn you that he's a bit of a boring fucker. I really need to pick someone more interesting next time. Maybe a magician or a mime or something."

The suggestion that a mime of all things would be more interesting than V made me offended on his behalf. I almost started to argue with it. But then 'Wild World' finished and V paused to tune up. This was probably the best chance I was going to get.

"Wait here. Don't come near us." I walked away before The Nothing could formulate a response.

My eyes were so fixed on V that I managed to bump into no fewer than three people. I didn't even bother to mutter apologies, they were insignificant. I was about to say goodbye to my only friend so I could go ahead and die for him – I felt I was allowed a little protagonist moment. It was just a shame the absence of music meant I didn't have my own theme song.

V was facing away from me. He played the first few bars of a song before deciding the guitar needed further messing with. Someone just ahead of me dropped some change into the waiting guitar case. The coins *clinked* as they collided with the rest of V's earnings and he turned to thank the donor. His eyes landed on me.

V smiled, face lit up with hope. My heart shattered into a million pieces. A quiet voice in the back of my head told me to stay with him, that he needed a friend just as much as I did. V stepped forward, knocking the case on the ground in front of him. Coins jangled.

"Mask? What's going on? Are you..."

I shook my head, tears filling my eyes. The envelope bent in my hands. I dropped it into the case. There was the unmistakable sound of keys hitting the floor.

V looked down at it, then back up at me. He knew, obviously; it was written all over his face. He swallowed, then looked away and sniffed. I backed away for a few steps. Then I turned and walked in the direction of The Nothing.

Behind me, V started to play again. Not the song he had just been tinkering with. It was something else that sounded familiar, but weirdly uncanny as cover versions sometimes do. And then he got to the opening lines.

It was not his usual cover fare. This was a fantastical song about dragons soaring across the sky.

I spun back to face him and our eyes met. He gave me a smile and a wink, his voice wavering for just a moment. Somehow, I laughed. Tears began to spill down my face. The crowd milled around us, oblivious to the moment we were sharing. I gave V my biggest, bravest smile. Then I turned and left.

By the time I got back to the bench, my tears were mostly under control. They were still coming, but just the odd one here or there, easily wiped away with the heel of my palm. To my surprise and relief, The Nothing kept its mouth shut. We sat and listened to the rest of the song.

When exactly had V learned to play it? I had never overheard him practising or even listening to the original song. Yet, at some point between being forced to watch my grainy VHS and tonight, he had secretly perfected it. Perhaps it was a surprise for me that he'd never got round to sharing. I liked to think that I knew what the gesture meant. If nothing else, I was finally certain that he truly had been my friend. And here I was about to abandon him.

I jumped when I felt a hand on my shoulder. The Nothing's voice was impossibly gentle in my ear.

"Let me know when you're ready to make a move, okay?"

Still singing, V had found us in the crowd. There was no doubt he knew what I was about to do. The struggle as he tore his eyes away from us was visible even from this distance.

"He'll be fine, won't he?"

"Of course. Born survivor, that boy. Must be used to losing people by now."

Obviously, that was bullshit; I knew you never really got used to losing people. I had even lost the same person twice and it was just as painful the second time around. And with Nan being terminally ill, I'd felt myself slowly losing her every day for an entire year. With Sam, it had been so obvious it was coming that I started grieving weeks before he even died. Just loss, upon loss, upon loss. And I'd never even had that much in the first place.

Fuck, I needed a subject change.

I nudged The Nothing. "Do you wish you'd got V?"

"Not if it meant not having you."

Oh, of course, that touched my needy little soul. I did my best to shake it off.

"The one that got away, eh?"

It snorted. "Oh, there's been plenty of fuckers who got away, they just never knew how close they came. Your nan, for instance, she was next on my list after dear Kath."

It went on, either not noticing or not caring that I'd stiffened in its arms.

"I was aiming for the whole row, just for my own sense of satisfaction. I probably still would have had to kill that nosy bitch on the end, unless I could've done something to her son instead and left her vulnerable. Debbie, though…"

"Deborah," I correctly automatically.

"She was perfect: dead kid, shitty grandkid – no offence – and I'd just eaten her best friend. We could have had something special."

"When you came round as Doris that day, you were after Nan." It seemed so obvious now.

"Yes and no. I'd watched you first – I'm a professional – and I'd seen that she hadn't been around for a while. I knew she'd been ill, so I popped round on a fact-finding mission. Had to gamble on you being too self-absorbed to recognise our Kathy and, boy, didn't that pay off! Then, of course, I found an even greater prize." It squeezed me in an awkward side hug. "You're my crowning glory, Mask. My greatest achievement. Never have I ever got someone to hand themselves over to me so willingly. Not with such a clear picture of what I was and what they were in for. And the fact you're doing it because you think you'll save a bunch of lives worthier than yours is just exquisite. Honestly, I wish I could cum."

I sat up, yanking myself out of its hold.

"Sorry, that was crass, wasn't it? Oh well, it's not like that's going to be the thing that makes you change your mind."

I stood, legs trembling slightly. I glared down at The Nothing. "You think you can just say all that shit about my nan and I'll still come with you?"

It shrugged. "What else are you going to do?"

"Tell you to go fuck yourself! It's what she would have wanted."

It leaned its head back and raised an eyebrow at me. "Let's say I'd managed to take Debs; how long do you think it would've taken you to notice she was gone?" It unfolded itself to a standing position, towering over me. "Christmas? Her birthday? Not Mother's Day, no way you'd have turned up for that. Maybe just the next time you needed someone to put you up for a while. You'd have turned up to find her disappeared and your dog's corpse mummified. Mummy being the operative word."

I slapped The Nothing's face so hard the sound reverberated across the square. Half the crowd turned to look as they passed by.

My voice came out as a hiss. "You can stick this deal up whatever you have instead of an arse."

"Oh, that's lovely. And what about all those lives you were going to stop me from taking?"

I spread my arms out wide. "Take 'em! As many as you want, but you'll never have me."

There was a "Good for you, luv," from someone watching nearby. I glanced around and saw that we had a small audience. The Nothing noticed too.

"Might we discuss this elsewhere, my sweet?"

"No, we mightn't. I'm leaving. Stay the fuck away from me." I turned and walked away.

"So I'll see you at home, then?"

I stopped, risked a look over my shoulder.

"You don't get to just walk away from this, Mask. I'm the best thing that's ever happened to you – not that there was much competition – finally, a chance to do something worthwhile with your pathetic little life."

I turned back. In doing so I caught sight of a couple of girls filming us on their phones. Plenty of others were watching as well; perhaps I'd give them all the show they so clearly wanted. Head held high, I stepped towards The Nothing.

This just seemed to amuse it. "What's this now? Are you going to do the climactic speech from *Labyrinth* again? It would be suitably dramatic."

A memory popped up then: V's bit of trivia about how *Labyrinth* could have ended. Beating the monster into a tiny little nothing. Far more climactic than just talking to the fucker.

I reached The Nothing. "Speaking of *Labyrinth*..." I watched the monster's head tilt in confusion. Then I watched my fist smash into Ginger's nose.

That earned us a collective gasp from the audience. The crowd around us began to solidify into a circle. A few more people took out their phones.

The Nothing held its hand up to its nose. It forced a cheery laugh for the onlookers. "I'm fine, folks. Nothing to see here!"

I booted it so hard in the shin that I hurt my own toes. Someone tittered at that. Then I got sick of holding back and launched myself at its face. A tiny ball of fury, just like it had said.

All the more furious for having been called tiny.

Apart from a couple of weak shoves, The Nothing didn't fight back. How could it, without exposing itself? At one point, an onlooker grabbed me around the waist and attempted to drag me away. He just about managed to jerk himself back a second before my teeth made contact with his cheek. No one messed with me after that.

Finally, I reached the limit of the monster's patience.

From its place cowering on the floor, it shot a hand out to grab my throat. It climbed slowly to its feet, lifting me over a foot in the air. I dangled, choking and slapping pathetically at its arm. It snarled as it watched me struggle for breath.

The crowd began to panic, thinking they were about to witness my death. The noise that rose up around us was a mixture of shouts and gasps, and at least one person calling the police. There was even a small chuckle of nervous laughter. And underneath it all, I could almost hear the cogs turning in The Nothing's mind as it realised it had fucked up. Its face slowly shifted from the lion scowl to a deer caught in headlights.

It dropped me. Pain shot through my ankle and I crumpled. My palms slapped down on wet, dirty pavement as I struggled to catch my breath. Feet moved around me, but I lacked the wherewithal to grasp what was going on. There were footsteps and shouts and then an almighty crash.

The Nothing landed next to me on the floor. I flinched, then looked up.

V, stood in a hero pose, held his guitar's shattered fretboard. The rest of it lay in pieces all around us from its collision with The Nothing's face.

The crowd exchanged glances, unsure how to react to the latest development and this last-minute introduction of a new character. Muttering came in waves, but I could hear no solid words. Then again, I had just been choked and my ears were mostly filled with the sound of my own blood pumping frantically through my veins.

With a groan, The Nothing pushed itself to its feet. Since its feet were all I could see from my position, I had no idea why the crowd collectively gasped. Then The Nothing stumbled backwards away from me and in the direction of V. I crawled after it, intent on doing something. The chatter around us built into white noise. Finally, The Nothing came to a stop. The whole crowd held their breath. Silence. I looked up.

My eyes passed Ginger's jack-ups that exposed a pair of hideous socks; to the belt he'd clearly had to add another hole to; to the braces under his jacket because the belt was somehow not enough; to the long, ginger hair trailing down his chest.

His head was backwards, twisted at an unnatural angle like Doris' leg. I looked to the crowd. They were watching in horrified silence as The Nothing leaned awkwardly forwards/backwards to get in V's face.

I reached up and tugged on his trousers. His head shot round to face me, snapping back into its rightful place. The crowd freaked out anew: shouting, crying out, stumbling backwards. That appeared to bring The Nothing back to its senses. Ginger's eyes widened as the full scope of what had just transpired dawned on it.

There were two dozen or so witnesses to an apparently ordinary man pulling a full Linda Blair. Some of them had phones out filming it. As the shock gradually wore off, it glanced around at the horrified crowd and appeared to make a decision.

It ran, bursting through the crowd with supernatural speed. It was out of sight in seconds.

More gasps, more mutterings, more people looking to one another for some kind of answer. I was pulled to my feet and only realised it was V when he spoke.

"We need to get out of here."

I nodded, not capable of words, and he helped me over to his busking spot. I leant against the wall, he packed up his earnings and slung the case over his shoulder.

"Are we going home now?" I asked, desperate to defer to someone else. My brain was mush.

"Not a good idea. You might have to spend some time sleeping rough for a while."

"With you?"

The question caught him off-guard. His eyes met mine for the first time in a while. He smiled.

"Yeah, you're with me."

36

LEACH, ARCHIBALD ALEXANDER

Despite my insisting several times that I wasn't hungry, V ventured off to get us something to eat. He left me sitting on a low wall where I eyed everyone suspiciously. As much as I thought The Nothing was likely to lie low right now, I knew how angry it must be. And I knew I was one of two very big targets for its rage. We would be lucky to make it through the night un-gruesomely murdered. It was probably burning my bungalow down right that second.

V returned with subs and crisps and drinks – a veritable feast. He took note of my surprise.

"This guy who caught the end of the fight wanted to know what happened and offered to buy the guitar-wielding hero a decent meal for his trouble."

I pouted. "Well, if he'd caught the beginning and middle of the fight, he'd have seen me being a bare hands-wielding hero and offered to buy me a meal for my trouble."

V rolled his eyes and held a sandwich out towards me. He rolled his eyes again when I made him wait while I found my hand sanitiser first.

"No, seriously," I said, taking my sub. "I kicked its ass first. You just finished him off."

V grimaced. "I beg you don't phrase it like that."

"Would it be better to say we double-teamed him?"

The look that earned me was more than worth it. My first bite of sandwich was seriously delayed due to laughing at my own shit joke. My second bite was delayed by my belatedly remembering something.

"Oh yeah, I tried to fuck The Nothing yesterday."

Being a complete bastard, I had waited until V was drinking to make my announcement. Poor fucker nearly choked to death.

He slapped a hand against his chest as he swallowed. I penitently rubbed his back for him. Finally, the spluttering subsided and he was able to croak out, "Dare I fucking ask?"

I shrugged. "It was a very strange time in my life."

"Yesterday was?"

"Yeah, it was." I grinned and went back to eating.

V finished before me – probably because he hadn't been pissing himself laughing – and sat humming to himself as he waited for me. It took me a couple bars to recognise it again.

"Can't believe you learned 'The Flight of Dragons'."

He shrugged. "It obviously meant a lot to you."

"And I obviously mean a lot to you."

He shook his head. "Eat your crisps or I'll chuck 'em for the seagulls."

V waited until I was making a disgusting show of licking salt and grease from my fingers before he spoke again.

"Serious question?"

I made a blah noise.

"Why did you agree to let it take you? Were you just tired of resisting?"

I eyed him as I tried to decide how honest to be. I was pretty sure he would hand the letter over unread, given the circumstances. Thus, I was free to tell him whatever I wanted. He would probably politely pretend to swallow whatever lie I told him. We could go on bullshitting each other for as long as we were together.

"I tried to… you know." My gestures were as vague as they were emphatic. He might well have thought that I was talking about trying to fuck The Nothing again. "It stopped me, told me if I was going to give up on life anyway I might as well do it in a way that benefited other people."

"Who would fucking benefit from your death?"

"You, for one. It wouldn't come near you because you knew my name. And then there was anyone else it would have taken instead of me." I shrugged. "It just seemed worth it. An objectively good trade."

V looked at me for a moment. "I should smack you round the head."

"I'd deserve it," I said, cheerfully.

Instead, V wrapped an arm around my shoulders. The Nothing had done the same thing, of course, but this felt comforting rather than possessive. I could lean against V for as long as he would let me.

His head came to rest on top of mine. "How you enjoying homelessness so far?"

I snorted. "It's really not all it's cracked up to be. I was expecting far more glamour."

"Yeah, I watched *Oliver!* at an impressionable age too. I was a year in before I accepted that no pickpocketing orphan gang was coming for me. Far less singing than I was expecting an' all."

"Is that why you became a busker?"

"Shit! I can't believe I never put that together. See, this is why we're good for each other, this back-and-forth mutual therapy thing."

My arms snaked around his waist and we hugged properly. Were it not for the fact that it would have eventually become incredibly socially awkward, I never would have let go.

I accidentally put some weight on my bad ankle as we separated. I startled V with my hiss of pain.

"How bad is it?" he asked.

"Pretty bad by the feel of it." I fished my phone out to look at it with the torch.

It was a little on the red side. It was also two or three times the size of my other ankle.

"Fuck." V whistled. "Think it's worth getting it looked at?"

"Nah. Not worth sitting in A & E for five hours just to have someone tell me to keep it elevated. Unless you want to, just for somewhere to go?"

He shook his head. "This really isn't a fantastic time of night to be in A & E. Plus, how're we even getting there? Can't call an ambulance out just for this."

I hummed in agreement. Then I held the torch up for V to see my neck. "How's it looking?"

He leaned in. "Starting to bruise. It'll look awful tomorrow." He looked sombre for a moment. "What if people see us together and think I did that to you? Like I'm your abusive boyfriend or something?"

There was an uncomfortable silence as the reality of that sank in. I placed a hand on V's arm.

"If anyone says anything, I'll tell them the monster who wants to steal my body did it."

V smiled, but it didn't come anywhere near reaching his eyes. He drifted off in thought.

Naturally, I started to piss about on my phone. It had been in my hand for well over a minute, how was I supposed to resist? I hit all the usual shit: emails, YouTube and then did the rounds of social media. Mindlessly scrolling is a bitch of a habit to break, even in the most absurd of times. I scrolled past something interesting and had to go back up: a video of what looked like people fighting in the middle of a crowd. I let it play through. It was not people fighting. It was one person and The Nothing. Then it was two people and The Nothing.

"Fuck, we're going viral." I turned my phone to show V.

"Shit. Do you think the police will be after us?"

I shrugged. "People mostly seem to think it's some weird hoax because of the whole body horror aspect. Some people think it's a real fight and the OP just messed around with it for whatever reason. Except, no, hang on, there's another one from someone else. Completely different angle."

"We might be best off avoiding town for a while."

"Agreed." I continued reading through the replies until I stumbled across one that seemed important. "Looks like a guy I went to school with," I read aloud.

"Do they mean you or me? Don't know about you, but I sure as fuck wasn't out at school."

My thumb hovered over the screen, wanting to scroll on. "They mean Ginger."

V's whole body turned towards me. "Have they said a name?"

I tried to steady my nerves as I clicked on the reply. "He tags his mate and says, 'Who does this look like to you,' then his mate replies, 'Swear on my life, that's...'" My heart stopped beating. I showed the screen to V again.

A quiet gasp slipped from his lips. "Fuck, Mask, we've got him."

*

Coming back to the house after I'd said goodbye to it for ever felt pretty anticlimactic. Silly really, as we most likely had one hell of an unpleasant climax coming our way.

I braced myself against the wall as V ventured into his case for the envelope containing the house keys. In hindsight, we should have done that earlier to save on freezing to death in the early-morning light as V struggled to fit the key in the lock. He managed just as I was reaching for my phone to use as a torch again.

The second the door was shut behind us, I had Nan's old cardigan wrapped around me. As I stood there hugging myself,

V had the bright idea to unhook the walking stick and hand it to me. Even with it, I still needed help to make it to the living room and the relief of the sofa.

I settled back and looked down at the photos I had assembled on the table. Despite everything, I smiled. I was back, I was home. I had a plan to defend myself. I hadn't let anyone down. Yet.

V remained on his feet, waiting for The Nothing. He could barely keep still.

"Is it here, do you think?"

"Probably. It'll turn up when it turns up. You might as well sit down."

Before I even reached the end of the sentence, The Nothing emerged from the kitchen.

The host body formerly known as Ginger stepped into the room. The monster snarled at us.

"Wanted to die at home, did you? Crawled back to your den like a wounded animal. Very fitting."

I looked up to V. He levelled his gaze at The Nothing. He stood tall and proud, his breathing level.

"I want to speak to Ginger."

The Nothing tilted its head. "What do you think this is? I'm not a fucking medium."

"No, but he's in there, isn't he?" V didn't wait for an answer. "You made my life hell for months. Obviously, you had your own shit to deal with, but you dealt with it by picking on someone smaller and weaker than you. I'm not even sorry for getting The Nothing to take you instead of me. If anything, it was karma."

The Nothing, still scowling, crept forward as V spoke.

"That said, no one really deserves what you must be going through right now. It's time for your suffering to finally end, Grant Carry."

The Nothing froze in place, Grant's eyes going wide. Its mouth dropped open like it was going to order V to take it back, but all that came out was a thin, watery gurgle. I got the impression it had no energy left to scream.

Cracks splintered across Grant's face like his reflection in a smashed mirror. A silver light shone through the gaps. They grew wider and wider until the broken diamonds of his face began to fall away, dissolving in the air. The Nothing's skull beneath was revealed piece by piece. Finally, there was a loud crackle and the last of Grant Carry's form vanished, leaving only the nightmare creature.

It was looking decidedly worse than the last time I'd seen it. From its right shoulder, it had split down to around waist level, one arm dangling off on its own. The big empty triangle widened its body considerably, but didn't make it look more robust. There were huge gaps in its skin, revealing far more dark, cracked bone than before. There were holes in its chest I could have put my fist through, the edges of them crackled. The image that came to mind was of holding a lighter under a sheet of paper and watching as it began to burn. I had to wonder if that was what it felt like.

The Nothing staggered towards V.

I pulled myself up with the stick and got between them. I was eye level with the creature that had once towered over me.

"It's over," I told it.

Its jagged mouth stretched into an undecipherable expression. "Forget I'm immortal, did you?"

I made a point of looking it up and down. "Doesn't look like it from where I'm standing. You look like an ancient thing that's used up all its strength and has no more fight left."

A claw-like hand reached for my face, but never made it. The Nothing's arm fell down by its side.

"Let me tell you something, Mask. I was not ready to wake up after our Kathy. Could've slept a few more years. But, for the first time in my existence, *someone* woke me up early."

It was most likely talking shit, but I couldn't help asking, "How exactly?"

It made a noise that could have been a laugh. "You wanted me. Your soul sang my name. Half-slipped into your own form of nothingness. I was worried you'd disappear down the plughole before I even got a taste of you. Such a waste of good food."

I pictured myself stretched up to write on my own ceiling. Had that been the exact moment it had awoken? *Your soul sang my name.*

"And that," The Nothing continued, "is why you pathetic children will never beat me. You yearn for me."

I shook myself out of my musings. "We don't need to beat you, time already has." Somewhat unwisely, I got closer to it. "You can barely stand. Doesn't it hurt?"

Its intact shoulder rose in a half shrug. "Living hurts."

"But you can stop that anytime you want, can't you? If you just let go?"

It eyeballed me, but remained silent. I knew I was onto something.

"You told me you'd lived for centuries, lost count of the people you'd taken. I can't imagine living anywhere near that long, especially not the way you do. Not even the part where you torture and kill people, just the monotony. Repeating the exact same pattern over and over." There I smiled, cocky as hell. "It must have been such a relief when you met me. And now you're not even going to have that anymore. Whether you kill me or walk away, this is over. It could all be over. On some level, don't you want that?"

It raised its head up to stare me down. "You arrogant child. You're barely an infant compared to me – an ant in the desert attempting to reason with the blazing sun. You have no idea what I am."

"I know exactly what you are. I called for you, didn't I?" Its head tilted, intrigued. "You've been telling us who you are over and over: nothing we've ever seen before; nothing we could possibly imagine. You were nothing before, so you draped yourself in corpses until you resembled something living. Layer after layer of lives sacrificed to prolong your miserable existence. But you used them all up and then we snatched the last few from you. Stripped you to the bone. You know what's left, don't you? What you are now?"

I reached out to it, my fingers resting lightly on its cheek. With the gentlest of voices, I named it, "Nothing."

There was a moment when I was certain I saw genuine pain in its lack of eyes. It stumbled back from me, gasping for breath.

"You… you can't just…" It seemed to lose its breath. Then its legs gave out and it fell to its knees.

V stood at my side. Together, we watched The Nothing fold in on itself.

The rest of its skin went first, crackling away as though burnt. Then the warped skeleton began to shatter from the limbs upwards. The Nothing had time to look down and watch the trail of destruction travel up its body until it reached the head.

Finally, the remaining skull dropped to the floor. It peered up at me for a moment. I didn't know what it was trying to communicate with its eyeless stare – hatred, a plea for help, or even acceptance. I could only watch as the last of The Nothing crumbled to dust on my nan's best rug. Then the dust itself faded away into nothing.

I suddenly realised I'd been holding my breath. I gasped for air, making V jump. When I turned to face him, he looked worried.

"I'm fine," I managed to gasp out. It was somewhat undermined by the tears that began to leak steadily from the corners of my eyes. "Fuck, V, it's over."

He grinned at me. "Yeah. Yeah, it fucking is!"

We laughed together, V practically holding me up. I leant forward to rest my head on his collarbone.

"What do we do now?" I asked his chest.

"Whatever we want, I suppose."

"Sleep then?"

"Oh, for a day at least."

"For a thousand years."

I straightened up with his help. Both my throat and my ankle were burning. My whole body felt like an overripe banana, but I was too tired and relieved to give a shit. I looked up at V.

"You haven't given yourself a new name in a while."

"Suppose I haven't. I'm feeling Victor right now."

I snorted. "It's a bit on the nose."

"It's extremely on the nose, but tough shit, it's my name now."

I laughed until it turned into weary tears. Then I left V to get settled back into his old room. I shuffled off to bed and slept for a thousand years.

The only dreams I had that night were of my mother and hers walking a tired old Border Collie through the park.

37

MASK

There was once a young idiot who decided to name themselves after their dog. At the time, it seemed like a great idea: they loved Sam more than anything and his name was perfectly acceptable for a human of any given gender. Their nan – the woman who had raised them – laughed herself silly when she heard. They had brought it up in a way that could be written off as a joke, just to test the waters. They obviously didn't go into why they even needed a new name. As much as the dismissal stung, they had to concede she was right about it being ridiculous. So they did the only sensible thing and flipped it. Mas. When they decided they also needed a new middle name, they went with Kelly. They didn't admit to themselves why that was. Then, over the years, Mas Kelly had evolved into Mask.

Mask liked to pretend Sam was aware of the tribute and was even touched by it. Ditto, with the middle name. It became something to cling to when everyone they loved began to leave them. First the mother, who never even knew their name; then the nan who had laughed at the name; finally, the dog from whom they took their name. Then they were left alone.

That's a common enough story. It happens to a lot of us. It isn't entirely unheard of for a lonely person to fall victim to a predatory monster. It's just usually not as literal as what happened to Mask over the craziest period of their life.

Still, they defeated their monster and lived to fight another day.

Mask learned the true meaning of friendship or something to that effect. Maybe something that sounds a bit less like the narration at the end of a Care Bears movie. It occurred to Mask that they'd never forced V to watch a Care Bears movie; they intended to remedy that as soon as possible.

One lesson they might have internalised was: you are not nothing. Even if there's not a single person in the world who cares about you, you still matter. Of course, having someone who cared about you certainly fucking helped. Especially if it stopped you attempting to narrate your life in third person. At least I wasn't berating myself in the second person anymore.

Victor stayed. He stayed Victor too. He's still V for short, as he says Vic is how cops refer to murder victims in terrible American crime shows. Kathy's money got him some bedroom furniture and a new guitar. Plus, he opened the first bank account he'd had in years. He needed it when he started getting the odd temp job.

These days he works as a barista in a nice vegan bistro where he has a regular slot at their open mic nights. I've been a bunch of times. His colleagues initially thought we were a couple. Now they're convinced we've got a mutual pining thing going on where we're both too scared to make the first move. This was not helped by the surprise birthday celebration he threw for me there. He sang both 'The Flight of Dragons' and a Yeah Yeah Yeahs cover where he switched the word 'maps' for 'Mask'. Swear to God, half his co-workers have written fan fiction about that night. He knew exactly what he was doing, as well. I should have fucking booed him off the stage.

Secretly, V's working on some original music. I know because he told me. Then he told me it was a secret, even from me. He's a complicated guy. I've not heard any of it, but I got a sneak peek at some lyrics when he left his notebook out and open. To be fair, the only thing I really saw was the title: 'Irene'. The only time I've seen that notebook since then was when he ripped out a page to draw up a cleaning rota. He is strict but fair.

As for me, I've found an admin job I can just about bear. It's only while I'm figuring out what I want to do with my little life. Maybe I should have had that down before I stumbled into my thirties but I doubt I'm alone in that regard. Plus, the thing about destroying an ancient, invincible monster is it convinces you that you can pretty much do anything. So that's what I'm going to do, once I've figured out what that entails.

We somehow managed a decent job of fixing my bedroom ceiling ourselves (there was no way I was letting a professional see it) and then we repaired the damage The Nothing did to the living room as best we could. I framed the picture of my mother and put it on the wall with the ones of Sam and Nan with Kathy. There are also a couple of new ones of me and V, plus an old one of V's sisters. He's seen them a few times, but it's still early days. I'm rooting for him.

At the moment, Victor and I are trying to figure out if we could manage a dog on our schedules. He doesn't have a wealth of experience with them, but the two of us have been walking the elderly Terrier of the even elderlier man who moved in next door. His name is Randolph, of all things. The dog is called Mr Smith.

A considerably younger disabled couple called Myrna and Louise are renting Peter's old house. We've been over and introduced ourselves. Let them and old Randy know that they can always drop in on us if they need to. There's a 'For Sale' sign outside the house on the end of the row, but I'm not sure if there will be any takers given the history. Maybe after sufficient time has passed. Whoever it is, we'll be sure to welcome them.

I do sometimes wonder if I could wake The Nothing again, undo the only death I wouldn't want undone. On those joyless days when all the progress I've made seems pointless. When, out of nowhere, I stab a screwdriver into the functioning clockwork of my brain and bring everything to a grinding halt. When I wrap myself in my duvet and stare up at the unblemished ceiling. Sometimes it feels inevitable that I'll invite destruction into our lives, ruining the happiness we forged. I just have to remind myself what happened last time: I killed my monster dead. It came down to me or it, and I chose me. I could do it again if I had to. As many times as it took to make it stick.

So I get dressed every day, I go to work, I hang out with my housemate, in my spare time I read or watch television. I'm on speaking terms with all my immediate neighbours. When we get post, it's usually addressed to either Mx M Whitehurst or Mr V Thomas. Soon enough, we'll most likely adopt a rescue dog together. It's all so disgustingly normal that it breaks my heart.

And they lived happily ever after. Probably. I don't know, I'm still living it.

All I know right now is that I have several reasons to get up in the morning, and there is seldom anything I need to feel bad about.

ACKNOWLEDGEMENTS

Firstly, I am eternally grateful to Rebecca Wojturska for taking a chance on me. Bringing *Benothinged* to life has been a bright thread through some pretty dark times and it would not have been possible without her tireless work.

Next, I want to thank Lydia/Phasemoth for the gorgeous cover art. It's been amazing to see her process from initial ideas to final form.

Thanks also to Kirstyn Smith and Ross Stewart for copy-editing and proofreading *Benothinged.*

Thanks to my sister, Emma, for her help with describing the shitty bureaucracy that Irene comes up against.

Finally, I want to thank my good friend Alex. She was the first person I told when the offer came through and has been with me throughout this whole crazy journey. Thank you for always making me feel better about my writing and for enduring the 'reversible plushie' conversation. I'm sorry the old lady wasn't okay in the end.